MW00604981

THE TRIDENT SERIES

SKITTLES

Book 7

Jaime Lewis

This is a work of fiction. Names, characters, business, events, and incidents are the products of the author's imagination. Any resemblance to actual persons, living or dead, or actual events is purely coincidental.

The Trident Series - Skittles
Copyright © 2021 by Jaime Lewis

All rights reserved. No part of this book may be reproduced or transmitted in any form or by any means without written permission from the author.

ISBN: 978-1-952734-21-2

TABLE OF CONTENTS

PROLOGUE

Ten years ago

Anna Grace got out of the truck and stood in front of the tall, black iron gates leading into her family's driveway. Noah got out of the driver's side and met her in front of his truck.

Noah Young was the older brother of her best friend, Nicole, whom she'd had a crush on for a few years. He was three years older, and was leaving for Navy Basic Training the next day.

She had been surprised when he called her and asked to go to the County Fair with her. She was meant to go with Nicole, but she had come down with the flu. At first, she thought it was a joke, but when he showed up on her doorstep five minutes later, she realized that he hadn't been kidding.

She started out feeling awkward, but by the time they arrived at the fair, she had begun to loosen up and felt more relaxed. She honestly had no reason to feel nervous or uncomfortable around him, being that she was a staple at the Youngs' house. They lived a street over from her house, but the sad part was that the Young's acted more like her family than her own mom and dad did.

She and Noah spent all day and evening at the Fair, going on the rides and filling their stomachs with all the delicious fair food.

Something had changed during the course of the day. There had been a shift in Noah's attentiveness towards her. Normally he would act like the playful annoying big brother. But as the day went on, he became very attentive, and at one point, he held her hand as they walked around.

Now, as they stood in front of her driveway, she felt those nervous butterflies invading her belly again. She shifted nervously on her feet as she tilted her head way back to look up at him. She was fun-sized compared to his six feet plus height. It was strange that she was so short, considering her parents were both very tall.

"Thanks again for hanging out with me today," she told him, and he grinned. He was so sweet.

"Thank you for saying yes to going with me. I had a lot of fun. And it's definitely something to remember and think back on while I'm at Basic Training."

"How long will you be gone?"

"Basic is eight weeks. From there, I hope to head to pre-BUD/s training. It's a long grueling training. Not many guys make it."

"That's for the SEALs, right?" She thought she remembered him telling his parents about that one night when she had been over their house for dinner.

He gave her a boyish smile, and she could see the spark in his eyes at the mention of the SEALs. For as long as she could remember, Noah had always dreamed of being one of America's elite soldiers. She knew deep down that he had the mindset and the dedication to succeed.

"Yeah," he said and then stepped closer to her before he reached for her hand. He must have felt how bad she was shaking because he chuckled, and his eyes continued to sparkle.

"You're trembling. Why?" He asked.

She licked her lips nervously. She didn't know what to tell him, but sometimes when she got nervous, her mouth tended to speak before her brain had a chance to filter her words. "I like you!" She blurted out, then immediately slapped herself in the forehead as she realized how stupid she sounded. *Jeez, could I be any more of a spaz?* She thought to herself.

She heard Noah snicker, and she couldn't even bring herself to look at him.

"Hey," he said, putting his pointer finger under her chin and lifting her head.

When their eyes met, his whiskey-colored eyes danced in amusement. She tried to turn her head away in a bashful way, but he held her chin firmly as he continued to stare into her eyes.

A slight smile appeared on his lips. "I like you too, A.G." He released her chin, then placed one hand on her waist and the other on the nape of her neck before he pulled her in close to him in a possessive hold.

Her breathing increased, and she swore she was going to pass out. This was like a dream of hers—to be held in the strong arms of Noah Young. She swallowed hard as she wondered what he was going to do next. She didn't have to wait long as he leaned down then stopped as his lips hovered over hers. Her lips parted just slightly. She was in awe. His warm puffs of breath were felt against her wet lips.

"Don't ever be afraid to speak your mind, especially to me. I really like you, A.G. My only regret was not stepping up to the plate sooner." He admitted before gently pressing his lips to hers and kissing her softly.

Her eyes closed as she absorbed the feel of his firm, warm lips as they tenderly swept over hers, leaving her breathless. It wasn't a long kiss, yet it wasn't short—it was perfect.

When he released her lips but still lingered over them, she didn't open her eyes but said, "Noah, please tell me that this is real. Because if it's all one big joke—"

He cut her off with another mind-blowing kiss. This one, though, was short-lived, but it was still amazing. When she opened her eyes, he smiled.

"That was definitely real," he told her.

"I don't understand—why now? I mean, after all this time," she asked, continuing to stare at him.

"Because I always thought I'd get over the crush I had on you. But I can't, A.G. You're too adorable, funny, smart, and you have one hell of a personality that I love and admire. I thought that my leaving after graduation would deter me from giving in and asking you out. You're still young and have the rest of high school to look forward to, and I didn't think it would be fair to ask you to wait for me."

She tilted her head to the side as she looked up at him. "Don't you think that should've been my decision?" She asked with a hint of amusement in her voice. She understood where Noah was coming from. She did have three more years of high school, but it wasn't like she had boys swarming all

3

over her. There was no doubt in her mind that if he gave her a chance that she'd wait for him. No matter how long it took, she'd endure the wait.

He scratched his head and smirked. "I guess I didn't think it through all the way."

She placed her hands on his chest. "If you give me a chance, I'll wait for you."

He stared at her, and she thought he would try and argue, but she was prepared to fight. But then he pulled her into a bone-crushing hug.

"Will you come with my parents and Nicole to my graduation?"

"Of course." She knew her parents wouldn't care. In fact, they'd probably be thrilled that she was out of their hair for a few days.

He pulled back. "Are you sure I can't walk you up to the house?"

"I'm good. I promise," she assured him.

He stepped forward and hugged her one last time. She heard him take a deep breath before he exhaled.

"I'm going to miss you."

"I'll miss you too." She looked up at him with tears in her eyes.

He bent his head and gave her one last kiss—one she would savor for the next eight weeks until she'd see him again.

"Mom…dad…I'm home!" Anna Grace called out inside the monstrous home she shared with her parents in Potomac, Maryland. It was a seven thousand square foot home with six bedrooms and seven bathrooms and all the bells and whistles you could think of. She always thought it was a little excessive, considering it was only the three of them.

She was still floating on cloud nine after the day she had with Noah.

Not getting any response from her parents, she started walking toward the back of the house where her dad's study was and where he spent most of his time when he was home. Her parents were introverts, meaning they hated socializing, which was odd because she was the total opposite. Anna Grace loved life. She loved hanging out with her friends, which was why she spent almost every waking moment at the Youngs' house with Nicole and her family. The Youngs actually enjoyed life and family time, and actually left their house to do fun activities. Thankfully, they always invited her to come along.

As she started down the hallway, she noticed a vase which had been filled with fake flowers and marbles that sat on the console table, had been shattered on the floor. An eerie feeling crept up inside her, almost like a warning to turn around and seek help. But her need to know had her feet moving closer to her dad's study.

"Mom? Dad?" She called out again, though this time she could hear the nerves in her voice. But all she got in return was silence.

She felt a bit of anxiety as she slowly pushed the heavy wooden door open. The first thing her eyes landed on was her mom sprawled on the floor in a pool of blood. "Mom!" She screamed out and ran to her. She dropped down onto her knees and felt for a pulse. Her mom's skin was cold to touch. Tears poured down her face, and she started to panic. She looked around the room. For reasons she wasn't privileged to, this was the only room in the house with a landline phone. She spotted it on the end table next to the couch. She jumped up and ran to the phone, but that was when she saw her father's body behind his desk. He too, was covered in blood and lifeless. She didn't need to touch him to confirm he was dead.

She felt sick. The room was straight out of a horror movie. She stumbled backward, needing to get out of the room and seek help. When she turned, two hands came down onto her shoulders, startling her. She screamed, but the person quickly turned her around, securing their strong arm around her waist while the other hand covered her mouth. She tried struggling with her attacker, but his hold just tightened. When she managed to bite the guy's hand, he shouted and released her. Her freedom was short-lived however as she made it only a few steps before she was hoisted into the air and secured back in her attacker's grasp.

"Wrong move, chica," the guy snarled close to her ear. His voice was rough, and he spoke in a thick Hispanic accent.

He clamped his big sweaty palm over her mouth to muffle her terrifying screams. Her body shook with fear in the man's hold. She didn't want to end

5

up like her parents. She tried everything she could to pry herself from his tight grasp, but it was no use. His power and muscles were too much for her to overcome.

Movement out of the corner of her eye had her head turning towards the doorway. All the tears in her made it difficult to see, but she was fairly certain it was another man. She thrashed her body again, but the arms around her midsection only squeezed her tighter to the point she thought he would crush her ribs. She gave up and fell limp hanging in his arms.

The second man appeared in front of her. He too, was large and bulky.

"We are going on a little trip," he told her. "But we need you to be cooperative for both your sake and ours." He offered a smug smile before he lifted his hand and jabbed her in the neck with a needle. Soon she felt the fight leave her body; her vision started to falter, and she became pliant in the man's arms.

Just before the black curtain fell over her eyes, the last image she saw was her parent's lifeless bodies on the floor.

CHAPTER ONE

"That's it, Grace! Tighten your grip and close the racket a little more."

Anna Grace tuned out the critique of her tennis opponent and focused on the return hit. Her eyes watched the ball as it sailed over the net. She set her body and readied for the return. She swung the racket and struck the ball on a short bounce. It was a line drive shot as it flew in the air, skimming over the net and right into the left corner of the baseline—match point.

"Damn Grace, awesome shot!"

She smiled as she walked toward the net and met Max, her tennis partner for that day, and she shook his hand.

He smiled. "You're really good. Remind me again why you never went pro?"

She gave him another smile with a shoulder shrug, not wanting to venture into that conversation. She had the opportunity, but that type of commitment came with fame and a high price tag. And she couldn't afford either one. The cost because she lived paycheck to paycheck, and fame because it could ultimately cost her, her life. She had risked revealing her true identity while she was in college by taking a part-time job at the country club and helping with their tennis program., and she had been questioned by many at the club about why she hadn't played in college. If her life hadn't been altered, she might have had the opportunity to go pro. It was a dream of hers, but even though it didn't pan out, she still had the opportunity to play the game in her spare time.

Since graduating college, she lived a quiet, non-adventurous life and preferred it to stay that way. She had plenty of adventures in her high school years, though they were adventures she'd never talk about. Those days were a dark time for her, and a time she would like to forget, but she knew that would never happen. She relived that nightmare practically every night when she fell asleep.

Max called her name, bringing her out of the fog she let her mind go to.

7

"What?" She asked, looking up at him.

He took her hand into his and brought it up to his lips, kissing it.

"How about having dinner with me tonight? Let's celebrate your birthday together."

She cringed inwardly, knowing that Max had the hots for her. She liked Max a lot, and he was fun to hang out and play tennis with, but she wasn't interested in anything beyond a friendship with him. Plus, he only knew it was her birthday because the club had posted it on the bulletin board.

She pulled her hand from his, took a step backward, and began putting her racquet and balls into her bag. "I can't. I promised some friends of mine that I'd meet them for dinner." That wasn't a total lie, though she wasn't really sure if Arianna and Mia were actually considered friends. She didn't have friends. She never had the desire to form friendships with others. She could thank her past for that. She learned long ago that so-called friends only hung around until the next "friend" came along, and then they would leave you in the dust.

"Well, if you change your mind, I'll be at the Country Club around eight o'clock."

Of course, he would. The Country Club was the only place Max ever went.

"I'll give you a call if my plans change," she told him before they both went their separate ways.

She walked over to her bike and slipped the straps of her tennis bag over her shoulders before she hopped on. As she pedaled her way through the back roads toward her apartment, she started thinking about this evening and what it may entail. The unknown began to make her feel a little anxious.

She had thought about giving Xavier a call to see if he wanted to meet her at Bayside as well. That way, if she felt uncomfortable around Arianna and Mia's friends, she would have an excuse to leave. But on such short a notice, he mostly couldn't make it.

Anna Grace considered Xavier and his wife Melanie her guardian angels. Xavier Mayfield, an Air Force Veteran, was a prominent attorney in the Norfolk area who was also locked in a fierce battle with incumbent

Senator Stan DeSmith in the U.S. Senate primary election. Senator DeSmith had a bad reputation amongst not only his colleagues in the Senate but also his constituents. He was one of those people who would go to Congress with all the wrong intentions. He was only there because of the glory it gave him. He wasn't there for the people of the State of Virginia. It was perplexing that he'd won as many terms as he had. Many people had come forward with election fraud claims, but when the time came to prove it, things had a way of mysteriously disappearing, including the people who dared to cross him.

Many election analysts were saying that Xavier had a really good shot at pulling off an upset. Xavier was a man who always put others before himself. Grace herself was a perfect example. When she was just shy of her eighteenth birthday and at a point in her life where she would have to make some significant decisions, Xavier and Melanie had shown up out of the blue and literally put life back into her.

Once she had slipped back into the United States after a terrifying two and a half years of being held against her will by a wealthy, controlling liquor tycoon in the little fishing town of Yelapa, Mexico, she spent another year evading law enforcement and trekking across the United States until she found herself in Wheeler, Virginia. Wheeler was the southwestern most populated place in Virginia. On her first day in the town, she befriended an older woman, Cathy, a widow who owned an extended stay motel along Route 58. It wasn't the most glamorous place, but Cathy offered her a roof over her head and a job. She didn't make a lot of money cleaning hotel rooms, but her room and board were included. And in her situation, beggars couldn't be choosers.

Before she ended up in Wheeler, she had traveled a few months with a guy named Scott she had met at one of the homeless shelters shortly after she started the journey cross-country. With his help, she had changed her name from Anna Grace Silver to Grace Montgomery. She didn't ask questions when Scott had come back to the homeless shelter one evening with a brand-new social security card and ID for her. Some days she still wondered whatever happened to Scott. One day he left the shelter, telling her he was going for a job interview, but he never returned. After a couple of days of waiting around, she finally realized that she would have to move on because staying in one place for too long wasn't safe.

Xavier and Melanie had been passing through Wheeler when Anna Grace met them inside the small diner across the street from the motel. She had been sitting at the counter studying for the GED test when the couple stopped in for dinner. They had sat at the counter two seats away from her and had immediately struck up a conversation with her. She wasn't sure why she felt compelled to converse with them, but she did. The more they asked about her current life, the more she found herself being more open with them than she would anyone else. She kept mum about the murder of her parents and her time in captivity, but she did admit she had been homeless until she ended up in Wheeler and was offered the job at the motel in exchange for room and board and some pocket change. She told them how she wanted to finish high school and was studying for her GED. That seemed to make them happy, though Anna Grace could tell that her living arrangements had upset the pair. They had bought her dinner that night, even though it was just a five-dollar grilled cheese and tomato soup meal.

After Xavier and Melanie had left the diner, she finished her sandwich before heading back across the street to the motel. Just as she entered the motel's parking lot, a light grey sedan pulled up next to her. When the window rolled down, she was surprised to see the couple again. They asked if they could talk with her inside the motel's lobby. At first, she was hesitant because it seemed weird. But again, her intuition had her agreeing, though there was one condition; that Cathy, the motel owner, could be there as well. She trusted Cathy and knew Cathy wouldn't let anyone take advantage of her.

Once they were inside, Cathy brought everyone into her office. To this day, it still baffled Anna Grace how her brief and vague story had touched Xavier and Melanie so much that they felt compelled to help her out. And she wasn't talking about here's a hundred bucks to help you get through the week—no, they had literally offered her a second chance at a semi-normal life.

Xavier and Melanie were big donors within their community, and a few years prior, they had set up a scholarship fund in honor of Melanie's dad. A little over an hour later, Anna Grace found herself in the back of the Mayfields' car with her two small bags that held all her belongings, on her way to Norfolk.

The Mayfields gave her a life she never thought she would ever have again—normal. That still didn't mean she ever let her guard down. She still walked around always looking over her shoulder.

She spent the next four years studying at Old Dominion University on a full-ride scholarship, courtesy of the Mayfields, which included room and board. She graduated with a bachelor's in Sports Management. She wasn't sure she'd ever use her degree. She was content with her job at the animal rescue shelter. She had stumbled across the job accidentally while she was in college. Originally it was meant to be a volunteer position, but shortly after she started, the person who ran the shelter quit. Nobody else stepped forward, so she raised her hand.

It was hard to explain to someone else, but she felt connected to the dogs that came through the shelter. They were how she once was—homeless. But she busted her ass to find each one a good home. Some she even rehabilitated. She took courses and attended several seminars on behavioral rehabilitation, helping dogs through traumatic experiences.

To this day, Xavier and Melanie had never pushed for her to tell them more about her life before meeting them, and she never offered them any details either. Maybe one day she'd be brave enough to confide in them, but until she knew she was not a suspect in her parents' murder, she'd keep her secrets to herself. In order to clear her name, she needed to find the one person who could—Noah Young.

She had tried searching for Noah using computers in libraries, but all that she could find was information before he went into the Navy. She wasn't even sure if he was still in the military. There had been many times she itched to seek out his parents, but her friend Scott had convinced her not to. Scott had a lot of trust issues. He constantly warned her that nobody could be trusted, and she learned the hard way in the year she spent living on the

11

streets that he was right. His paranoia had rubbed off on her. But she knew that if she found Noah, he was the one person she could trust. However, the hope of locating him dwindled every year that ticked by, and she started to wonder if she'd ever see him again. Just recently, she thought of saying screw it and just showing up at his parents' house. She knew they still lived in the same house in the neighborhood she grew up in.

A chill shot through her body as she thought back to the last memory she had of Mexico. It was the day after her seventeenth birthday, and all she could remember was waking in the doctor's office and being treated for a busted lip, a broken nose, two broken ribs, bruising on most of her body, and a concussion. She was pretty messed up. To this day, she couldn't remember a single event of what happened the night of her birthday. Whatever it was had been bad enough for her subconscious to keep it tucked away.

Doctor Martina Hernandez was the only person who Anna Grace respected and who treated her with respect and seemed to care about her wellbeing. She remembered how upset Dr. Hernandez had been when she had to help her get dressed because she had been in so much pain that she'd been unable to complete that simple task herself.

She kept asking her if she remembered anything that happened the night before, and Anna Grace had just shook her head no. But something deep in the pit of her stomach told her that something catastrophic had gone down, and it wasn't just because she had been beaten to a pulp; it was something in her subconscious held under lock and key. Thankfully Dr. Hernandez hadn't pushed and just nodded her head when Anna Grace spoke. But the one thing she told Anna Grace was that nobody would ever lay another hand on her again. At least nobody with the last name of Castillo.

After Dr. Hernandez treated Anna Grace's injuries, she had fed her lunch before she drove her approximately one hundred sixty-two miles south to Manzanillo to the shipping port. At first, Anna Grace wasn't sure what was happening. She was confused as to why Dr. Hernandez hadn't taken her back to Senor Castillo's estate. When they arrived at the port, she put the car in park and turned off the engine. She then gestured for Anna Grace to get out and follow her. Anna Grace did, reluctantly, because she still was apprehensive of what may happen next. She met Dr. Hernandez at the back of the vehicle, where she began pulling a backpack and a small cooler from the trunk of her car. Anna Grace was both surprised and confused when the doctor handed the bags to her.

When Anna Grace questioned it, Dr. Hernandez just took her hand and began to walk her down toward one of the long piers where a large shipping boat was docked. As they walked out onto the pier, a man dressed in jeans and a polo shirt met them, and he hugged Dr. Hernandez. Dr. Hernandez then introduced Anna Grace to the man. His name was Mario, and he seemed very friendly.

Dr. Hernandez then turned toward Anna Grace and gave her the biggest shock of her life since she'd been held by Senor Castillo, telling her that she was free. Mario would see to it that she made it back to the United States. When she questioned why this was happening, Dr. Hernandez told her that there was nothing left for her in Mexico and that she was free to return to the life that had been stolen from her. This had surprised Anna Grace, considering all Senor Castillo talked about was how she would make a perfect wife for one of his sons. For two and a half years, they had been grooming her to take that role.

At first, she was hesitant to believe the doctor and thought it might be a trap. Once she was placed in Senor Castillo's estate, she had learned quickly not to trust anyone. But there was something in Dr. Hernandez's eyes that made Anna Grace believe that this was right. With one last hug and some words of wisdom from Dr. Hernandez, Anna Grace boarded the large boat with Mario and was on her way to the United States.

Anna Grace pulled her bike into her apartment complex. She carried the bike up the two flights of stairs like she did daily and let herself into her apartment. She went straight to the tiny bedroom that was just big enough to hold an extra-large twin bed and a small bedside table.

On her way into the bathroom, she pulled out her favorite light blue hip hugger jeans and a dark purple long-sleeved shirt. It was supposed to be chilly this evening, so she'd wear a jacket since she'd be riding her bike part of the way.

13

She looked at the time and blew out a big breath. She needed to calm herself down before she worked herself up into a tizzy. Mia and Arianna knew she wasn't a fan of crowds, and she trusted both of them not to do her wrong. Something kept nagging at her, but she countered the feeling and pushed it aside.

She needed to do this. She needed to live a little.

CHAPTER TWO

Her leg nervously bounced up and down as she sat near the front of the bus waiting for it to stop. Anna Grace was one stop away from where she was due to get off. After she had gotten dressed, she had sat in her living room, contemplating if she was going to go. She came very close to calling Mia and canceling, but decided against it. Not just because it was impolite considering Mia and Arianna had put in the time and effort to make sure she had a nice birthday, but also because she needed to get over the fear that everyone was untrustworthy. Up until now, her life consisted of working at the shelter, playing tennis, or barricading herself in her apartment. It was time to expand on the new life she had built.

The bus began to slow down. She took a deep breath trying to ease the nerves zipping through her body. As soon as it came to a stop and the door opened, she stepped off. She wasn't sure how far Bayside was from the bus stop, so she brought her bike along with her.

She walked to the front of the bus and unhooked the bike from the bike rack on the front of the bus. She gave the driver a wave before she crossed the street and hopped on, pedaling in the direction of where she needed to go. If she remembered correctly from the directions she looked at before she left, Bayside should only be four streets away. The roads were beginning to darken as the sun went down, but at least the roads up this way weren't as busy as the ones near her neck of the woods.

As she rode her bike and the cool air hit her face, she thought about how much she had changed over the years. The main change she had noticed was that she had become somewhat of an introvert. She hated it because that was the type of people her parents were, and she had sworn she would never become what they were. But long were the days when she was that vibrant girl who loved life and all people. Those responsible for her parents' murders and the mental and physical abuse she had suffered since were to blame.

Since her days of becoming a hermit, she did one of four things. She either wrote in her journal, built LEGO sets, played tennis, or went to the air base to watch the fighter jets.

She found that writing in her journal had become very therapeutic. She had taken a few writing classes in college and found that writing provided her an outlet for her emotions. When she couldn't sleep at night because of the nightmares from her past, she would write. She wrote about her time in captivity and her time living on the streets. She hadn't realized how much hatred she had built up within her until she read back over some of her entries.

She focused back on the road in front of her, and soon the rundown building with the big sign that read Bayside came into view. She almost thought she had misread the sign until she got closer. From the looks of the place on the outside, she wondered if she was at the right place. She had heard a lot about the bar and restaurant and knew that it was a hangout for many service members who lived in the area. She was also told that the place served some of the best food in town, and she was looking forward to trying it out.

She saw the bike rack on the far side of the parking lot and rode over to it and parked her bike there. Her hair probably looked a complete mess from riding, so she pulled out the ball cap she always kept in the small basket on the front of her bike and put it on. Once she got it adjusted, she blew out a big breath as she started walking toward the front entrance.

Skittles looked at the time on his phone and sighed. If he was going to be at the birthday party that Mia and Arianna were throwing for their friend, then he needed to head out. His apartment wasn't too far from Bayside, so he could still make it before the birthday girl was supposed to get there.

He grabbed his keys and headed out to his truck. As soon as he closed the door to his apartment, he heard the door one down from his open, and he closed his eyes, hoping that the woman who lived there didn't step out into the hallway.

"Skittles! I thought that was you." The prissy voice behind him said, and he knew he had to say something to her.

He turned, and the moment he saw her, he wanted to roll his eyes. Could she be any more desperate, he wondered? Who in the hell walked out into a public hallway in a sheer red nightie? The material was so transparent that he could see everything, noting she wasn't wearing any undergarments.

He regretted that one night a few weeks ago when he had too much to drink at Bayside, and she had been there and offered him a ride home. He didn't remember much except waking up in her bed the next morning. Ever since that night, she'd become a royal pain in his ass. He had even politely explained to her that he wasn't interested in having a girlfriend. Still, she wasn't getting the picture because she was constantly showing up at places where he was, or in this case, conveniently deciding she needed to come out into the hall barely clothed.

"Hi, Monique."

Her eyes lit up, and she smiled wide. Her lips were painted in a fire engine red lipstick, and he wanted to cringe. A little lip gloss was okay, but he despised dark lipstick, especially red.

She hugged her door, trying to act all seductive, but she looked desperate and stupid in his opinion.

"Where are you running off to? I saw your truck was parked downstairs, and I was going to come over and see if you wanted to hang out. I ordered enough takeout for two." She licked her lips.

He shook his head as he looked at her. "I told you, Monique, nothing is going to happen between the two of us."

She squinted her eyes, and he could see the inner bitch in her starting to come out. She had a reputation around town for her bitchiness. She thought she was queen bee, considering she was one of Senator Stan DeSmith's top aides. She worked in his local office in town. Senator DeSmith was an asshole, so it was no wonder his staff followed his lead.

"I'm willing to give you a little more time," she told him with a slight pout.

"You could give me all the time in the world, but I'm telling you, nothing you do or say will change my mind. Move on because I have."

He heard her dramatic gasp as he turned on his heel and walked toward the stairwell. Jesus, he needed to find a new place to live. Maybe he'd start looking around. His lease was going to expire in a couple of months.

He pulled into the parking lot at Bayside seven minutes later and found a spot right near the front door. He exhaled and closed his eyes. He wasn't up for company tonight. All he wanted to do was sit in his apartment and sulk.

Over the last few days, he'd been beating himself up over whether he should continue to seek answers in A.G.'s disappearance or just leave it be. He had pretty much exhausted all his leads, and any new information was few and far between. It still came back to the same major detail—she was the main suspect in the murder of her parents.

But giving up made him feel as if he was giving up on her. What would happen if she was still out there somewhere and in need of help? Sure, it'd been ten years since she vanished without a trace, but there had been cases of people in the same situation, who had been gone even longer, and were eventually found.

He ran his hand down his face. What made matters worse was that today would've been her twenty-fifth birthday.

He closed his eyes and leaned his head back against the seat. He could still remember his last day with her like it was yesterday. The bright smile on her face as they rode the Matterhorn, to the adorable little noises she made while savoring her boardwalk French fries that were doused in vinegar and old bay. How could he forget that day? Especially when he kissed her goodbye. It had been his first and last kiss with her.

The day he graduated from basic, he had been so excited. He had already been selected for pre-BUD/s—and one step closer to his ultimate goal.

When he finally met up with his family, he knew right away something was wrong. Nicole tried to tell him, but she couldn't get a word out without breaking down. But she did manage to get out A.G.'s name. His mom looked to his dad who then gave him the dire news. He didn't believe it at first. It

18

had literally shocked him into a daze. There was no way that A.G. was gone or had committed the crime that the FBI accused her of.

He didn't even care about his career at that point. His focus was finding A.G. But it took Nicole sitting him down later that night in a hotel room and convincing him that A.G. wouldn't have wanted him to give up his dream.

Nobody, not even his family knew how special that last day with A.G. was for him or how important she had become to him. He gave his sister his word that he would go forward with his training, but he vowed to never give up searching for Anna Grace as long as he lived.

He made a decision the day he was told about A.G.'s disappearance, and he was going to stick to it. She was out there somewhere, and he was determined to find her and bring her home.

As he got out of the truck and walked towards the door, he saw a girl riding her bicycle through the parking lot. He watched her park it at the bike rack that Paul had installed last summer.

A sudden wave of realization hit him that she must be Grace, the person's birthday they were all there to celebrate. He remembered that Arianna mentioned she rode a bike. That made him wonder where she lived, considering Arianna and Dino had seen her near the airbase watching the jets. If she lived over that way, she had to have ridden miles along some pretty dark and busy roads. That didn't sit right with him. Not that the town was bustling with crime, but certain areas had their problems as with any other town. She didn't need to be around those places, especially when darkness fell and she was alone.

He caught up to her and walked behind her; her platinum blonde hair visible under the ballcap she was wearing. She reached for the door handle, but being the gentleman he was taught to be, he reached around her and grabbed hold of the door.

"Here, let me get that for you," he offered.

She turned her head and looked up into his eyes, and Skittles thought he felt the earth shake. There was no mistaking those violet-colored eyes that haunted his dreams almost every night he fell asleep.

"A.G.?" He whispered, then he reached out and tried to touch her face. Had he been hallucinating? The woman recoiled and slowly started to back away from him as if she was afraid of him. But her low gasp and wide eyes told him all he needed to know. Then without any word or warning, she spun around and took off through the parking lot as if her ass was on fire.

Skittles couldn't move. His feet felt like cement blocks, and his body was numb.

The front door flew open, and Arianna and Dino were there.

"Was that Grace that just took off running? We saw her through the window," Arianna asked, looking concerned.

Dino stood in front of him. "Skittles, what the fuck happened? You look like you just saw a ghost."

He looked Dino in the eye and managed to get out a few words. "I think I just did."

"What in the hell does that mean?"

Skittles looked at Arianna and shook his head. He was still trying to come to grips with what just happened. "Your Grace is my A.G. The girl I've been searching for, for the last ten years."

Dino's eyes widened in surprise. "You're positive?"

Skittles ran his hand through his hair. "One hundred percent," he said as seriously as he could.

"That doesn't make any sense. Why would she run? Did she recognize you?" Arianna asked him.

"I don't know. But judging from her reaction, I think she did."

Now everyone had poured out into the parking lot as they, too, were wondering what was going on. While Dino and Arianna explained what happened, Skittles scanned the area in the direction that Anna Grace had run off to. He'd admit, she still had a quickness in her step, and with darkness impeding his sight, he knew he wasn't going to find her tonight. The main question he kept asking himself was, why would she run?

He turned toward the others and could see the concern in their expressions.

20

"What do you want to do?" Ace asked, taking charge just like he did with the team.

"I honestly don't know," Skittles replied. This wasn't something he had planned for. And, if he was honest, he never thought this day would come.

"Why don't we all go back inside and talk this through? If she took off the way you described, then she's probably spooked. And, if she's been hiding out this long, then the odds of finding her today are slim," Ace said to Skittles, and Skittles had to agree, even though he wanted to search high and low for her.

As he went to walk inside with the others, he took one last look around the area. She was still out there. He could feel it. At the moment, all he had was questions, but only ones she could answer.

Once everyone was back inside and sitting around the table, Skittles looked at Mia. "What about her employee paperwork? She had to have listed an address."

Mia gave him a sympathetic smile. "She doesn't have a physical address. When Arianna and Dino voiced their concerns about her being at the air base on New Year's Eve in the middle of the night, I checked her file and all she listed was a P.O. Box."

"What about her I-9 form?" Arianna piped in. "You have to list a physical address on that form. The government won't accept a P.O. Box."

Mia shrugged her shoulders. "I can go into the office tomorrow and check." She looked at Skittles. "Or I can go now."

Skittles shook his head. "No. But thank you for the offer. Let's wait until tomorrow. Ace is right; I don't want to spook her."

"What about her bike? It's still outside, and that is her main mode of transportation," Mia asked.

"I'll take it," Skittles said.

"I'm more concerned about how she's going to get home tonight, wherever that may be," Dino said.

Alex looked around the table. "Why don't we leave her bike where it is? If we want to gain her trust, let's leave her alone for tonight and let her retrieve her bike. Most likely she's still in the area, and if she relies on her bike as her means of transportation, then she isn't going to leave without it."

"She does take the bus too," Mia said.

"Plus, if we were to leave her bike here and she doesn't come back, there's a slight chance that it may not be there tomorrow morning," Arianna stated.

Skittles was shaken up. He wanted to know answers now. He wanted to go out and search for her. That was what they were paid to do. Their job was to find people. He ran a hand through his hair.

"Did she say anything to you?" Stitch asked.

Skittles shook his head. "No. But I know, without a doubt, she knew it was me."

While the others discussed what to do, Skittles couldn't stop the replay of her backing away from him and the fear in her eyes.

What in the hell happened to you, A.G.?

Anna Grace couldn't control her breathing nor her trembling body as she lay flat on her belly under an SUV parked in a driveway just down the street from Bayside. Tears poured from her eyes, and she tried hard to keep them at bay. She had so many emotions running rampant through her.

She had been totally blindsided seeing Noah. For ten years she wished for this moment to come, and when it did, she had totally panicked and ran like a scared rabbit. She couldn't explain why she had done it. Instead of running into his arms as she had imagined herself doing when she got that opportunity, she froze, then ran the opposite way from him.

She saw Noah and a group of people standing outside the bar looking around. Mia and Arianna were out there too. She knew they were looking for her. She couldn't go back there. Not right now. She felt too embarrassed. She'd see Mia on Monday and knew she could talk to her, and possibly have her get in touch with Noah.

She waited, and as soon as she saw the group start to head back inside, she slid her body out from under the SUV. She looked down at her clothes. They were filthy, covered in dirt, and God knows what else. She tried to brush off what she could, but it only seemed to make it worse. She eyed her bike sitting next to the bike rack. There was no way she was going to be able to go over there and get it. Hopefully, nobody took it. Maybe Mia or Arianna would realize it was there and grab it for her.

She reached into her pocket and pulled out the thirty dollars that she had brought with her. That should be enough to get her home. If she took the bus, it would be more than plenty, but the bus would take forever to get back across town, plus she'd have to walk from the bus stop to her apartment. A cab ride sounded much better and consumed less time. She walked along the sidewalk toward the opposite end of the street. Once she was there, she pulled out her cell phone. It was one of those pay-as-you-go phones. She pulled up the number of a local cab company she had save that still operated in the area. She gave them the cross streets of where she was, and they told her they would dispatch a driver to her location. She put the phone back in her pocket and waited. Tomorrow was going to be a very interesting day.

CHAPTER THREE

Anna Grace slid down onto the floor inside Biscuit's kennel at the shelter. Biscuit was a sweet, gorgeous white, brown, and grey Australian Shephard who loved everyone. The friendly pup walked over and stuck his head in her face, making her smile.

She scratched him behind his ears, knowing that was what he was searching for. Then suddenly, he just flopped onto her lap. She laughed as she continued to pet him.

"I know the feeling, boy." She was exhausted herself, and if she could close her eyes, she'd probably fall asleep right where she was. It had been one hell of a restless night. Once she had gotten home, she tried to lay down, but between her nerves and the fact that her mind wouldn't shut down, sleep was hard to come by. When she saw the first sign of the sun starting to rise, she pulled herself out of bed, got dressed, and headed to the shelter. She'd do anything to keep her mind busy.

She wasn't supposed to work the weekends, but she always came in on either Saturday or Sunday just to make sure the animals were okay. Usually, the volunteer staff handled feeding and cleaning up on the weekends along with any adoptions.

She closed her eyes and leaned her back against the chain-link fence. In a matter of seconds, images of Noah's face appeared. She was still in denial at seeing him. What were the odds that both of them had been in the same town and that her new boss was friends with him?

She felt the tears start to build behind her eyelids. She hated crying. She had cried every day for the first few months after she had been locked behind the gates of Senor Castillo's estate. Finally, one day after talking with herself, she realized that crying wasn't going to help her. So, she stopped and never cried again—until last night. She had gone through hell down in Mexico before living on the streets for an entire year and never shed a tear. But for the last twelve hours, that was all she had done. She was surprised she even had tears left.

Knowing her reunion with Noah hadn't gone over well, she knew she needed to find a way to reach him. She already had a plan in place to call Mia later in the day and ask her to get in touch with him for her.

The door leading to the front reception room opened, and Anna Grace glanced at her watch. It was close to the time when the volunteers arrived. She gave Biscuit another pat on the head before she gently slid him off her lap and got to her feet. She exited the kennel and secured it. When she turned to see who was there, she was shocked to see Mia walking towards her. As soon as Mia caught sight of her, she smiled as she approached.

"I thought I heard someone in here," Mia said as she stopped and stood right in front of her.

Anna Grace envied Mia. She was young, just a few years older than herself and was already an established veterinarian. Not to mention she was beautiful and had a gorgeous husband who adored her. Just from the few occasions she'd seen them together at the clinic, anyone could see the love shared between them. She and Arianna were both lucky women who had men that loved and cherished them. Even though Mia had just recently taken over ownership of the animal clinic and shelter, Anna Grace enjoyed working for her. She was the type of boss who didn't micromanage as long as you did your job, plus she was big on updating things around the clinic, like technology. That was huge. Dr. Katz, the former owner, was old school. Everything was handwritten. As soon as Mia came on board, she installed a top-of-the-line system for the clinic and shelter. It made everyone's job so much easier, not to mention more efficient.

"I stopped by to check on the animals and to make sure everything was ready for the volunteers," Anna Grace told Mia.

Mia started to nod her head but then scrunched her nose up. "Wait, do you always come in over the weekend?"

"Most of the time. I know that's what the volunteers are for, but I just feel better knowing firsthand the animals are okay."

"But you don't get paid for that, do you?"

Anna Grace waved her off. "It's fine. I don't do it because of the money. I do it because I care about the animals. And it's not like I have anything else to do with my time."

The statement could not have been truer. Her life outside of work, especially on the weekends, was zilch unless she picked up a few tennis lessons at the country club.

"Well, I care about you, and you should get paid for the hours that you put in. This place stays running mostly because of you. Promise me that you'll start putting down all the time you come in."

"But then that'll cause me to go over forty hours, and it'll be considered overtime. Dr. Katz had been adamant that nobody worked overtime."

Mia smiled. "Well, I'm in charge now, and if you work overtime, then you need to get paid for it."

"You don't mind paying overtime?"

"Of course not. I know you're not just coming in and sitting around doing nothing. You're a hard worker, and someone who I appreciate around here."

Mia's comment warmed Anna Grace on the inside. She didn't like to disappoint people, so knowing how well Mia thought of her made her feel good about herself. But her joy started to fade, knowing Mia probably wanted to ask her about last night.

Anna Grace pulled her bottom lip between her teeth. She may as well bite the bullet and bring it up first.

"So, last night didn't exactly go as planned. I guess you probably have a lot of questions about what happened," Anna Grace said to her, feeling guilty, though she knew she shouldn't be. In all honesty, she had panicked.

Mia looked her over, and Anna Grace wasn't sure what Mia was thinking or would say next, but she sure hadn't been expecting the question she asked first.

"Are you alright?" Mia asked. It had shocked Anna Grace, considering for the last ten years nobody really cared about her. She had Xavier, who checked in every so often, but other than him or his wife Melanie, there was nobody else. She couldn't remember when anyone asked her if she was okay.

Well, except for Dr. Hernandez. *No! Don't let your mind wander back there,* she silently told herself.

"I think so, now that I'm over the shock," Anna Grace answered honestly.

Mia smiled. "I don't think you were the only one." Mia shook her head. "I still can't believe you're the girl who Skittles has been searching for."

Anna Grace wrinkled her forehead.

"What are you talking about, and who's Skittles?"

Mia laughed. "Sorry, I'm used to calling the guys by their nicknames. Skittles is Noah. It's his nickname, but don't ask me how he got it. The guys won't tell me, and Skittles always blows the question off when I ask him. Anyway, I'm getting off track. For as long as I've known him, every free moment he's had, he has spent with his nose in his laptop looking for something or someone to lead him to you."

Now that shocked Anna Grace. She had just assumed that he had moved on as everyone else had. She had read a few newspaper articles. Everyone was quick to blame her because of the evidence. She still had no clue what type of evidence the police had that made her their main suspect. All she had done was walk into her home and find her parents lying in a pool of blood.

"I don't know what to say. I'm really embarrassed about last night. I didn't mean to run. I was just caught by surprise, and then a million things went through my head, and I panicked. I'm sure he's probably furious."

Mia's expression softened. "Furious, no. Worried, yes. I've known him for a few years, considering my brother is his team leader."

"Are you talking a SEAL team?" Anna Grace asked and wondered if Noah had achieved his dream.

Mia smiled. "I probably shouldn't say anything because they don't like it when people talk about them, but in your case, I don't think he'd mind. Yes, their SEAL team."

Anna Grace smiled. "Noah always talked about wanting to be a SEAL."

"He's a really nice guy."

"He always was."

27

"He's really worried about you and wants to see you."

"I'd like to see him too. Though I'll admit, I'm scared."

Mia squinted her eyes. "Scared?"

"Maybe not scared—more so nervous." Anna Grace began to fidget, twisting her fingers together.

"Stitch is here with me. Do you want me to have him call Skittles and have him come up here?"

Anna Grace took a deep breath. "I think that would be okay."

Mia sent off a text to Stitch, and then she smiled at Anna Grace.

"Want to go outside for a bit and talk until he gets here? Though I don't think it'll take him long."

Anna Grace nodded. "I think some fresh air would be good."

They walked out to the yard, where they let the dogs run and sat down at one of the picnic tables. It was a gorgeous day—not too cold and not too hot. The season was at that in-between stage where you didn't really know the temperatures from one day to the next.

"So, the question I'm most interested in is—what is your actual name?" Mia asked her.

"My real name is Anna Grace, but I changed it to Grace when I was seventeen."

Mia smiled. "Anna Grace is a beautiful name. Now I get why Skittles called you A.G."

Anna Grace turned toward Mia, surprised to hear her nickname that Noah had given her years ago.

"Has he really been looking for me?" Anna Grace asked.

Mia nodded her head. "Sweetie, he cares for you a lot. I don't know the history between you two or what really happened, but I know that he has pretty much exhausted every lead."

"He didn't tell you anything that happened?" Anna Grace felt as if that was hard to believe.

The somber look on Mia's face told her the answer. "Only that your parents were murdered. I'm so sorry."

"Mia, I'm not the same person he used to know. Some things changed me—changed how I see people. There is a period that I can't remember. I know he's going to ask me questions, and I don't even know how to start a conversation with him."

She started to think about how her conversation with Noah would lead to even more conversations that would include other people like the police. She began to get a sickening feeling in her stomach, realizing that her time had somewhat run out and that she was going to have to finally face the group of people she had been trying to avoid the most—the police. The same people who blamed her for her parents' death. What if they didn't believe her and arrested her?

Anna Grace's eyes got big, and her breathing started to increase. Nobody could know her whereabouts, at least not until she had a chance to explain things to Noah and he could help her. She still had no idea why her parents were killed or why she was taken. As if sensing her panic, Mia took hold of her hand.

"Anna Grace, calm down."

She tried sucking in a few deep breaths to calm herself. She looked at Mia. "I'm scared, Mia."

"Scared of what?"

"As I said, I'm not the same girl he used to know."

Mia gave her a reassuring smile. "Why don't we let him decide that for himself?"

Anna Grace still wasn't convinced. Ten years was a long time, and people change.

"Look, how about if I promise you that Stitch and I won't leave? We'll stay inside, and if at any time you feel uncomfortable, you just come inside and get me." But then a sly smile appeared on Mia's face. "But once you talk to Skittles, I don't think you'll need anyone else."

Anna Grace wasn't as confident as Mia seemed. But the one thing she did know was that her life was about to change in a big way. That made her think that she would have to come forward and talk to Xavier about her past, especially now that he was a candidate for the U.S. Senate. That was the last thing he needed for his campaign.

"I think I'll be okay. I want to see him. He's the only one who can really help me."

"Are you in trouble?"

The images of her parents' bloody bodies reappeared in her mind. For so many years, she had tried to scrub her brain of those gruesome images, but to no avail.

"They think I did it. I swear I had nothing to do with it. They were already dead when I got home that night." She felt that familiar tightening in her chest, signaling the first signs of a panic attack. The tears begin to burn her eyes, but Mia pulled her into a hug.

"It's going to be okay, sweetie. I promise you," Mia whispered to her.

Mia looked over Anna Grace's head and saw Stitch standing there with Skittles. Both were frowning, maybe because he had heard some of what Anna Grace said. Between all their friends, Mia knew that they would help Grace—or—Anna Grace get through this difficult time. She knew that Skittles would be her advocate.

Skittles didn't waste any time in getting to the shelter. He'd been sitting by his phone since five o'clock in the morning waiting for the call from Mia, but when Stitch called about ten minutes ago and said that Anna Grace was at the shelter and that she was asking for him, he didn't think twice before grabbing his keys and running out the door.

He pulled into the shelter's parking lot and saw Stitch standing outside. He got out and walked over. His stomach felt like it was in knots. Never in his life, even going into battle, had he ever felt as nervous as he was at this moment. For ten years, he had waited for this day to come.

"She's outback in the yard with Mia," Stitch told him but then stopped him before he went in. "Mia said in the text that A.G. seems to be in a very fragile state right now."

His gut clenched. But that was good to know because the last thing he wanted to do was push or say something that would make her bolt again.

He shook Stitch's hand and thanked him. Stitch told him that he and Mia would stick around and be inside Mia's office over at the clinic just in case they were needed.

They both walked inside and down the small hallway toward the back door. As soon as Skittles opened the door his eyes immediately locked onto the woman with platinum blonde hair sitting with Mia at the picnic table. Mia was hugging her, and his gut clenched. As he moved closer and more of Anna Grace came into view, his chest tightened. He could hear her sniffling and knew she was crying as Mia consoled her.

Jesus, A.G., what happened to you?

Mia met his gaze over Anna Grace's shoulder. He could even see the emotion in Mia's eyes, and he could only wonder what details Anna Grace had shared with her.

He watched as Mia pulled back and released A.G. before whispering something to her. Seconds later, Anna Grace's head whipped around, and as soon as her face came into view, he nearly dropped to his knees. Her eyes were red and puffy from crying, and his heart broke for her. He was afraid to approach her, fearing she may take off again, so instead, he left it up to her, and he stood in place.

As they just stared at one another for a few seconds, he could see the internal battle she was facing. She appeared timid, and he knew he would have to be the one to make the first move. All he did was take one step forward, then opened his arms as if telling her that it was okay. And that was all it took because he saw the spark in her eyes just before she leaped off the table and sprinted into his arms. She hit him with such force that she almost knocked him over. He wrapped his arms around her tightly, and he nearly shed a tear himself as she snuggled into his chest. He closed his eyes as he relished the feel of her in his arms. He was filled with excitement yet nervousness as he'd waited ten years to hold her again.

She was shaking terribly, and he could hear how her breathing was unsteady. It almost sounded like she was hyperventilating. He needed to get

31

her calmed down before he did anything else, but he didn't want to let her go. So, he did the next best thing—he picked her up and carried her over to the picnic table, and sat down with her. That was when he realized how light she was. She had always been petite, but she was too thin, in his opinion.

Holding her in his arms, he gently rocked her, and he whispered to her that everything was going to be okay. As the minutes ticked by, her breathing started to even out more, and her sobbing became more of a hiccup, and he started to relax a little more. After another minute or two, she finally pulled her head from his chest and peered up at him.

"I can't believe it is really you," she croaked out as she wiped her eyes and nose and stared up at him.

"I feel the same way," he admitted looking down into her violet eyes that were glistening with tears.

She covered her mouth, still appearing in a state of shock, and she took a deep breath.

"I have so many things I want to ask you right now, but I don't want to scare you off or overwhelm you," he told her, and he could see from her expression that he was on the right track and that she would definitely feel overwhelmed if he bombarded her with questions. Especially with the way he'd been trained to interrogate. He needed to keep that in the back of his mind—she was not the enemy.

She smiled. "I was just telling Mia that I didn't even know what to say to you first."

He took a quick glance over his shoulder and saw Stitch and Mia watching. Stitch had his arm around Mia, who had tears flowing down her cheeks. He mouthed "thank you" to her, and she nodded before she and Stitch turned and walked back inside the building, leaving him and Anna Grace by themselves.

He turned his attention back to the woman in his arms. Not just any woman either; she was his woman. He still couldn't believe she was sitting here in his arms. He ran his knuckles down her cheek then used his thumb to wipe away any lingering tears.

32

"You okay?" He asked, and she smiled, and damn, he felt it all the way to his heart. Jesus, he hadn't realized how much he missed seeing that smile of hers. She always knew how to bring a smile to his face.

"I think so. I'm still in a bit of shock," she admitted as she tried to sit up and move to the seat next to him. He helped her but kept a hand on her leg. He needed that connection—to know that she was really there, and this wasn't a twisted bad dream that he was going to wake up from.

Anna Grace was fidgety as she moved off Skittles lap and took the seat next to him. The nerves were overbearing. When Skittles placed his hand over hers, she realized that she wasn't alone. She could feel the slight shake in his hands. She looked over at him, and when he grinned, she wondered how in the world his smile still made her belly quiver after all these years. He looked really good. He'd gotten much more muscular. Even his neck had muscles.

"You don't know how long I've waited for this moment, and now that you're actually here in front of me, I feel..." She didn't really know how to explain what she was feeling right now. "I feel sort of clueless. I know that sounds silly and strange, and I know you have many questions you probably want to ask, and believe me, I want to tell you everything, but I need you to be patient with me." That was what she was afraid of—reliving the darkest moments of her life. Years of abuse and loneliness still haunted her. But doing so would hopefully bring her peace.

"Have you had breakfast?" He asked her, totally throwing her for a loop, and she scrunched her forehead up. *What the hell kind of question was that?* She thought to herself. After everything she had been through; missing for ten years and being held captive, and the first question he asked her was if she had breakfast?

She snorted a sarcastic laugh. "That isn't the first question I imagined you asking me."

He grinned. "I figure we could eat while we catch up. Would you feel more comfortable?"

She smiled. "I could eat a little bit. I'm not much of a breakfast person," she told him, and he frowned.

"You need to eat breakfast. It's the most important meal of the day," he barked, and she widened her eyes to his response.

He took her hand and pulled up from the table. "Let's go," he ordered nicely in a deep voice. She didn't remember his voice being that deep or raspy. It was a voice that she could get used to listening to.

Skittles drove them to a little diner near the shelter. Neither one had touched their breakfast. He had lost his appetite when she told him how she found her parents and how she was taken just moments after he had been with her. He had stopped his mind from playing the "what if" game. She explained her version of what had happened during the years that followed, though he had a feeling she only gave him the cliff notes. There were many holes in her story and he was trying his damnedest to hold in his temper and let her finish without interrupting her. His patience was being tested, and he felt he was doing a damn good job of not rushing to any sort of judgment.

Every word she spoke angered him even more. Boy, had the police and FBI been so fucking wrong. Yes, she had disappeared without a trace, but they were so quick in their investigation to close the case before they even really tried to search for her. He remembered when they suggested that she was a disgruntled teenager and may have killed her parents. It sounded good, and with no other leads, it was the story they stuck with.

Knowing now that she had been kidnapped and taken to Mexico had him boiling mad. But questions remained.

"Why didn't you go to the police when you got back into the states?" He asked her knowing that was the first thing he would've done had he been in her shoes.

She stared at him, then looked out the window. "I tried to when I got off the boat in Southern California."

"Southern California?" He interrupted her and she looked across the table at him.

She nodded. "San Diego," she said, and he closed his eyes. He was probably still in Coronado when she came through. Jesus, she had been right there.

"What do you mean you tried to go to the police?"

"I was seventeen years old; I had been kidnapped, then two and a half years later I end up on a boat with a bunch of men I didn't know and brought back to the United States. I didn't know where to go or what to do. San Diego was really crowded, so I took a bus with some of the money that Dr. Hernandez had given me and ended up in a little town in New Mexico. I found my way to the tiny Sherriff's department. When I walked in there and told them who I was and what happened, they put me in a small room with a desk. I waited and waited. Finally, I had to use the restroom. As I was heading down the hall, I heard the Sherriff talking with someone on speakerphone. They were talking about me, so I stopped and listened. He couldn't see me out in the hall, and there was nobody else around. I heard the person on the phone say that I was wanted by the FBI for questioning in the murder of my parents." She looked up at Skittles, and he saw the tears in her eyes and could tell how scared she was. "I didn't murder my parents, Noah. I told you what happened. I found them, and then someone grabbed me. The next thing I knew, I was in Mexico. I got scared when I heard that, and I bolted. From there, you know the rest. I made my way across the U.S. until I met Xavier and his wife, and here I am."

He reached across the table and took her hand.

"I believe you, A.G., but you're going to have to go to the police." He felt her start to pull her hand back, but he held on tight. She wasn't going to run. She was done having to deal with all of this on her own.

"I swear to you, I will be there to help you through it, and I know my parents will too. Jesus, they've been so worried about you. None of us ever gave up hope that you were still alive."

He could see the emotion building in her eyes. "You were the only one I could trust."

"My parents would've helped you. You should've gone to them."

"Believe me, I thought about it plenty of times, but my anxiety and trust issues prevented me from doing it. I figured that I had been living under the radar for seven years without my true identity being challenged; why risk it."

"They and Nicole are going to be so happy when I tell them about you."

He watched as her eyes widened. "You can't tell them yet. In fact, nobody can know yet."

"Why the hell not?"

"There's something that I need to do before news of my appearance breaks. Please, can you give me at least a week?" She was practically begging him.

He eyed her over and wondered what was so important. His gut clenched. Was she going to try to run again? He shook those thoughts from his head. She had already given him a watered-down version of what happened. He could easily go to the authorities himself. She placed her hand over his.

"Noah, I promise I'm not trying to hide anything. There are people I'm close with that I need to explain this to before it goes public."

He thought about it, and then he realized what it was or who she needed to speak to. Xavier Mayfield. Considering he was running for U.S. Senate, her connection to him could affect his campaign.

He nodded his head. "You have one week," he told her, and she smiled. Then she surprised him when she slid out of her side of the booth and slid in next to him and gave him a big hug.

He embraced her and kissed the top of her head. "I'm here for you A.G."

She squeezed him tighter. "I missed you," she whispered.

"I missed you too."

CHAPTER FOUR

The next day Anna Grace found herself sitting on her sofa trying to focus on the paperwork in hand, but it was hard. Every time she'd start to read over the contracts, she felt her eyes start to droop. Again, she had trouble sleeping. After tossing and turning for over an hour, she spent some time jotting down some of her thoughts in her journal. Because of Skittles, she finally got to write about something that made her smile. God help anyone if they ever got a hold of her books. They would probably think she was some sort of nutjob.

She knew Noah was upset at her when they parted ways yesterday because he had wanted to take her home, but she wasn't yet ready for him to see where she lived. It wasn't because she was embarrassed, because, hey, that was all she could afford. She didn't want him to see the place because she knew he would go ballistic. Her apartment wasn't all that safe, but she took precautions and made the best of it for the last three years.

She smiled, remembering their conversation after she gave him a summarized version of her last ten years. Surprisingly she got through it without breaking down. But that could be attributed to the fact that she hadn't really gone into too much detail on her life in captivity. They had spent about two hours sitting together as he caught her up on his life. She was so proud of him for succeeding in the SEALs, and she told him so, which had made him blush.

She had been glad that he had her bike with him in the back of his truck, considering that it was her mode of transportation. She didn't have a driver's license. However, that didn't mean she didn't know how to drive. Back in Mexico, Senor Castillo's estate was so big that they had golf carts and Gators all over the place. She had learned to drive pretty quickly. She remembered early on in her captivity when she thought she had snuck out of the main house and hijacked one of the carts and took off, thinking she could find an exit on the backside of the estate. She had been mistakenly wrong, and she paid for it too. Senor Castillo had allowed his oldest son Jorge to administer her punishment with a belt. She still had a few faint scars from that night on the back of her upper thighs.

She pushed that memory aside and focused on the paperwork she was getting organized for tomorrow. She had two families coming to finalize their adoptions. Adoption days made her happy because that meant there were two fewer dogs in the world needing shelter.

She looked at her watch and saw it was already close to eleven. Normally, she would skip the shelter on Sundays and spend the morning at the farmer's market picking up her fruits and vegetables for the week. The farmer's market was a whole lot cheaper than the grocery store for produce.

Noah had wanted to see her and offered to take her to breakfast again, but she told him she had some work she needed to complete, and then she had to pick up some food. He had seemed disappointed, and deep down, she was too. She enjoyed spending time with him yesterday. She could see how much the Navy had changed him. He wasn't the nerdy kid that she had grown up knowing. Noah was hot! But he was still sweet, even though she could see he had a fierce temper lying under his demeanor that could explode in the blink of an eye.

She finished up the paperwork then prepared to head to the market.

Just as she hopped on her bike, she heard her phone ring. She didn't recognize the number, but she answered it.

"Hello?"

"A.G.?" She heard the deep voice, and her insides instantly melted.

"Noah?" She asked as a smile formed.

"Hey. I know you told me you have some things to do today, but I wanted to see if you had plans later this afternoon?" He asked, sounding hopeful.

"Not really."

"Not really? Either you do, or you don't."

Her eyes widened, and she pulled the phone away from her ear and looked at it. Jeez, the Navy really brought Noah out of his nerd shell. He was blunt.

38

"No. I just finished up my work for the shelter, and I was getting ready to head to the farmers market and get my produce for the coming week. It's cheaper, and the fruits and veggies are fresher." She could've kicked herself in the butt mentioning money. He didn't need to know she lived paycheck to paycheck.

"How about I meet you at the farmers market? You can get what you need to pick up, and then we can head to that little Mexican place right there on the corner for lunch. You do still like Mexican food, right?" He asked, and she knew why he asked—because of her past. That was nice of him.

Of course, she liked Mexican food. However, the closest she'd had to Mexican food since she had returned to the states was Taco Bell. That was the only Mexican food she could afford. She supposed she could cook, but the ingredients weren't cheap, and she didn't see a need to cook for just herself. She stuck with a lot of frozen meals and her fruits and veggies.

"Okay. I should be there in about fifteen to twenty minutes."

"I'll see you in fifteen to twenty then," he told her.

"Okay. Bye."

Skittles watched Anna Grace closely as she interacted with the merchants. She laughed and smiled with them as if they were friends. But the one thing he noticed was that she hardly bought anything she looked over. She looked at a lot of items, but he didn't miss how she would put the item back after looking at the price tag. His chest tightened, thinking back to their conversation yesterday and everything she had been through. There were still some parts to her story that he wanted to press her on, but he promised to be patient.

She hadn't seen him yet. He had gotten there before she had, and he'd followed her through the maze of vendors. She was cute ten years ago, but she had matured into a beautiful woman. He didn't miss the guys that would look her over as she passed by them. However, she seemed oblivious to it.

She approached another vendor who sold jewelry. He was within hearing distance and heard the lady who worked there greet Anna Grace by name. However, he frowned when she used Grace. They chatted for a few until the lady asked Anna Grace if she was ready to buy yet. He immediately wondered what the item was that the lady was talking about. Anna Grace responded and said no but that she was close. Another month and she'd have the full amount. The lady had assured her that the item would stay behind the counter. Anna Grace thanked her and hugged her before she wandered down the aisle toward the produce.

As soon as Anna Grace was far enough away, he approached the jewelry counter. The lady working smiled.

"Hi. Can I help you today?"

He smiled. "I hope so. The woman who was just here. What was she looking at?"

The lady eyed him funnily, and he could understand. "Are you talking about Grace? The woman that just left?"

He nodded. "Yes. She's my friend, and I'm trying to figure out what to get her for her birthday. I'm supposed to meet her here to take her to lunch, but I don't want her to see me here with you. Was she looking at something in particular?"

The lady smiled again then held her finger up. "Give me just a minute."

He watched as the lady dug through a cabinet behind the counter before returning with a necklace box. When she opened the box and he saw the white gold heart pendant on the white gold chain, he felt his heart rate speed up. *It couldn't be*, he thought to himself until he flipped over the pendant and saw the small A.G. that his mom had engraved on the back. It was a one-of-a-kind necklace and pendant that his mom had given Anna Grace on her thirteenth birthday.

"She's been saving for months to buy it," the lady told him. "She said she used to have one just like it, but this one looks as if it was specially made." She turned the pendant around to show him where the initials were.

Because it was specially made for Anna Grace, he wanted to tell the lady, but she didn't know its history.

"Where did you get this?" He asked.

"Oh my...It had to be ten or so years ago—too long ago for me to remember. Someone brought it into the shop I used to run with my husband up near Alexandria. I had many buyers look at it, but they didn't want it as soon as they saw the initials on the back. There were many times I almost sold it off to those companies who melt the metals down. But something in my subconscious told me to hang on to it. When we closed our shop up there and moved to the area, I started selling here on the weekends. I had forgotten about this piece until a few months ago. The day I put it out, Grace had come by and saw it. I could tell she was interested the moment she laid eyes on it. Her eyes lit up like a Christmas tree. She wanted it badly but told me that she couldn't afford it then. So, I made her a deal. I told her that I'd keep it hidden until she could afford it."

Skittles smiled. "That was very kind of you to do that."

The lady smiled. "Grace is an amazing young woman. She comes through here every weekend. I enjoy seeing and talking to her."

"She is amazing. I'd like to buy the necklace and pendant for her."

The lady's eyes widened, but then a smile formed on her face. "That's very thoughtful of you."

She told him how much it was, and he didn't even bat an eye as he handed her his credit card. If that put a smile on A.G.'s face, then it was all that mattered. And, she'd have a piece of her past back.

After she wrapped it up, he stuck it in his pocket and went in search of A.G. He found her not too far away picking out vegetables and fruit. She had a basket-full—so full it looked like she was struggling with its weight.

He walked up and took the basket right out of her hand. He had surprised her, and she went to reprimand him when she looked up and saw it was him, and then she smiled.

"Hi," she said, and he winked at her.

"Hi."

"I'm almost done. I just need to pay for those."

"It's fine. Take your time," he told her. He didn't care; he had all day.

She picked up a bag of almonds and added them to her basket before telling him that she was all set. Even though she was thin, it seemed that she

41

ate healthily. They walked up to the cashier, and he set the basket down on the counter. Before she could get her wallet out of her little purse, Skittles had already handed over his card to the young kid at the register. He wanted to laugh at her expression. She narrowed her eyes at him but then said thank you.

He thanked the kid then grabbed the bags off the counter.

"Are you hungry?" He asked, and she smiled up at him. God, he'll never get tired of her smile.

"I could eat," she told him.

"You didn't have breakfast, did you?" He asked wryly.

"No," she replied and then laughed. "I told you yesterday that I'm not a big breakfast person."

He rolled his eyes. There were more battles to fight in order to win the war, so he let it go for now.

"Where's your bike at?" He asked.

"Right at the front entrance where the bike rack is."

They walked there to get her bike, then to his truck. He set the bags in the back seat, then lifted her bike and put it in the back of the truck.

"Your produce will be fine in the truck while we eat since it's a little chilly out," he told her, and as he opened her door and let her get in. His truck was tall, and she was having trouble getting in. He chuckled as he bent down and lifted her in. As he held her close, he closed his eyes as the smell of her shampoo wafted into his nostrils. She smelled like springtime. He knew that thought sounded a bit corny, but it was true. It was a light flowery scent. He set her down onto the seat and stared into her eyes.

She licked her bottom lip, and so badly he wanted to kiss her. But they still had a lot to discuss. Hell, he didn't know if she was involved with anyone else. He didn't think so, and he sure as hell hoped not.

"Buckle up," he whispered to her before he closed the door and ran around and jumped in the driver's side.

The Mexican restaurant was only a few miles down the road, and since there was no traffic, they made it there in minutes.

He helped her out of the truck, then took her hand and led her inside. The young hostess smiled as they walked in.

"Hi, Skittles." Then her eyes widened. "What, no laptop today?" She asked, and Skittles felt his cheeks heat up. He looked down at Anna Grace and saw her smiling back at him because now she knew what he had been doing on his laptop. He looked back at Ashley and smiled. "Nope. I found what I've been looking for." He squeezed Anna Grace's hand and boy did she feel those flutters in her belly.

Ashley then looked at Anna Grace. "I'm Ashley. I normally just like to give him a hard time. I'm glad to see he brought along someone to have a meal with other than his computer."

Anna Grace smiled. "It's nice to meet you."

"Do you want your regular table?" Ashley asked him, and he nodded.

Once they were seated by the back door, Anna Grace looked at him.

"I take it you come here often?" She teased, and he grinned.

"Now and then."

Their waiter came over and took their food and drink order since they both knew what they wanted.

"So, what do you have planned for this week?" He asked, hoping she would have that discussion with Xavier earlier in the week so they could move forward with her situation, plus he was itching to call his parents. He also wanted to talk to her about attending Alex's charity foundation event with him next weekend. It was a black-tie dinner. And he knew that Mia and Arianna wanted to reschedule the surprise birthday party for her as well.

She took a drink of her water. "Well, let's see," and she pulled out a small pocket calendar from her purse, "Tomorrow and Wednesday, I have a tennis lesson after work."

That surprised Skittles. Before she disappeared, Anna Grace had been one hell of a tennis player. As a freshman in high school, she led her team to a state championship. She had a private coach and everything. She had been on her way to a professional career. In an instant, he felt the anger start to re-emerge, and he tamped it down. That had been another gift taken from her.

"You still play?" He asked, and he could see the spark in her eyes as she answered.

"I do. After I started college, I got back into it. I didn't play for them; I was the team manager. I was afraid to put myself out there."

Skittles knew that had to have sucked. Not playing the sport you loved all because you had to protect your real identity wasn't fair.

"During college, I met a guy who was a country club member near the university. He got me an interview at the club to teach tennis lessons. Once I finished college, my boss at the club in Norfolk gave a call to his buddy who ran the tennis club here in Virginia Beach and put in a good word for me. I interviewed and was hired on the spot."

He reached across the table and took her hand.

"I'm sorry things in the tennis world didn't work out for you. I know you would've gone far."

"It's fine. I've accepted it. I like helping out at the tennis club a couple of days a week. Besides the money I make from the lessons, the club lets me play if there are courts available. Usually, though, I go and hit balls at the courts at my apartment complex since it's free."

Skittle frowned. "Speaking of your apartment, where do you live?"

She looked away just for a brief second, and Skittles knew she wasn't going to tell him. "Close by. How about you? I'm sure you live closer to Little Creek."

Before he could ask her anything else, their food arrived, and they both dug in.

Skittles pulled up to Anna Grace's apartment complex, and immediately he was pissed. He'd heard about this place, but he'd never actually been there. He never had any reason to come until now. He couldn't believe she lived here, although he already knew her days were numbered. She wouldn't be staying for long.

As they exited the truck and he went around to get her bike out of the back of the truck, he scanned the area both out of habit having to know his surroundings and also trying to see if this complex was even safe for her to stay in. Just a few seconds looking around, and he was ready to demand her to pack her shit up and move in with him.

She met him and took the bike from him. She seemed still kind of peeved at him. They argued as they were leaving the restaurant. He didn't want her to have to ride her bike back to her place, but she didn't want to accept the ride. Now he knew why. She knew he would be furious seeing where she lived. He understood she didn't have a lot, but Jesus, he'd seen better places that she could most likely afford better than the shithole he was looking at.

He pulled the two bags of fruits and vegetables out of the back seat and met her at the front of the truck. She offered him a smile, and he gave her the best one back that he could muster up. He loved seeing that smile of hers, but he couldn't take his eyes off the group of men who were huddled around the entrance of the stairwell and were now staring at them. He took her hand, and apparently, that gesture shocked her because he heard the low gasp emit from her.

As they neared the men, his alert heightened, and his grip tightened around her hand. He was ready to pull her out of the danger zone in a heartbeat. But what came out of her mouth shocked the shit out of him.

"Hey, Ziggy. How's it going?" Anna Grace greeted the first guy they approached.

Did she know these people? Was she friends with them? He wondered and hid his astonishment.

"Hey, blondie. You, okay?" The main guy dressed in a brown t-shirt and dark jeans asked Anna Grace.

Blondie?

She smiled. "Yeah, just catching up with an old friend. Have a good day."

He looked down just as Anna Grace had glanced up at him, and immediately, she started to bite her lip. *Oh yeah, sweetheart, you bet your ass we are going to be catching up.*

45

She grabbed her bike and hauled it up the flight of stairs before he could even offer to do it. He followed, and they came to an end unit on the second floor. He had to bite his tongue, seeing how shitty the lock was on her door. Anybody could pick it. Or better yet, one swift kick, and they could break down the door.

She rolled her bike inside and leaned it up against the wall by the door. He followed and closed the door behind them, locking the shitty lock, but he was at least happy to see that she had installed a deadbolt on the inside.

When he turned, he got his first look at how she had been living, and it made him hurt inside. She had the bare necessities. The apartment was tiny. It was smaller than Autumn's—Frost's wife's apartment before she met Frost, and Skittles thought that place was tiny. This was miniature everything. Hell, he could practically sit on her sofa and cook on the two-burner stove in the so-called kitchen. He set the bags down on the one counter. Before he got into her living arrangements, he needed to know about the guys they ran into downstairs.

"Are you friends with those guys out there?" He asked.

"Umm…not so much friends, but acquaintances might be a word to describe them."

"Jesus, you're not sleeping with them, are you?"

Anna Grace felt this conversation was going to go south as her eyes bugged out of her head. *What the hell?* That question she didn't see coming nor had it ever crossed her mind. *Eww…*

"What? No…"

"Then explain your relationship with them. Especially that Ziggy guy. Christ, A.G., he looked like he was ready to go all caveman and pick you up and take you to his hideaway."

"Why do you care?" She asked him, and she knew right away she had hit a hot button of his.

"Don't push me, A.G. Answer the fucking question."

46

Ok, note to self: The new Noah is total alpha-male, and why in the world did his abruptness turn her on? Jesus, she really needed help.

She ignored him as she walked to the fridge and started to put the vegetables away. She was using the few minutes to think about how to explain how she met Ziggy and why she acknowledges him and his crew.

She put the last cucumber in the drawer, turned around, and ran smack dab into a hard chest. She went to take a step back, but Skittles' large hands wrapped around her biceps, holding her in place. She looked up at his intense gaze and fierce expression.

"Holy crap…I didn't even hear you," she told him.

She caught a small smirk on his lips. But his eyes told her a different story. She needed to give him some information. So, she opted for the cliff notes version, something she was well versed in doing.

"Ziggy is harmless." When Skittles gave her a look with his eyebrows raised, she elaborated. "At least he won't harm me."

"Like that makes me feel so much better," he stated dryly. Then he pressed on. "So, you are, or you've slept with him?"

She rolled her eyes and huffed out a sigh. "Will you just shut up and let me finish."

"One night last year, I was out by the courts, and some guy was bothering me." She wasn't going to go into the full details because that would just piss him off even more, knowing the guy almost got her into his apartment. "Anyway, Ziggy and his crew happened to be hanging out by the tennis courts when the guy approached me. Ziggy intervened, and since that night nobody has ever bothered me. I know better than to associate myself with criminals. And trust me, this complex is filled with them. However, I also know to keep my head down and be cordial when needed."

"He harassed you how? And what happened to the guy?"

She should've known he'd ask for more. "Umm…He started following me, and when I was right near his door, he tried to pull me into his apartment. Ziggy and one of his guys got to me in time. His friend pulled me out while Ziggy gave him a beatdown.

Skittles was flustered as he ran his hand through his hair and gave her the stare-down that parents give their children when they're upset with them.

"Jesus Christ, A.G. Do you know what could've happened to you?"

"Yes. Yes, I do. I wasn't born yesterday. But now you know why I'm 'friendly' with Ziggy and his crew. He saved my life, Noah. I don't give a shit what they do so long as they leave me alone. Although I think Ziggy makes someone from his crew wait outside until I get off the bus and get into my apartment every night."

"Does the guy that attacked you still live around here?"

She grinned. "No. As a matter of fact, he moved out two days later."

She saw him relax, even if it was just a wee bit, and he took her hand and led her two steps to the sofa and sat down.

"I need to sit for a bit. I want to learn more about Mexico and the year you spent on the streets," he told her, and she swallowed hard.

Skittles was furious that Anna Grace was on a first-name basis with a gang. And she could spew all that shit about how friendly they were to her, but he knew the motives of people like that. They would suck you in before they struck. He didn't like it.

He took a seat on the sofa and pulled her down next to him and could see she was leery.

She surprised him when she spoke first. "Noah, I know that you still have questions about my past, and I really want to answer them, but there are things that I can't forget, though I wish I could. Things I carry around inside of me I don't like to think about."

He could relate. Being a SEAL, there was a lot of bad shit he'd been a part of and seen and had to carry around the images after missions. But he was more interested in her baggage right now.

"Like what?" He questioned.

"Noah…" She shook her head and turned away. But not before he noticed her eyes tear up.

48

He touched her shoulder and turned her toward him. She had her head down, and he lifted her chin with his fingers.

"Christ, Anna Grace. What happened to you?"

"It was so bad," she whispered out. "Bad enough that I'm even embarrassed to tell you."

"You know you can tell me anything. You don't need to be embarrassed. I'm not a judgmental guy."

She raised an eyebrow. "Really? You're a SEAL. Don't you guys judge people all the time?"

"Some. But I would never judge you."

He reached up and wiped the few tears from her cheeks. When she met his gaze, he wanted to remove the sadness from her eyes. She tried to pull her hand from his, but he squeezed it tighter, letting her know that he'd support her. He wouldn't turn his back on her no matter how bad she thought her life was, but he could see the frightened look in her expression and her eyes. He wouldn't force her to talk. He'd wait until she was ready to.

He looked across the room and saw a few LEGO sets. They were the adult Creator sets, and he got an idea. He'd apply his knowledge from his job, improvise, adapt, and overcome. He'd do whatever it took until she was comfortable telling him.

"How about we put a LEGO set together?"

She looked at him in surprise but then realized what he had just done for her. She smiled and leaned up and hugged him. And as she did, she whispered in his ear, "thank you."

CHAPTER FIVE

Senator Stan DeSmith exited the elevator on the fourth floor of the Russell Senate Office Building in Washington, D.C. Steve, his Chief of Staff, had sent him a cryptic text message while he was on the floor voting on a bill. All it said was, *get back to your office as soon as the vote is cast.*

Whatever it was had Steve worked up, but he trusted Steve with his life. There were secrets about his life that he knew Steve would take to the grave with him.

He walked into his office suite, and his secretary and scheduler both greeted him. Linda was not only his long-time secretary, but she was also his late wife's best friend. She looked at him.

"Steve's waiting for you in your office." Linda wasn't a fan of Steve. Many people weren't because of his no-nonsense attitude, but that made him the perfect Chief of Staff.

DeSmith nodded and turned to enter his private office when she stopped him. "I need to know if you've decided to attend that function in Virginia Beach for the Veterans foundation."

DeSmith wanted to roll his eyes, but he didn't. He couldn't afford not to make an appearance, considering he needed all the votes he could muster. He knew his opponent was scheduled to attend. Xavier Mayfield was gaining in the polls, and now election analysts were predicting that he could pull off the win.

There was no blood loss between the two candidates. They both had blamed each other for Sue Ellen's death, though only one was actually responsible.

His beef with Xavier stretched back to over twenty-five years ago when Xavier had been involved with DeSmith's now-deceased wife, Sue Ellen. Xavier and Sue Ellen had been close friends since they attended law school together. But it was DeSmith's infidelity that ultimately drove Sue Ellen into Xavier's arms.

DeSmith had found out that Sue Ellen saw Xavier between his Air Force deployments before she had confronted him on his cheating scandal, which had been occurring for most of their marriage. He never was a one-woman guy. But he loved money, and Sue Ellen, who was many years younger than him, was loaded.

A few months before that special election, Sue Ellen informed him that she was filing for divorce because of his indiscretions. The problem was that his career couldn't afford to go through divorce publicly, especially when he was the one at fault and especially not during an election year. It would have been a career killer. Plus, he knew what he stood to lose, monetary-wise, if she divorced him.

After her parents had died, she inherited their entire fortune. Her dad was a technology inventor. He had patents to many things that made him millions and would continue bringing in money for whoever the patents were willed to. If Sue Ellen had divorced him, he would have lost all that money he had access to.

He knew that the divorce was imminent, and she had hired a private investigator who had obtained photos of him with other women. He had actually been impressed that the mousey woman had some backbone. What she hadn't known, or at least if she did, she never called him out on, was that he had been slowly withdrawing money from a few of their shared bank accounts. That way, if she ever did leave him, he'd have a large amount of cash on hand.

Unfortunately, that wasn't the biggest news she had shared with him that day. Sure, divorce was a big thing, but there was something much more significant. She informed him that she was pregnant. Knowing that he and Sue Ellen rarely ever had sex, he was pretty positive that the baby wasn't his. He despised children and never wanted any of his own. But he knew who the baby's daddy most likely was—Xavier Mayfield considering the timing matched up during one of Xavier's trips back home.

They both agreed to separate and work through the terms of the divorce quietly. With the help of a few people in his trusted circle that included his attorney, his Press Secretary, and Steve, his COS, he had been able to thwart

51

her plans of filing anything related to the divorce until after the election. She moved out of their Alexandria waterfront home and moved south to the Hampton area, where she still had her parents' house. During the final three months of the campaign leading up to the election, Sue Ellen's absence was noticed and had been a large topic of conversation. His press secretary kept the details quiet but also pacified the press. They were told she was dealing with responsibilities relating to her family's estate. She kept her pregnancy quiet and didn't venture out too much. Nobody had a clue she was with child. He knew she hadn't been in contact with Xavier during that time because he had been watching as well as having her phones tapped. He knew it was illegal, but he had some friends in high places who owed him a favor or two.

During the campaign's home stretch, he found out that she was planning to cut him off financially. One day, she transferred most of the money out of their shared accounts and into her personal one.

That had infuriated him. Sure, he had padded his account, but he thirsted for more. He was greedy and wasn't afraid to admit it. When his attorney informed him that she was going to go after him for child support, that was where he drew the line. He didn't want anything to do with that child, let alone support it. One evening during dinner and drinks with Steve, a plan was devised, and it made sure that Sue Ellen would never be a hindrance in his life again. Nor the child who wasn't his.

He shook that time in his life from his devious mind and looked back at Linda. "I'll let you know tomorrow if I plan on attending."

"Okay. Steve left me strict instructions to not interrupt."

DeSmith quirked an eyebrow as if asking what she knew, but she just shrugged her shoulders and went back to doing whatever she was doing on the computer.

He opened the door leading into his office and saw Steve sitting in one of the two chairs positioned in front of his desk. He had a drink in hand as his foot bounced. That was never a good sign.

He walked around his desk and shrugged his suit jacket off, flinging it over the back of his chair before loosening his tie. As he looked at Steve, he

52

could already tell that whatever news he was here to deliver wasn't going to be good.

"What's going on?" He asked as he took a seat in his leather chair. It creaked as he leaned back.

Steve motioned to a folder sitting in the middle of his desk.

"Bobby delivered his latest round of material on Xavier Mayfield."

Bobby was a friend and private investigator that DeSmith used to gain dirt on his opponents during election time. He had a way of getting the nitty-gritty on anything and anyone.

"Considering the fact that you summoned me here, I'm guessing he found something significant."

When Steve didn't reply but tightened his lips, DeSmith became even more curious. He picked up the folder, and as soon as he flipped the folder open and laid eyes on the photograph sitting on top, he swore his heart stopped beating.

There was no possible way it could be her. She should be in Mexico or somewhere far from Virginia serving as someone's bitch. Once DeSmith's transaction with Senor Castillo was complete, he cut all ties with Castillo, making sure nothing could be traced back to him.

"Where was this taken?" He asked Steve as he unbuttoned the top two buttons of his shirt. He felt his body temperature rising, meaning his blood pressure was rising at a seemingly alarming rate. He reached for a bottle of water sitting on his desk and took a slug of it.

"Last week, when Xavier was delivering food to the homeless shelter. She was there volunteering."

DeSmith stared at the picture, still in disbelief. He wondered if this could be someone's form of a sick joke and had the picture photoshopped. That couldn't be it either, because only a handful of individuals knew the details surrounding that time in his life, and all of them, except for one currently sitting in front of him, were dead.

He raised his eyes to where they met Steve's. "How is she even here, let alone connected to my opponent? Senor Castillo assured me that she would never be a hindrance to me."

He began to feel a little squeamish. Could she know the truth and was here and working with Xavier to bring him down in front of the world? *Jesus, this could be a disaster in the making.* He could already see the headlines now, not to mention the charges that could be brought against him.

When Steve removed his wire-rimmed glasses and pinched the bridge of his nose, he knew it was only going to get worse.

"After Bobby showed me all that he found and I saw the picture, I started searching for answers." DeSmith raised his eyebrows. "There was an incident about ten years ago involving Senor Castillo and his sons. The details are sketchy, but it appears that all three were gunned down in cold blood. It was rumored that Jorge had been involved in the cartel that controlled that part of the state. The news down there says it could've been a hit from a rival cartel."

"What about Anna Grace? Any idea how she ended up back here and what she's doing?"

"Bobby said she goes by Grace Montgomery now, and she works at an animal rescue shelter in Virginia Beach."

"Got an address?"

Steve shook his head. "No. We can't find anything in her name. However, she did attend Old Dominion. According to the university records, she graduated three years ago."

DeSmith quirked one of his bushy eyebrows. "She graduated three years ago? Tack on four more years of getting through college, and that amounts to seven years in total that she's been right here under our noses?" DeSmith questioned in an angry tone.

"She attended on a scholarship. And not just any scholarship, I might add. She was the recipient of the Ralph Mickens Scholarship."

DeSmith drew in his eyebrows. That was a familiar name, but he couldn't place it.

"Why do I know that name?"

"Ralph Mickens was the former State's Attorney. He passed away years ago after a brief battle with pancreatic cancer. He was also the father of the now Melanie Mayfield."

54

DeSmith's eyebrows jumped at that detail.

"Interesting," DeSmith said as he took another look at the picture of a very grown-up, Anna Grace Silver. She had matured into a gorgeous woman. But he learned long ago that no matter how pretty a woman was, their beauty couldn't hide the mayhem they could cause. And DeSmith was quite sure that Anna Grace Silver shared the same trait as her mother, Sue Ellen, who was beautiful and brilliant.

"I don't like it that she's close to Xavier."

"What do you want to do?" Steve asked, and DeSmith gave him a deadpan look.

"You took care of the problem once before; make it happen again."

CHAPTER SIX

Anna Grace was mopping the floor where Astro, one of the dogs, had an accident when she heard the bell ring signaling that someone had entered the main door.

She couldn't stop the smile from sweeping across her face, knowing it was most likely Noah there to pick her up.

She was a little nervous because even though she knew they were supposed to go to dinner at Bayside, he had told her there was another surprise. She didn't have a good track record when it came to surprises.

She rinsed out the mop and put it away in the closet, then made one more pass through the kennels, making sure all the dogs were good for the night. She got to the door and dimmed the lights. She took one last look around before she entered the front room.

She pushed open the door and came to a stop when she saw a woman standing at the counter with her back toward the door. When she turned, Anna Grace was in awe. The woman was beautiful. She had dark brown hair that fell below her shoulders and was cut into long layers, but it was her sparkling green eyes that drew attention toward her. They were stunning, especially with how the black pantsuit brought the color out even more. She was very put together, whereas Anna Grace wasn't.

The woman smiled. "Hi, are you Anna Grace?"

The sound of her biological name rolling off the woman's tongue had Anna Grace taking a step backward and making sure she put the counter between them. Just because the woman was pretty didn't mean she couldn't be the enemy. That was another lesson she had learned back in Mexico; the friendly ones were the least ones to be trusted. She often found herself in hot water and at the mercy of Senor Castillo because she was naïve and was played by smarter people who disliked her and thought she didn't belong there.

"Can I help you?" Anna Grace asked cautiously. It wasn't like she had anything around to protect herself with unless a pooper scooper was considered a weapon.

"I'm Alex." She stepped forward extending her hand and instantly Anna Grace took another step backward.

The woman must have noticed because she dropped her hand and her smile quickly disappeared.

"I'm sorry. I didn't mean to frighten you. Skittles sent me. He's running late at work and asked if I could swing by and pick you up."

Anna Grace looked her over.

"How do you know Noah?"

Alex smiled. "Mia's brother, Ace, is my fiancé. He works with Skittles. Err, Noah." She smiled. "Sorry, I'm used to their nicknames."

She pulled her bottom lip between her teeth, feeling slightly embarrassed. But in her defense, she had major trust issues and still had to be on guard.

"I had to take something over to the base, and I ran into the guys. They said they were called in for a meeting, and Skittles knew you'd be waiting on him. He wasn't sure how long he'd be, so he asked if I could swing by and get you. He said he would try to call to give you a heads up. But I'm guessing from your reaction that he didn't get around to doing that."

Anna Grace realized that the phone calls she received while cleaning the kennels were probably Skittles trying to reach her. Then she felt embarrassed that Skittles had asked someone to pick her up. Sometimes she hated not having a driver's license and a car.

"I'm sorry, you didn't have to do that. I can just ride my bike home."

Alex grinned. "He said you'd say that. He gave me strict instructions to not take no for an answer."

Of course, he did, she thought to herself.

"Are you sure?"

"Positive," Alex stated with a smile on her face.

As Alex and Anna Grace drove through town, Alex could see Anna Grace fidgeting giving away that she was nervous. From what Skittles had shared with her, her heart broke for the young woman. Knowing what Skittles had planned for her tonight, Alex wanted to get that nervousness out of her system, but she understood how hard it could be.

"So, this will be your first dinner with the whole gang."

Anna Grace turned her head toward Alex and nodded. "Yeah, but I'll be honest, I'm nervous."

Alex gave her a reassuring smile. "Don't be. There's no need to be nervous around any of us. Just think of everyone tonight as family. You know Arianna, Mia, Dino, and Stitch already. Now you know me. Everyone is super nice."

Anna Grace just nodded her head, and Alex could still see that she wasn't breaking down any of the walls.

Alex pulled into the shopping plaza that was on the way to Bayside and parked her Escalade in front of the bridal shop. She wanted to laugh when Anna Grace scrunched her forehead up as she looked through the windshield at the store. Then she turned toward Alex.

"Why are we here?"

Alex pulled Skittles' credit card out of her purse and held it up for Anna Grace to see, though she wasn't sure how Anna Grace would react to Skittles wanting to buy her a dress for the black-tie charity event this weekend.

"Another direct order from Skittles was to take you shopping for a dress for the charity event this weekend. The one he invited you to."

Anna Grace's eyes got huge, and she started to shake her head, but Alex intervened before she could argue.

"This was Skittles' idea. He said that you didn't have a dress to wear. I tried to tell him that you could borrow one of mine or from one of the other ladies, but he insisted that you have your very own."

"Alex, I can't afford a brand-new dress. I was planning on going to one of the consignment shops in town that I know sells secondhand dresses."

Alex smiled. "That is why I have this." She held up the credit card again. "This is Skittles', and he said for you to pick out a dress and that he's paying for it."

"Why would he do that? Good god, the man stocked me up on groceries a few days ago, and now he wants to buy me a dress?"

Alex laughed. "Get used to it. He cares about you. And believe me, when the guys get something in their head, there's no stopping them."

Anna Grace grabbed Alex's hand as she went to exit the vehicle. "I don't want to be a charity case for him."

Alex frowned. "Skittles would never treat anyone like that. You don't get it yet, but you will in time. I understand a little about how you feel. When I first met the guys during a mission, I was a little stubborn and set in my ways like you. But over time, I realized how caring each of those eight men on that team is—Skittles included."

"You were on a mission with them?" Alex chuckled at how big Anna Grace's eyes got.

"Yeah. One day I'll tell you a little about it." She smiled. "Well, at least the parts that aren't classified."

Alex hated reliving that trip to Afghanistan, but if it helped Anna Grace realize that these guys were the real deal and cared for women, then she'd suck it up. She patted Anna Grace's hand. "Come on, let's just go in and see what we can find for you. Who knows, maybe they won't have anything you like."

❧

Skittles stood at the bar with Dino as they waited for Alex to arrive with Anna Grace.

Alex had sent him a text about ten minutes ago letting them know that they were on the way. Since the last birthday party for Anna Grace sort of went haywire, Skittles wanted to make it up to her. So, he planned another birthday dinner. This time it was sort of a surprise. She thought they were just having dinner with the team.

"Hey, isn't that Xavier Mayfield, the guy running against Senator DeSmith?" Dino asked, and Skittles turned towards the entrance as Xavier walked in with his wife, Melanie.

Skittles nodded as he watched Derek greet the couple. Once again, Alex had come through. She apparently knew Xavier through her connections and had given him a call to invite him to the little surprise party for A.G.

"It is. Anna Grace knows him and his wife," Skittles responded to Dino's question.

"Sounds like there's a backstory to their relationship."

"There is. If it weren't for Xavier and Melanie, there's no telling where A.G. would be right now. Anna Grace volunteers for his campaign."

"Well, if he didn't already have my vote, he'd have it now. Did you hear that fucking DeSmith voted to slash the military's budget?"

Skittles had heard about that, and the primary election couldn't come fast enough. DeSmith needed to be voted out. All he did was tell people what they wanted to hear, and as soon as he was re-elected, he'd renege on every promise he made to the people of the state of Virginia.

"I know it's only been a few days, but has she opened up anymore? You know, specifics of what went down in Mexico?"

Skittles shook his head. "No. And I don't want to push. She asked for patience, so I'm trying my best to oblige."

"That's understandable. Have you talked with her about going to the cops?"

"I have, and she asked to wait until she could talk to Xavier, which I hope she'll do tonight. That's partially why I wanted to invite him. I also knew she'd be more comfortable around people she knows."

Skittles felt his phone vibrate and saw the message from Alex letting him know they had arrived, and he quickly got everyone in place.

Anna Grace was talking up a storm with Alex when they arrived at Bayside. Alex was very easy to talk to, and she appreciated that she didn't try and ask questions. She could definitely see herself becoming friends with her. Alex was genuine and not one of those women who would blow smoke up your ass just to get them to like you. She was honest and straightforward.

Alex had given Anna Grace a tiny peek into her life and told her about when she was a little girl and her dad was killed during a mission, and how Derek, the team's commander, who was also her dad's best friend and teammate at the time, adopted her.

She had been so engrossed in the conversation with Alex as they walked through the doors of Bayside that she hadn't seen all the people standing there or all of the balloons until everyone shouted, SURPRISE, and nearly sent her running back out the door again. Thank goodness Alex had looped her arm through hers and had held her in place.

Skittles was the first one to approach her, and even though he was smiling, she could see the concern in his eyes. He greeted her with a big hug, and she immediately hugged him back.

"You, okay?" He whispered to her, and she couldn't help but be touched by his caring words.

"Yeah, just a little surprised," she whispered back, and she pulled away to look up at him. He gave her that boyish grin that made her stomach do flips.

"I figured since your first birthday dinner didn't fare well, that we'd have a re-do."

When he said, "I," that was when she realized that he had coordinated this for her. She looked around at all the smiles that everyone offered her, and for the first time in ten years, she felt wanted and part of something. She looked back up at Skittles and smiled. "Thank you."

"You're welcome. Come on. Arianna put together a buffet consisting of grilled chicken breast, sliced prime rib, mashed potatoes and gravy, green beans and rolls."

Her stomach growled as he ticked off each food item. She hadn't had much to eat that day, so she was more than hungry.

She held onto his arm as he walked with her over to the two large tables set up for the party. On the way, he introduced her to everyone who she hadn't met yet.

61

The first couple she was introduced to was Potter and Tenley, their daughter Alejandra who was seven years old, and their babies Kensi and Kelsey. Diego was standing nearby, so she met him next. She then ran into Frost and Autumn and their eleven-year-old son Cody. Autumn, the fiery redhead, as Skittles called her, was almost six months pregnant, and she was glowing. As they went further down the line, they came to the next family of three who were all blonde and blue eyes. Skittles introduced them as Irish and Bailey and their six-year-old daughter Sienna who was freaking adorable. When she reached out to shake Sienna's hand, Sienna had asked her if she was her Uncle Skittles' "special friend." Hearing all the kids call everyone affiliated with the team Aunt or Uncle stated just how close this group was to one another, and it touched her deep inside.

Alex walked up with a man who she assumed was Ace based on his striking blue eyes. Earlier, when she was trying on dresses, Alex explained to her how Ace's eyes had captivated her the first time she had met him, and now Anna Grace understood why. He was a very handsome man, and she could see the love he held for Alex as he held her close to his side.

Ace reached his hand out. "Hi, Anna Grace. I'm Ace."

She shook his hand. "Hi, it's nice to meet you."

With everything she had read in the last few days about SEALs, she had the impression she'd face a bunch of muscle heads with egos the size of the earth. But she was wrong. These men were the complete opposite. She couldn't believe how gentle and caring all of them were as they spoke with her.

Another couple walked up next to Ace and Alex, and they appeared older than the rest of the group. Alex introduced them.

"Anna Grace, this is Derek and Juliet. Derek is the one I told you about on the way here. And Juliet is Tenley's mom."

Anna Grace smiled at the couple and shook their hands.

"It is so nice to meet you both," she said.

"It's a pleasure to be able to meet you too, honey," Derek told her. "If you ever need anything, don't hesitate to reach out. We all sort of look out for each other. It's how we operate here at home."

Anna Grace didn't think her heart could grow anymore before it would burst out of her chest. It was like living in a real-life fairytale with how the group interacted.

Skittles leaned down close to her ear, and when he spoke, his warm breath hit her skin, making goosebumps break out along her arms and other parts of her body tingle.

"There's two more people who want to say hi."

She looked up at him, wondering who else there could be. When he took her shoulders and turned her around toward the bar, and she met the gaze of the two individuals standing there, she felt the waterworks turn on.

"You invited them?" She asked Skittles while motioning to Xavier and Melanie.

He smiled. "It was my idea to invite them, but it was Alex's connections that made it happen."

She squeezed him around his waist, then walked over to Alex and pulled her into a hug.

"Thank you," she whispered to Alex as she got choked up.

Alex hugged her back. "They were thrilled to come."

Anna Grace pulled back and wiped her eyes as Xavier and Melanie came over and hugged her and wished her a Happy Birthday.

She couldn't stop smiling. This was the best birthday she'd had in the last ten years.

She glanced over at Xavier. "So, I hear you know Alex."

"Sure do. Alex is a staple in this community with everything she's doing to help out veterans and their families."

"Speaking of that, it's only fair that I warn you that Senator DeSmith is attending with a group. His scheduler called yesterday and confirmed." Alex said with a smile. "But I have them sitting in the back while your table is reserved upfront with all of us."

"Thank you, Alex. And that's fine. It'll be nice to see him squirm."

"I'm actually surprised he even responded because every other invite I've sent him just as a courtesy, he's declined. He didn't even show up for the ribbon-cutting ceremony. He RSVP'd then never showed. No call, nothing. So, it is perplexing why all of a sudden now he has shown an interest in the foundation, not to mention, purchased a two-thousand-dollar table."

"Simple. He wants votes," Ace said as he put his arm around Alex's shoulders and pulled her close to his side.

"But everyone knows he never carries this area in an election. The military community dislikes him because of his stance on certain agenda items concerning their livelihood, not to mention how he's always looking to cut funds geared toward service members and veterans."

"Well, we'll just have to wait and see," Xavier said, and everyone agreed.

"You guys will get to meet Charlotte—well, Charlie, as she likes to be called."

"Who's that?" Skittles asked.

"She's the new office manager I hired for the foundation." Alex glanced up at Ace and smiled, and he winked at her. "I finally realized that I needed an extra person to help with some of the administrative tasks, so I recruited some help. Anyways, Charlie is awesome. She comes from a family with a strong military background, but unfortunately, she's had to deal with the not-so-good aspects of it. Her dad was a Lieutenant Colonel in the Army. On his last deployment, his helicopter was hit by enemy fire and went down. There were no survivors. She also had a brother who was a Ranger. Charlie said when he came back from his last tour, he wasn't the same person. He committed suicide a few months later."

"Damn. That's awful," Skittles said.

"Yeah, but that's why she's very active in educating people about PTSD."

Skittles smiled at Alex. "It's about time you slow down a little. You've done so much to help this community just in the short time since your foundation launched, but you've had to sacrifice a lot on a personal level."

Ace slid his hands down Alex's arms before he wrapped his arms around her waist. "Yeah, like maybe planning our wedding," he told Alex and Anna Grace didn't think Alex's smile could get any bigger as her eyes lit up looking at her fiancé.

As the conversation started to die down, everyone congregated toward the tables to eat.

෧

Skittles was in line with everyone else getting food when Alex walked up and stood next to him.

"Here," She said, handing his credit card back to him.

He eyed it then looked back at her. "You used it, right?" Before he took it back, he wanted to make sure that Anna Grace had bought a dress for the charity event.

Alex beamed. "She did, and you're going to love it. Remind me to get it out of my car before you leave tonight."

That made him smile, and he knew she would look beautiful in whatever she had bought. "Thank you again for helping me out with that."

She waved him off. "You know I'd do anything for you guys."

And that was a true statement. Alex was the backbone of their little unit here at home, though she also saved their asses in Afghanistan. He still got the chills thinking how close the entire team had almost been blown to smithereens. If it hadn't been for Alex's keen eye, none of them would be standing here right now.

Once everyone had food, they all sat around the tables talking and laughing. Many of the women told Anna Grace stories about the team.

He watched A.G. closely through the evening, making sure she was enjoying herself. There were times he noticed where she seemed to get a little quiet, and her eyes would glaze over, but she would quickly pull herself together and act as if it never happened. He was proud of her.

He heard Alejandra, Potter, and Tenley's little girl talking at the other end of the table. The moment he heard the word penis come out of her mouth, he wasn't sure if he wanted to laugh at Potter's shocked expression or keep quiet so he could hear the rest of what she had to say. Those kids made get-togethers very entertaining—especially for those who weren't their parents.

Skittles opted to listen to what the seven-year-old had to say to the table.

"Did you know that when an octopus reproduces, it removes its penis and throws it at the females so she can impregnate herself? But then he grows back another one? It's really cool."

Alejandra turned toward Potter, who had his face all contorted as he stared at his little girl in shock.

"Daddy, is that how mommy got pregnant with Kensi and Kelsey?"

The snickers at the table weren't subtle; in fact, some of the guys were chuckling, himself included.

Potter's head whipped around towards Tenley so fast that Skittles thought it might fly off his shoulders. Tenley was known to have a big mouth at times, though she was funny to listen to most of the time.

"Did you tell her that?" Potter asked, and Tenley's eyes widened as if she was guilty, but then she burst out laughing.

Alejandra jumped from her chair into Potter's lap and placed her hands on his cheeks. "Daddy, don't blame mommy. I was with Aunt Alex when I learned that." She scolded him, and holy shit, was this getting good. You just never knew what was going to fly out of these kids' mouths.

Before Potter could get a word in, Alex threw her hands up in the air. "Hey, I didn't tell her that. She and I were watching some show on the Animal Planet channel, and they were talking about it."

Suddenly, Sienna, Irish's little girl who was watching and listening intently, turned toward Irish, and Skittles saw the gleam and curiosity in her eyes. She was getting ready to interject herself into the conversation when Irish stood up and plucked Sienna from her chair and walked toward one of the video games on the other side of the room.

Skittles couldn't contain his laughter any longer and laughed out loud along with the others. Though Potter was still looking at his daughter as if she had two heads. Skittles turned toward Anna Grace and explained what happened during Christmas dinner when Sienna informed everyone that she had a pussy. However, after getting over the shock of that coming out of a six-year-old's mouth and a little coaxing, they all realized she was referring to her pussy cat, Mr. Whiskers.

66

Anna Grace covered her mouth to hide her laughter, and Skittles beamed as he looked around the table, seeing smiles and laughter coming from everyone. This right here was what Skittles loved about their little unit, and he was glad to have the opportunity to introduce Anna Grace to it. Over time, he knew she'd fit right in.

Anna Grace excused herself to go to the restroom. She had been having a good time and enjoying all of the conversations, but she needed a little break just for a few minutes.

She bypassed their table on her way back from the restroom, seeing the door to the back patio deck.

The cool night air felt good against her face, and she took a deep, cleansing breath. She walked over to the railing and stood there looking out at the ocean, watching the waves roll onto the beach.

She closed her eyes and tilted her head towards the sky. A slight breeze blowing in off the ocean caressed her cheeks, and she smiled. She felt free.

"Are you okay?"

Anna Grace turned around, surprised to hear someone behind her. Irish's wife, Bailey, stood there looking at her.

"I just needed some fresh air."

"I know I shouldn't tell you this, but if you ever need a breather and don't want anyone to know, there's a side door back by the bathrooms."

Anna Grace glanced over at Bailey, and the blonde hair blue-eyed girl gave her a sympathetic smile.

"I've been in your shoes before. It can be overwhelming when the group gets together."

"It's a great group," Anna Grace said. "But I think I've been a little on edge thinking that one of them would start to ask me questions about my past."

Bailey furrowed her eyebrows as if confused.

"I feel more comfortable about you and the other ladies. Almost as if you guys get it and can understand what I'm going through."

"That's because we probably do. I don't know what happened to you, but Alex, Tenley, Autumn, Mia, Arianna, and myself all have stories of our own survival."

Anna Grace knew a little about Mia's story, and from what Alex had told her in the car earlier, she figured something had happened to her, but she hadn't realized that all of them had something bad happen to them.

"Really?"

Bailey nodded her head. "Yeah, and I'll be honest. If it wasn't for that group inside, I don't think I'd be alive right now."

Anna Grace was intrigued. Bailey smiled. "Come sit with me for a few minutes. I'll tell you about it, and that'll give you a little bit of time to gather your wits."

They sat down at one of the tables. They were the only two out on the deck.

"Long story short, my parents were trying to arrange a marriage for me to gain access to my inheritance. They were and still are evil people. They are currently living the rest of their lives in a federal prison. There was a guy who my parents were trying to make me marry. He made my life a living hell for a few months. That's how I ended up here in Virginia Beach. I loved teaching and got a job at one of the elementary schools here in town. That's where I sort of met Irish." Bailey laughed and had a look on her face as if she remembered it all over again. "Well, I actually met Irish at this very place, out in the parking lot near closing time, in the pouring rain. My car got a flat tire, and while I was trying to change it, my prince charming appeared and literally scared the hell out of me." She laughed again. "Anyway, for a few weeks, I couldn't get him out of my mind, and I never saw him again—until he showed up in my classroom with his niece, Sienna."

Anna Grace was confused. "I thought Sienna was your daughter."

"She is now. Irish and I adopted her last year. I love her like my own."

Anna Grace had always dreamt of having a husband and family of her own one day.

"Needless to say, Irish and I were both surprised to see each other and come to find out, we both had been looking for each other. He was very aggressive but in a good way. I, on the other hand, I was scared to trust or get involved with a guy."

"Because of the guy back home who your parents wanted you to marry?" Anna Grace asked her.

"Yeah, but as you can see, it all worked out. However, it wasn't easy; my past returned with a vengeance. He tried to take both me and Sienna, but I wasn't bound to let him harm that little girl. I fought hard, and I paid the price, but I got her to safety. I ended up at a private airport being led to a private jet when the calvary arrived. The guy who had me tried to shoot Irish and the guys, but again, I wasn't letting anyone hurt my family, so I tried to take the gun away. The guy and I struggled, and we both fell to the ground. The gun went off, and I ended up with a bullet in my lower stomach."

Anna Grace covered her mouth. "Bailey, I'm so sorry."

"Don't be. I'm alive, and I have my family. The odds of having my own baby are slim because of my injuries, but what matters most is I'm here today."

"Thank you for sharing your story with me. And I'm glad you recovered from your injuries and found love and a family."

"That's what friends are for. I'm sure Alex already told you that we're all sort of our own little unit. We look after each other and help one another if need be. I can tell you right now that every single one of those people sitting at that table inside would have your back in a heartbeat."

Anna Grace looked through the window at the table where Skittles and the others were all sitting. Could it really be that great? She wondered.

Bailey placed her hand on Anna Grace's arm. "Give it a chance, and you'll see how good things can be."

Bailey stood up. "I'll let Skittles know you'll be in shortly."

Anna Grace thanked her and followed her with her eyes as she walked through the door back inside and watched with envy as Irish went right to her and wrapped her in a hug.

She turned back toward the water and thought about everything Bailey shared with her. She was like the others, but now she just had to learn to let her guard down.

Moments later, she heard the door open and knew it was Noah—or Skittles, as his friends call him. She needed to ask him how he managed to get a nickname like that.

❧

Skittles was on his way toward the patio door when he saw Bailey come back inside. As their paths crossed, he stopped her. He had seen Anna Grace skirt the table and head outside while on her way back from the restroom. As he was getting up to go and make sure everything was okay, he had seen Bailey follow her, so he gave them some time to talk.

"Is she okay?" He asked, motioning toward where Anna Grace was sitting outside with her back turned away from them.

Bailey smiled. "Yeah. She just needed some fresh air. You know how we girls can get a little overwhelmed, especially when one of us is the newbie." She winked, and Skittles understood what she was saying. And Bailey wasn't wrong. He knew it was hard for an outsider to come into a group or family such as theirs and not feel intimidated.

"She's hurting inside and holding back, but just from what I've heard about her ordeal, which isn't a lot, it's understandable. I told her a little about what I went through with my parents and Randy. I thought maybe opening up to her and letting her know that she isn't alone may help her come to terms with what she's holding in."

"Thank you, Bailey." He leaned down and kissed her cheek.

"I like her a lot, and I hope she becomes a permanent member of our family," Bailey told him, and Skittles smiled.

"Me too," he replied and looked out the window where Anna Grace was sitting by the railing, looking out at the water.

"Just give her some time to open up. She will eventually," Bailey said before she walked back over to the table.

70

Skittles knew Bailey was right, and as much as he wanted to know all about what Anna Grace went through, he had to be patient and not force it. But it wouldn't hurt to keep reminding her that he was always there for her.

He pushed the door open and walked outside. He took the seat next to her but didn't say anything. She continued to stare at the horizon. The moon was large and was a sight as it hovered over the rippling water.

"Xavier and I are having lunch next week. I told him there was something I needed to talk to him about and that it was important," she said, then looked over at him. "I know you were probably hoping I'd speak to him tonight, but it just wasn't the right time or place to discuss that."

Skittles reached over and took her hand and placed their joined hands on his leg.

"It's a step in the right direction."

"You're not upset?"

His expression softened. "Why would I be upset?"

"Because I know how badly you want me to talk with the police."

"I do. But it's because I want you to have your life back. But I'm not going to push you."

She gave him a small smile. "I won't ever get back the ten years I missed of being Anna Grace Silver. I missed out on a lot of things, but you know what, that's okay because I'm still alive. I may not have the life I imagined I'd have, but I've come to terms with it."

Skittles leaned closer to her and placed his palms against her cheeks and gazed into her unique violet-colored eyes.

"Now that you have me, let me help you close the door to your past life of the last ten years, and let's together pick a new door to open."

She grinned. "I might be able to do that."

He smiled, then leaned toward her and kissed her forehead. Again, he really wanted to kiss her on the lips, but he wasn't sure if she'd be ready for that yet. He was content, for now.

CHAPTER SEVEN

Skittles sat on the couch in his living room, fiddling with the television remote. He wasn't really interested in anything that was on; he was just buying time while he waited for Anna Grace to call him so they could go to dinner. He looked down at his watch. She should've called by now since she had told him last night when he dropped her off that she got off work at four. It was now six, and he was a little worried.

Since last Sunday he had spent all his free time with her except for the two nights she had tennis lessons. Those nights he settled for talking to her over the phone. He'd admit that it killed him to be away from her.

He waited another fifteen minutes before he tried calling her cell phone, but it went straight to voicemail. He debated on what to do. Should he go over to her apartment to see if she was there or just wait for her to reach out?

Waiting around when he knew he could do something wasn't his forte. In his line of work, they got in, got shit done, and got out. At least that was how it was supposed to work. Sometimes the shit hits the fan, and their plans were altered—sometimes even multiple times.

He paced his apartment. "*Screw this,*" he mumbled and picked up his phone and car keys.

As he walked down to his truck, he called Arianna, thinking maybe she had heard from her.

"Hello?"

"Hey Arianna, it's Skittles."

"Hey, what's up?" He could tell from the music and chatter in the background that she was working at Bayside.

"You don't by chance know where Anna Grace might be, do you?"

"No, why?"

"We were supposed to have dinner, but she hasn't called."

"Did you try calling her?"

"Yeah, but it goes straight to voicemail."

"My only guess would be that she's still at the shelter. Maybe call there or drive over and see if she's there."

Of course, that was what any average person would think to do, but he was flustered, and that was impeding his commonsense thought process.

"Thanks. I'll drive over there."

"Let me know if you don't find her."

"Will do."

Skittles parked his truck in front of the shelter. For a few seconds, he felt a sense of relief when he saw Anna Grace's bike leaning against the side of the building.

He got out and walked inside. He was surprised when he saw Mia still there.

She smiled. "Hi, Skittles."

He gave her a chin lift. "Hey."

"Are you here to see Anna Grace?"

"Is she here? I've been worried. She and I were supposed to have dinner when she got off work, but she never called."

Mia's eyes widened. "Shit!"

"What?"

"She sort of had a little accident today."

Skittles chest tightened, wondering how significant 'little' was in Mia's terms.

"What happened? Is she okay?" He fired on the questions, and Mia held her hand up.

"She's fine, and yes, she's here. Beretta got a little too playful today and knocked her down, and she hit her head on the edge of the picnic table."

"Did she get checked out?"

"Yeah, I drove her over to Alex's clinic, and one of the doctors took a look at her. He thinks she just has a mild concussion."

"She has a concussion, and she's still here?" He questioned, wondering why she hadn't gone home. He was sure that was what the doctor probably told her to do. Jesus, she was still stubborn.

Mia walked closer. "She's still here. In fact, she is out back with Beretta right now. She felt bad that she hadn't gotten to work with him."

Skittles stared at Mia as if she had grown horns. "He's a dog. I'm sure he wouldn't have minded."

Mia shook her head. "You don't understand. Anna Grace thinks of these animals as if they're just like you and me. She isn't someone who likes to disappoint nor let others down if she can help it." She offered him a small smile. "If it helps settle your nerves, I've been checking on her since we got back. I promise you that she's fine."

He ran his hand down his face thinking how foolish he probably seemed. He needed to take a step back and breathe. It wasn't until now that he realized he was afraid. He was terrified of losing her again.

As if knowing what he was feeling, Mia nudged his arm. "Come on, I'll walk with you."

As soon as Mia opened the door to the outside, he heard that sweet laughter that brought an instant smile to his face, and it hit a soft spot in his heart. He wanted to listen to that sound all the time.

Neither Anna Grace nor the dog had heard them come out. Anna Grace was taking the dog through some sort of makeshift obstacle course. As the dog made his way towards the end and crouched and crawled through a tube, Skittles realized who the dog was.

He looked at Mia. "Is that Beretta, the dog from Team Four who was injured a few months ago, that they were going to put down?"

Mia smiled and nodded. "Sure is. Amazing, isn't it?" She asked as she stood next to him and watched the pair.

"Anna Grace is a natural with animals, especially the dogs."

"I can see that."

"Stitch had told me about the dog's injuries and what they were planning to do, and it broke my heart. I knew I had to try and fight for the pup even though I knew my chances were pretty slim to convince them to let me *adopt* and rehabilitate him. I asked Stitch to give the base vet my number. They had flat out told me no at first. But I kept pestering them, and finally, I sort of used an ally, or maybe two, who helped me win my case, and they made an exception. But the agreement is that we have to provide reports every week on his progress, and they are free to pop in whenever they want to come in and evaluate him."

They both watched in awe as a dog who had been deemed unrecoverable ran around the yard as if he hadn't just months ago been a victim of a horrific IED blast that left three members of the team critically wounded.

A lot of people don't realize that animals can suffer from PTSD just like humans. They just show it differently. Beretta hadn't been the same dog since coming home from that traumatic ordeal on the outskirts of Bagdad, Iraq.

"Beretta and Anna Grace formed an incredible bond from the get-go. It's too bad we can't adopt him out. That was part of the agreement. He has to stay here."

At that moment, Anna Grace turned, and the smile on her face hit him hard in the gut. She seemed so happy, as if in another world while she worked with the dogs. It was indeed a sight to take in.

Mia's phone rang, and she excused herself to answer it. He, on the other hand, walked toward where Anna Grace stood with Beretta by her side.

As he approached, he saw her say something to the dog, and he sat down right beside her and eyed him as he moved closer. Beretta's tongue was hanging out of his mouth as Anna Grace stroked his fur.

She smiled. "Hi," she said, looking up and giving him that megawatt smile of hers.

"Hi."

She looked down at Beretta, and he followed.

"Can I pet him?" He asked.

"Sure." He went to reach his hand out, and she followed up with, "He only nips a little." He pulled his hand back quickly but then saw the amusement on her face. He smirked and pointed his finger at her.

"Trouble."

She laughed but then told him it was fine to pet him.

He gave Beretta a scratch behind the ears.

"Beretta, meet Noah. Noah, meet Beretta."

She said something to the dog in a different language, and the dog lifted his left paw.

Skittles grinned and reached to shake the paw. He noticed the area on the dog's leg where the fur grew back around the long scar.

He released the dog's paw then Anna Grace walked over to the nearby tree and sat down on the ground. Skittles followed.

"Mind if I sit?"

Instead of answering, she peered over at Beretta. "What do you think, boy? Should we invite him to join us?"

The dog barked then licked her cheek, making her giggle, and it was music to Skittles' ears. She looked up at him, and her eyes were sparkling.

"I think that means yes," she told him with a grin.

She scooted over, making room for him under the tree. He lowered himself and mimicked her position, stretching out his legs. When their thighs touched, it set off a sensation that traveled throughout his body.

She leaned over and nudged his arm.

"What brings you here?" She asked, and he tilted his head to the side as he looked at her. Then he glanced at his watch.

"I thought we were meeting for an early dinner."

Watching her eyes expand was amusing. But then, when she lowered them and appeared sad, he wasn't sure what to make of it. Until he remembered what Mia had said earlier about how Anna Grace hated to disappoint people.

He lifted her chin with his fingers, and when her eyes met his, he recognized the emotion swirling around her purple irises. She felt as if she had let him down.

"What's the matter?" He asked.

"I'm sorry. I got caught up working with Beretta, and I completely forgot."

He smiled, trying to put her at ease. "It's okay."

She shook her head. "It's not okay. It frustrates me when I feel like I've disappointed someone. Especially those close to me."

"A.G., look at me." She turned her head in his direction and tilted it upward to look at him. "You didn't disappoint me. Nor am I upset. I was worried."

"You were?"

"Yeah. More so when Mia told me that you bumped your head and the doctor believed you had a concussion."

He watched as the redness appeared in her cheeks, and she looked away. She touched an area on the back of her head.

"Yeah. Beretta got a little excited when he and I were dancing."

Skittles scrunched his eyebrows together. "Dancing?"

She smiled. "Yeah, dancing. You get the dog up on their hind legs, and while you're holding their front legs, you sway side to side, and then you start to 'dance' by taking steps forward, backward, and sideways. It's an exercise to improve mobility. However, my little dance partner here thought we were doing the Texas two-step and got a little carried away." She laughed again, and it made Skittles chuckle too.

She looked at him. "So, what did you have in mind for dinner?"

"Well, I did have this big elaborate—"

Anna Grace smacked him in playfully in the arm. "Oh, stop it. Now you're really trying to make me feel bad."

He put his arm around her shoulders and laughed as he pulled her into his side. He smiled to himself when she leaned her weight against him and rested her hand on his thigh. She had no clue what her gentle touch did to him. The warmth from her hand spread throughout his body.

He hadn't shown as much affection toward her as he had wanted out of fear of her reaction. Not really knowing what she truly had experienced during her time in captivity, he didn't want to cross any lines until he knew it was safe to do so. But to get to that point, he needed to get her to open up to him.

For now, he'd play it safe, and instead of kissing her like he really wanted to do, he opted for a compromise and kissed the side of her head.

Beretta then decided to join the party and collapsed on top of A.G.'s legs.

"I guess he felt left out," she said in amusement.

"Seems like you guys formed a pretty incredible bond. Especially considering what he went through and probably still deals with."

She stroked his fur. "He and I are a lot alike."

"How so?"

"We both were on our own with no future."

Her response jolted him, and he couldn't help but think where she'd be now, even months or years down the road, if he hadn't found her. But he fully understood what she was trying to say, and she was right. She was on her own.

"But you're not now. Not anymore."

She smiled softly. "And neither is Beretta because he has me." Her smiled faded and soon turned into a frown.

"What's the sad look for then?"

"I hate that he'll never have a real home again. I mean, yeah, he gets to stay here at the shelter, and I get to see him all the time, but it's still not fair. He deserves a real home and to be with someone around the clock who loves him." She looked up at Skittles. "Someone like me. I'd love to adopt this pretty boy."

Skittles wished like hell he could make that happen for Anna Grace, but the military was very strict when it came to their K-9s. They were already somewhat breaking their policy by allowing Mia to house Beretta at her facility to give him a little bit of normalcy as he lived out the rest of his life. Maybe with time, those overseeing those policies would have a change of heart.

Changing the subject, he asked, "Are you all set for the charity gala and dinner tomorrow night?"

"I think so."

"You think so?"

She grinned. "I'm not used to going to functions like that. So, I'm a little nervous."

"By the way, I never did thank you for my dress. You didn't have to do that."

"You're welcome. I want you to have a good time. Everyone who's sitting at our table you've already met."

"Your friends are really nice. I like them a lot."

He smiled. "They're your friends now too. All the ladies enjoyed talking with you, and they've already told me that they can't wait to see you again tomorrow night."

"Really?"

"Really."

"Hmm…" She hummed and looked across the yard. He knew she had something on her mind.

"What's racing through that mind of yours?"

"Sometimes I feel like this past week has been one big dream, and tomorrow I'll wake up, and it'll all be gone." She looked deep into his eyes and he felt it all the way to his heart. "Including you."

He turned his body more toward her and squeezed her hand.

"A.G., this is definitely not a dream, and I'm not going anywhere." He scrunched his face up. "Well, sometimes I have to if Uncle Sam orders me to. But aside from my job, it'll be hard to get rid of me."

He saw the emotion in her eyes as they filled with tears, but she was quick to dispel them before they breached her lower lids, and she leaned forward and kissed his cheek.

Baby steps, he thought to himself.

CHAPTER EIGHT

Senator DeSmith watched her from across the room. Anna Grace was even more stunning in person. In the pictures he'd seen of her that Bobby took, she always wore jeans and t-shirts. Tonight, she looked like a supermodel wearing a light purple evening gown. She shared many features of her mother, which included unique violet-like colored eyes. It was those eyes that had drawn him to Sue Ellen. But just like her mother, Anna Grace was a thorn in his side. How in the hell she managed to escape the grasps of Senor Castillo and find her way back into the United States was a story he'd love to hear. But then, to stay undetected for all these years was mind-boggling. And the biggest question was, why hadn't she gone to the authorities?

He looked up, and Steve was approaching the table. Steve had called DeSmith shortly before the event started and informed him that he was running late, but he had some valuable information to share.

Steve took the empty seat next to him, and DeSmith looked at him.

"Well, what did you find out?"

Steve glanced around the table, but none of the other staff members paid any attention to them.

"Our little escape artist now goes by the name of Grace Montgomery. She works for an animal shelter in Virginia Beach. She lives by herself in those rundown apartments near the airbase."

DeSmith looked toward the front of the room where Grace, as she now went by, sat.

"If she changed her name, then she's hiding."

"Well, she was and still is the main suspect in her parents' murder."

DeSmith smirked. "That scenario couldn't have played out any better."

"True, but we never imagined that she'd return," Steve stated very seriously.

"What about Castillo? What happened there?"

"Castillo and his two sons were gunned down ten years ago almost to the day."

DeSmith widened his eyes, surprised by that detail. "Who was responsible?"

"Nobody claimed responsibility, and if someone close to the family knows, they aren't talking."

The Senator rubbed his hand along his jaw. "Wow. Ten years ago."

"Ten years ago, on March 27th."

DeSmith's eyes shot to Steve. "March 27th? That's —"

Steve nodded. "Anna Grace's birthday. She would've turned seventeen that year."

DeSmith again glanced toward the woman who was laughing at something the guy next to her said.

"Who are the people she's sitting with up there? The guy next to her seems very attentive and protective of her."

"Military."

DeSmith rolled his eyes. "That would explain it. But what's the relation? Boyfriend? Friend?"

"I'm not sure. The woman, Alex Hardesty, who runs the foundation we are here supporting this evening, is engaged to the guy sitting next to Anna Grace's left. The others at the table and the table to the right are all part of the same team."

"Team?" DeSmith huffed out in annoyance. He hated these types of functions. He believed that the government wasted too much money on the military.

"They aren't just your normal military personnel."

DeSmith raised an eyebrow.

"They're SEALs."

"You've got to be fucking kidding me. The one woman who could destroy everything I've worked for has surrounded herself with a bunch of egotistical Special Forces soldiers? Just fucking dandy."

"I'm interested in the relationship she has with the guy."

Steve grinned wickedly. "I already have someone working on it."

When DeSmith eyed Steve, Steve gestured with a nod of his head in the direction of Monique, his senior aide at his local office in Virginia Beach. He noticed she kept her eye on the guy with Anna Grace.

"How does she fit into the picture?"

"She somewhat knows the guy. He's her neighbor, and she sees him at the local hangout often. He goes by the name Skittles."

"Skittles?" DeSmith said. "What the fuck kind of name is Skittles?"

Steve shrugged his shoulders. DeSmith was on the Armed Forces Committee, and he was sure that he could get some information if needed. He reached for his glass of water and took a drink.

"What about her connection with Xavier?" That was the one thing that had DeSmith more concerned about than anything. If Anna Grace found out the truth, there would be hell to pay.

"From what Bobby could find out, she's just a volunteer on his campaign, and again she was a recipient for he and his wife's scholarship."

DeSmith's gaze moved to the table next to where Anna Grace sat, and he eyed Xavier Mayfield before he turned his attention back to Steve.

"Do you think he knows?"

Steve's eyebrows shot upward. "No! If he did, you'd have heard about it by now."

"Did you coordinate the trip we spoke about and handle pulling together all the documentation to back everything up?"

Steve smirked. "It's all set. All she has to do is accept the offer."

"Well then, I guess I'll make my introduction tonight and make damn sure that I sell her on my new International Animal Cruelty bill I'll be sponsoring."

He glared at the sweet Anna Grace as she sat at the table with a smile on her face. It was too bad that beautiful smile of hers would be wiped away in due time. And he'd make sure she never smiled again.

Anna Grace excused herself so she could walk around a bit and go to the restroom. She was surprised by how good a time she was having. Since when she was getting ready for the evening, she felt like she would be put in front of a firing squad. Once she had arrived with Skittles at the venue and was around everyone, she felt a little more positive that the evening would be a success.

Though when they were seated at their table, and she found herself squeezed in-between two hulking and very skilled Special Forces soldiers, she did at one point start to feel a little claustrophobic.

She never used to have a fear of being in tightly confined spaces or large crowds. That anxiety disorder all started when she was whisked off to Mexico and was locked in a small closet as a form of punishment when she didn't follow the rules. Sitting in a five-by-five closet in the pitch-black had been an awful experience. Senor Castillo would lock her in there for hours until she'd beg him to let her out. After many times of him doing that, she concluded that Senor Castillo got off on hearing her beg.

As she walked down the tiled hallway leading to where the bathrooms were located, her mind traveled to Noah and the conversation they had yesterday while sitting under the tree with Beretta. When she revealed her biggest fear about this past week being a dream and potentially losing him, she hadn't been expecting Noah to react the way he had. Sure, when they were together, he was attentive and would grab her hand here and there and place a kiss on her head, but yesterday she felt something more. When he cupped her face and looked her in the eye, and stated that she wasn't getting rid of him, she felt his words all the way to her heart.

The thought that lingered in her mind was what Noah expected from her. Was there a chance at a budding romance? God, she hoped so. Everything she'd been through, her feelings for her best friend's older brother never wavered. Or could she just be overthinking things? He hadn't tried to make a move on her, and he'd had plenty of opportunities the last few times they were together. Maybe he was waiting for her to show interest. With that thought, she devised her own mission in her head: *Operation Kiss Noah.*

As she finished up and washed her hands, she looked herself over in the full-length mirror that hung near the door. The silk, lavender, floor-length gown looked amazing on her. She had been grateful that Alex had found the dress tucked back in the racks when they went dress shopping. She wasn't a fan of flaunting her assets, though she was a little light up top; the way the dress was designed gave her an extra lift in the front. It was just enough to look classy, not slutty. The last time she had worn a dress this fancy was the homecoming dance her freshman year of high school. Boy, had that been a night to remember. She and Nicole had almost skipped the dance, but Noah had convinced them not to, telling them both to experience as much as they could while they were still young because, in a blink of an eye, it would all be gone.

Boy, had he hit the nail on the head with that statement. Who knew that in six months, her entire life as she once knew it would be gone?

Thoughts of Nicole, Noah's sister, filtered through her mind, and she couldn't wait to see her best friend after all these years. She just prayed that Nicole and her parents understood why she didn't come forward and seek their help.

She pulled the door open and stepped out into the hall, ready to get back to the party. She thought she heard Noah's voice toward the right where there was a small sitting area, so she walked a few feet down the narrow hall. As she got closer, she was able to confirm that it was Noah, but there was another voice—a female. She peeked around the corner and had to cover her mouth to hold back the gasp that almost came out as she saw a woman standing very close to Noah with her hands on his chest and her face just inches from his.

"You know we're perfect for each other," the woman told him as she leaned in to kiss him. Anna Grace slowly backed out of the little niche as the tears burned her eyes. She felt like she'd been punched in the stomach. Here she was pretending that life would pick right back up where she left it ten years ago. It never occurred to her until now that Noah could be seeing someone. She never asked, and he never told her. God, how stupid of her! Of course he had moved on. He may have been looking for her all these years, but that was Noah—always the helpful one. He was just helping his sister try to find her best friend. He even admitted that she was family.

84

Maybe it was best she kept her new identity and put Anna Grace behind her once and for all.

She turned and followed the hallway back to the ballroom. She wasn't in the mood to go back to the event, let alone have to sit next to Skittles. But she'd suck up the pain because she was the better person and because it was the right thing to do.

Just as she was about to enter back into the room, a voice called her from behind.

"Excuse me."

When she turned around, Senator DeSmith stood there looking like the smug dick he was known to be. There was something about him that didn't sit right with her.

He gave her a half-smile. "You're Grace Montgomery, right?" He asked, and she took a defensive step back. She didn't like it when people she didn't know knew who she was. It put her on edge.

"Maybe. Who wants to know?" She said with a slight bite of attitude. She didn't know this guy other than his reputation in the government.

He reached his hand out. "I'm Senator Stan DeSmith. I was wondering if you had a few minutes so I could speak with you."

She wasn't going to lower herself to his standards, so she shook his hand. "I know who you are, but I don't believe we have anything to talk about, considering I don't really know you."

She started to turn away when he spoke.

"You work at the animal rescue shelter right here in town, correct?"

She spun back toward him, shocked that he knew that.

"How do you know where I work?"

DeSmith took a sip of the brown whiskey in his glass then licked his lower lip as his eyes bored into hers.

"I have a diligent staff that works for me. I believe you and I have something in common that I think we could work together on."

"What would that be?"

"Dogs."

"Dogs? I don't believe I've ever seen you with a dog, Senator."

85

He tried to blow off her comment with a slight laugh, but she knew it was all an act. It was how most politicians carried themselves nowadays. They'd tell you whatever you wanted to hear as long as they got your vote.

"I have a new bill I'm introducing in the coming weeks. It's an animal cruelty bill focusing on animal rights and abuse internationally."

Okay. He had her attention.

He gave her a smug smile as if he knew he had her hook, line, and sinker.

"You have my attention."

"How would you like to be a part of an operation that I'm leading in the Philippines that will see to the rescue of thirty-one dogs?"

"The Philippines? As in the country in the western Pacific Ocean?" She asked, just to clarify she had heard him correctly.

He nodded. "Yes. After research done by my staff, my bill will focus first on countries in Asia. My office is working and coordinating with organizations working to reduce the cruelty to animals, mostly dogs. Because of their locations, the organizations can't house the dogs for a long period of time once they are rescued. That is where my bill will come into play. We hope to work with organizations and shelters such as the one you work at all over the United States to agree to take in these abused animals and help rehabilitate, and hopefully adopt them out to loving homes."

It sounded like a wonderful idea.

He looked her over. "I'd love to partner with the Virginia Beach Animal Rescue Shelter and bring the first set of rescues to your shelter."

She stared up at him, and a part of her wanted to accuse him of being up to something but the more she thought about it, the more she realized she was just looking for an excuse to hate the guy more. His bill sounded amazing, and if it helped even one dog escape any type of abuse, she was on board. But she was curious as to what part she would play in it.

"I'll have to speak with Dr. Chambers as she owns the shelter, but what you want to do sounds amazing. Do you have a card with contact information in case Dr. Chambers has any questions?"

He smirked as if saying, *see, I can do something without being an asshole.* But he really was an asshole. He handed her two of his cards.

"Oh, I only need the one to give to Dr. Chambers," she told him and tried to hand back the additional card, but he pressed it back into the palm of her hand.

"That one's for you, so you can contact me with your answer." He took a sip of his whiskey and eyed her over the rim.

"What answer?" She asked, clearly confused with his comment.

"If you'll accompany me to the Philippines to kick off the project."

She jerked backward. "You want me to go to the Philippines…with you?"

"I believe that is what I just said."

Okay, she hadn't been expecting that. That was a lot to think about. She didn't even have a passport. She stayed away from anything that asked for her name out of fear that a background check or something would flag her as a fraud. She placed her hand over her stomach, and it began to hurt.

"Do you not want to go?" He asked.

She shook her head. "No. It isn't that. It sounds like a wonderful opportunity, but I don't have a passport, and it sounds like this trip is imminent. There's no way I could get a passport in time."

He grinned. "If I guarantee that you'll have your passport in hand by the time you board the flight, would you consider it?"

"Of course, I'd consider it. As I said, it's an amazing opportunity. When are you looking at going?"

"The plan is to leave next Thursday. My staff is still working on all of the logistics. We plan on being on the ground for roughly four or five days. It will consist of meeting with the organization and helping get the animals ready for transport." A smug smile appeared on his face. "And of course, photo ops to promote the bill."

Of course, she said sarcastically to herself. What politician could do a good deed and not have a photo op?

She nibbled on her lip. This was a big decision. Before she said yes or no, she needed to talk to someone about it. She damned her mind for going straight to Noah. Of course, her subconscious would go straight there.

She looked back up at the Senator, who was watching her intently.

87

"Can I have a day or two to think about it?"

He shrugged his shoulders. "Sure. But just remember this opportunity could lead to bigger and better things for the shelter."

She nodded her head in understanding. Just then, Xavier walked up and stood next to her. He looked between her and DeSmith.

"Is everything okay here?" Xavier asked as he eyed DeSmith.

Anna Grace looked up at Xavier. "Everything's fine. Senator DeSmith was just telling me about a new bill he's going to introduce with a focus on animal cruelty on an international level."

Xavier looked over at DeSmith. "Really?"

DeSmith smirked. "I am." He then turned his gaze on her. "I'm not here asking for your vote, considering we all know you've already made your decision on that. But what I am asking is for you to think wisely about the offer and consider how many dogs could be saved." He handed her another card. "That is the name and number of Steve. He's my Chief of Staff, and he'll be handling all the travel arrangements. If you're interested in helping be a part of this initiative, I'd love to have you on board. Oh, and all expenses are paid for."

She took the card and stared at it before looking back at him. "I'll give it some consideration and let you know in a day or two."

He grinned then turned toward Xavier. "Xavier. It's always nice to see you around." With those words, he turned and walked back toward the hotel bar.

Anna Grace looked at Xavier. "Well, that was weird." She explained everything to him and then asked him for his advice if she should go.

"Grace, it's a great opportunity and a way to get your name out there."

The only problem with it was that she wasn't looking to get her name out there.

"I need to think about it."

Just then, Skittles appeared from down the hallway. "Hey. I've been looking for you," he said and smiled, but honestly, she couldn't look at him right now. Not that she was angry or upset with him because he had his own life to live after all. She was more upset with herself, thinking she actually had a chance with him. Her mind was going in a million directions at the moment, and she started to feel overwhelmed. She needed to be alone.

"If you both will excuse me, I don't feel well."

Skittles watched Anna Grace turn her back and walk away toward the hotel lobby. Something was off with her, and whatever it was had to have happened between the time she left the table and when she went to the restroom.

When she had excused herself, he had given her a few minutes before he went in search for her. He hadn't gotten to spend as much alone time with her as he had wanted to. She looked stunning in the dress she wore. When he arrived at her apartment to pick her up, and she opened the door, it had taken a lot of willpower not to pull her into his arms and kiss her senseless. He wanted to use the time later in the evening to talk to her about them.

He just wasn't expecting Monique to pounce on him, throwing a wrench in his plans. He had noticed her eyeing him all night, but he ignored her. She had cornered him while he was waiting for A.G. to come out of the restroom. She questioned him about Anna Grace, and knowing Monique's track record, she most likely had a motive. Then she pissed him off when she tried to kiss him. Without getting physical with her, he managed to dodge her lips.

He looked at Xavier. "Is she okay?" He gestured toward the direction that Anna Grace went.

Xavier looked that way, then back to Skittles. "Senator DeSmith just offered her an opportunity that could launch her initiative of rescuing animals."

Skittles crossed his arms in front of his chest. "How so?" He asked, now curious because Senator DeSmith wasn't known to be the helpful Senator his office liked to portray.

"He's sponsoring a new animal rights bill, and he wants her to travel with him to the Philippines. There's a group there that his office has been working with, and they've got thirty-one dogs they've rescued and are holding at their center, but time is running out for the group to get them out of the country. He's offering to fly the dogs back here and use Dr. Chambers' shelter to adopt the animals out."

"Is Dr. Chambers aware?" Skittles asked, knowing that this arrangement wasn't going to sit well with Stitch because Stitch couldn't stand the Senator either. In fact, nobody on the team could.

"I don't believe so because he sort of sprung this on Grace just now."

Skittles had to bite the inside of his cheek, hearing Xavier call Anna Grace, just Grace. He couldn't wait until she could go back to using her given name.

"She said no, right?" Skittles questioned. There was no way in hell he was letting her go to the Philippines, let alone with Senator DeSmith. What was that old saying…*No matter how many times a snake sheds its skin, it's still a snake.*

Xavier shook his head. "I don't know. She told him she'd think about it and let him know. I personally don't think she should. The Philippines is a volatile country for foreign visitors.

Yeah, no shit. Skittles thought to himself. He'd spent time there before, and it wasn't for leisure. There were so many things that could go wrong with this trip should she decide to go. For starters, if she put herself out there like that, it was possible that someone from her past could identify her before they could get to speak to the police. The other thing that bothered him was that kidnappings of foreigners was huge in the Philippines. There were many gangs and terrorist organizations throughout the island-riddled country.

"I'll talk with her," Skittles told him.

Xavier eyed him. "I don't know a lot about Grace's past—just the basics that she was willing to share with my wife and me. I know she was homeless for about a year, but that is the extent of her background. Since you know her, I'm guessing you have a little more insight into what happened to her. Whatever it was, I can tell it was traumatic because she carries a lot of anger and distrust in her."

Skittles wasn't sure how to respond. He promised Anna Grace that he'd give her time to talk with Xavier, to get things straight before they went to the police. Obviously, Xavier cared for A.G., and that made Skittles happy knowing that she hadn't been totally alone all this time. But now that he had found her, he would be the one to care for her going forward.

"There's a backstory to her past, but even I don't know the full extent of it. I'm working with her to open up, and when the time is right, I'm sure you'll be one of the first few people that she'll talk to."

"She's amazing," Xavier told him, and Skittles couldn't disagree.

"Yes, she is. I'm just glad our paths crossed again."

"She asked me to have lunch with her next week."

Skittles offered an encouraging smile. "Maybe now's the time, and she's ready to talk to you."

"You care about her, don't you?" Xavier asked, and Skittles nodded his head instantly. There was no having to think about that. He more than cared for her. He loved her. Even after all this time apart, he still loved her as he had ten years ago.

"I do."

"You keep her close. She deserves some happiness in her life."

Skittles grinned. "I intend to." He looked around. "Now, I just need to find her."

Xavier laughed then shook his hand.

"I'll let you get to searching for her. It was good seeing you again this evening."

"You too. And I hope to be seeing a lot more of you when you win that primary election." He winked, and Xavier laughed again before he walked off.

Skittles walked back into the ballroom where the event was taking place. When he got to the table, he noticed that A.G.'s chair was empty. Then he saw that the small clutch she came with was missing from the table where it sat, and Alex said that she'd keep an eye on it while Anna Grace was using the restroom.

Ace turned and faced him. "Is Anna Grace okay?" He asked Skittles, and Skittles started to get an odd sensation in the pit of his stomach.

"I think so. She was talking to Xavier a little while ago, and when I walked up, she mentioned she wasn't feeling well and excused herself, but I thought she came back to the table."

"She did. She picked up her clutch and told Alex and me that she wasn't feeling well and headed home. We thought you took her."

Skittles ran his hand through his hair. He knew something wasn't right. He could see it in her eyes and her body language. *What the hell?*

"I didn't," he stated flatly. Then he wondered how she got home considering he had brought her. He pulled out his phone and dialed her number. He cursed when it went straight to voicemail. He was going to send her a text but then remembered her shitty phone didn't do text messages. *Fuck!* She could be upset with him all she wanted to be, but he would buy her a decent phone.

Mia walked up and asked him what was going on, and as he was explaining, Mia's phone rang, and he could see the name that flashed across the screen—Grace Montgomery. His chest tightened as Mia gave him a concerned while she answered it.

Anna Grace took a quick glance over her shoulder as she continued to walk as fast as she could in the high heels she was wearing. When she eyed the dirty blonde-haired guy with the goatee still walking about twenty or so yards behind her, her internal alarms sounded.

She could kick herself in the ass for forgetting to switch out the cash she usually carried in her purse to the clutch she used this evening. She realized that when she was standing in line at the hotel to catch a cab. Luckily, she found a few bucks in the clutch that must've been in there the last time she used it—God knows when that was. She had enough to catch a ride on the bus.

The guy she had her eye on had boarded the bus the same time she did. He sat five rows behind her and then got off at the same stop she had. Now he was following her, and she was a little frightened. She could see her apartment complex just up ahead, but she still had a ways to go. In-between the sound of her heels clicking on the pavement, she could hear the guy's heavy footsteps behind her. Every time she glanced at him; he was always looking away.

Damn it! She internally cursed at herself for letting her feelings get the best of her and leaving the event. If she hadn't, she wouldn't be in the situation she was in right now. She didn't even think about it as she pulled her phone from her clutch. She dialed Skittles, but it went to voicemail. She pulled up the following number and dialed Mia.

On the third ring, she answered.

"Anna Grace?"

"Hi, Mia. I'm sorry to bother you, but I'm kinda freaked out right now."

"Where are you?"

"I'm walking to my apartment. I tried to call Noah, but his phone went to voicemail."

"He was trying to call you. Wait…did you say that you're walking?" Mia asked as her voice raised, but then Anna Grace could hear voices in the background. *Was that Noah?*

Skittles voice then came over the phone. "A.G., where in the hell are you?" He asked in a harsh tone, and she wanted to cry. She could hear the disappointment in his voice. Either that, or he was just pissed off.

"I'm right by my apartment. When I left the hotel, I realized I forgot the cash I normally carry with me, so I scrounged up enough to take the bus. There was a guy who boarded the bus the same time as me, and then he got off at the same stop as I did, and now he's following me."

She heard him curse. "Is he still following you? How far are you from your apartment?"

She took another peek, but she didn't see him. He just vanished. "He's gone."

"Are you sure he's gone?"

She scanned the area and didn't see anyone around except for a few people hanging out by the entrance to her apartment building, people she assumed were Ziggy and his crew. "He's gone. He may have gone into the little corner store."

She turned around and continued toward her apartment. She needed to explain why she left so suddenly.

"Noah…I'm sorry I left without telling you."

She heard him take a deep breath. "Are you okay? You mentioned to Xavier and me that you weren't feeling well, and then when I got back to the table, Ace told me you left because you didn't feel good."

God, he sounded so caring now. "I started getting a really bad headache, and my stomach started to hurt." That wasn't a lie. Her head hurt from all of the thinking, and her stomach hurt because her head hurt. That may not make sense to some people, but it was the truth.

"I'm coming over," he stated, but she didn't want to see him right now. Right now, all she wanted to do was take some Tylenol and curl up in bed.

"I'm fine, Noah. You don't need to come. I'm going to take something for my head and then lay down. Please tell Mia that I'm sorry."

Suddenly, Mia's voice came back over the phone, and that was when she realized they had her on speakerphone. Jesus, she hoped not everyone could hear.

"Anna Grace, you had an instinct, and most times, our instincts are right. So never be sorry for calling your friends when you feel like things aren't right. Now, are you sure you don't want Skittles to come over?"

Anna Grace made it to her building, climbed the stairs to the second floor, and then let herself inside her unit. She locked the bottom lock before she slid the deadbolt into place.

"No, I'm good. I'm inside my apartment now."

"Are the doors locked?" Skittles asked, and she wanted to roll her eyes.

"Yes. Both locks are in place."

"A.G.?"

"Yeah?"

"As Mia said, don't ever be afraid to call any one of us—especially me."

"Okay."

"Are you positive you don't need me to drive over?"

She smiled even though he couldn't see her. "No. I'm good now. Thank you again for this evening, and I'm sorry for making you worry."

"I'll always worry about you, A.G. No matter what you think, I always will."

What could she say to that? *Worry about your girlfriend, not me.*

"Thanks, Noah. I'm going to go lay down."

"Ok. I'll give you a call tomorrow."

"Ok."

"Night A.G."

"Goodnight."

She disconnected the phone and threw herself onto her bed. Life was cruel. Just when she took a step forward, something comes along, and she finds herself taking two steps back. Would she ever get ahead?

CHAPTER NINE

Anna Grace rolled over onto her side. It was a little after one in the afternoon, and she was still dressed in her pajamas and still in bed. For her, that was unheard of. She had never been one to sleep in, much less just lie around in bed all day and think. She preferred her mind to be busy, so she didn't have time to think. Thinking for her always led back to her dark days. But most of today's thoughts were current situations she was facing. First, there was Skittles and what she witnessed last night. She couldn't understand why he hadn't said anything about the woman she saw him with. On the plus side, it was good she had stumbled upon them because if she had tried to kiss him last night and he rejected her, she wasn't sure if she could overcome that. At least now, she could still be friends with him, but she was going to have to talk to him about how touchy-feely he was. His actions clearly sent her mixed signals. But if he was happy, then she had to be happy for him.

She eyed the business card sitting on the table next to her bed. She reached for it and looked it over—Steve Johnson, Senator DeSmith's Chief of Staff. She wasn't much of a fan of him either. She had caught him a few times looking at her last night, but she had chalked it up to him knowing what the Senator would ask her.

As for the trip, she was still undecided. She had spoken to Mia earlier when she had called her to check on her. She really hadn't thought about how worried Mia or the others had been about her until Mia told her that some of the guys were on the verge of coming to her apartment whether she had wanted them to or not, just to make sure she was okay. Their thoughtfulness had sent Anna Grace's emotions into a tizzy. It was hard to realize that there were good people around her now who actually cared about her wellbeing. It was something she was going to have to get used to if she planned on sticking around. She had also talked to Mia about the trip and explained what it all entailed. Mia voiced her support for hosting the dogs at the shelter, but she wasn't thrilled when Anna Grace told her that she was considering making the trip with Senator DeSmith. She still had one day to decide.

She blew out a big breath. She hated making decisions as such. This trip had both pros and cons. She was a list person, so later in the evening, she would sit down and list all of the positives and negatives and compare the two, then use that information to make her decision.

She glanced at the clock, and now it was quarter to two. She really needed to get up and get a move on before she wasted the entire day. She needed to swing by the shelter and make sure everything was good there. By the time she got there, all of the volunteers should have left for the day. She'd be able to spend some time with the dogs.

She smiled, thinking about seeing her favorite Belgian Malinois, Beretta. God, she wished the military would reverse its decision and let her adopt him. Her apartment building allowed dogs, and they had plenty of land where she could take him outside. Plus, he could accompany her to work at the shelter every day, where he'd have free rein. She saw it as a win-win situation. But again, they had to abide by the military's orders. If they didn't, they could lose Beretta, and who knows what could happen to him then. At least now she got to see him every day at work.

She threw the covers back and went to climb out of bed when her phone rang. The sight of Skittles' name on the screen warmed her. She shook her head. She needed to work on her emotions and learn not to get all giddy when he called or when she saw him. She picked up the phone and answered.

"Hey."

"Hey. You doing okay?" He asked.

"Yeah."

"You sound down. Are you sure?" He pressed, and she wanted to tell him no, she wasn't because she had seen him last night. But now wasn't the right time to bring that up. She'd rather talk to him in person.

"Just tired."

"Your head isn't still hurting, is it?"

"No. I'm just feeling lazy."

He laughed. "We all have those days sometimes."

"True."

"Do you have plans later? I wanted to see if you'd like to have dinner with me."

Really?! She thought to herself. If he's with her all the time, when does he ever see his girlfriend? Her mind started to drift to an answer she really didn't want to imagine.

"Uh…I can't tonight. I need to swing by the shelter; then, I have a couple of lessons at the club.

"Oh." She could hear the disappointment in his tone. "Maybe tomorrow then?"

Okay, maybe she needed to come clean with him now because this was torture for her.

"Noah, I think—"

"Shit!" He blurted out and interrupted her. "I need to go. My commander is calling. Listen, I'll give you a call tomorrow when I get a free minute, and we'll go to dinner. Don't make any plans."

"Okay," she found herself saying.

"Later, A.G." She heard the click, followed by silence.

She set the phone down then rubbed her face. *Fuck me,* she thought. *Torture. Complete fucking torture.*

CHAPTER TEN

The rain clouds blocked out the setting sun just as Anna Grace pedaled her bike into the parking lot of Maggie's, a little local bar just down the street from her apartment building.

Since her second lesson got rained out and she wasn't quite ready to head home, she decided to stop by the little hangout. Not that she was there to drink. Alcohol was one drink she stayed clear of. She had drunk enough Tequila in the three years she spent in Mexico that she should be immune to it. That was how they kept her complacent and under their control, and most likely also contributed to her memory loss during certain periods of time there. She was actually surprised that she hadn't become an alcoholic as a teenager.

She shivered, remembering some of the times when one of Senor Castillo's men would hold her head back and pinch her nose so she had to open her mouth to breathe, and when she did, another man would pour the tequila down her throat. It burned so bad as the poison hit her stomach. Most of the time, she'd end up throwing it all up.

She walked into the little bar, and her eyes lit up when she saw the pinball machine was available. Every now and then, when Anna Grace needed to escape the confines of her apartment, she'd venture over to Maggie's. She didn't mind the majority of the people—mostly men—who frequented the bar. Most of them were Naval Aviators stationed at the airbase just down the road. For the most part, everyone was friendly and pretty much kept to themselves, which she liked. She smiled to herself, thinking how different groups of the military congregated at different places—the aviators at Maggie's and the SEALs over at Bayside. She was sure other groups hung out at other places.

Maggie and her partner Regina owned the place. They were also the bartenders, and both were super nice and didn't put up with any crap. Regina was a former Marine who was tall, fit, and definitely not someone that Anna

Grace would even think about getting into a scuffle with. She'd seen Regina literally pick up big men and throw them out on their asses.

As she made her way over to the pinball machine, she grabbed a stool and took it over with her. She waved to Maggie, who was deep in orders at the bar. The place had seemed a little more crowded than usual for a weeknight. All twenty of the bar seats were taken, and the majority of the high-top tables were filled by those who were playing pool at the four pool tables.

"Grace, honey, you want your regular?" Maggie yelled out over the loud rock music and chatter of the men around her.

"Please," she yelled back. It wasn't like her drink was hard to make. It was just club soda with two lemon wedges.

Anna Grace turned back toward the machine, set her tennis bag on the ground next to her, then reached into her purse and pulled out the red coin pouch that contained several dollars' worth of quarters. She put a quarter into the machine, then pulled back the plunger and let it fly. She was racking up the points when Maggie walked over and set her drink down on the small table next to the machine.

"Haven't seen you in here in a while," she said to Anna Grace, and A.G. picked up her glass and took a small sip.

"I've been preoccupied with work and some other things."

Maggie eyed her over. "You're doing okay though, right?"

"Yeah. It's all good. As I said, I've just been busy."

"Well, we've missed seeing you in here."

Anna Grace laughed. "Well, you can't get rid of me. I mean, you are the only place that I know of in town who has a pinball machine."

Maggie grinned. "Holler if you need anything else, hun."

"Thanks, Maggie."

The time ticked by, and Anna Grace was down to her last dollar. A group of six men stood around her watching and cheering her on as she played. She felt very uncomfortable with the audience she had. Maggie had brought over a fresh club soda for her. She put her coin pouch away in her pocket, picked up her drink, and stepped to the side, but first told the guys that she was finished and they could have the machine. One guy stopped her by grabbing her wrist, and she immediately tensed up. The guy must have realized because he let go and apologized.

"Please don't leave on our account. We were actually watching you play. You're really good."

She took a step backward and looked at the guy. "Thanks, but I'm done for the evening."

"I don't think I've seen you here before," another guy said as he leaned in close to her.

"I come in every now and then," she replied and lifted her glass to her lips. The carbonation bubbles tickled her lip as she gulped down a quarter of the drink.

"Well, I'd definitely remember you. You've got the coolest eyes," the tallest guy of the group told her, and he leaned forward to get a closer look. Anna Grace thought that he would try and kiss her for a moment, so she took a step back. A strong arm came around her waist, and she was pulled backward against a wall of muscle. When she went to give the rude person a piece of her mind about grabbing women, the voice that spoke over her head made her tense up, but her body came to life.

"There you are, sweetheart; I've been looking for you."

Skittles and Stitch were on their way back from the airbase after dropping off some equipment that Bravo Team needed for their flight out later in the evening. As they drove down the street, Stitch spotted the sign to Maggie's and commented that he hadn't been there in ages. They decided to stop in and grab a beer since they didn't have anywhere else to be. He wished he had a dinner date but understood that A.G. had job priorities just like himself, though it had been raining and he didn't recall tennis being a rain sport. Maybe after their beer, he'd give her a call and see if her plans had changed.

After talking with Stitch, Skittles wanted to speak with Anna Grace about the offer from Senator DeSmith. Stitch had told him that Mia had spoken with Anna Grace earlier and that she was still considering the Senator's proposal. Skittles didn't think there was anything to consider. He just didn't want her going, period.

As they walked in and their eyes adjusted to the dim bar lighting, Stitch whistled low. "Damn, it's crowded."

Skittles agreed as he looked for an open table. He found one and started for it when a group of guys huddled around the pinball machine started cheering.

"I wonder what's going on over there," Stitch asked as he sat down.

Skittles didn't care. He just wanted to drink his beer and head back to his apartment. Those thoughts quickly changed when he saw the mass of platinum blonde hair emerge from the crowd.

"What the fuck!" He exclaimed, and Stitch looked in the direction of his sight.

"Is that A.G.?"

Skittles didn't even answer as he hopped off his stool. Her back was turned toward him as he approached. He had a few questions filtering through his mind. What in the hell was she doing here? Had she lied to him about the tennis lessons?

He wasn't sure what was going on with her, but something was definitely off. Between her abrupt departure from the event last night and how she sounded on the phone earlier, she wasn't acting like herself.

He saw red as the one dude bent down and appeared as if he was going to kiss her. Those lips were his lips. Just as she took a step back, he was there and wrapped his arm securely around her waist and pulled her against his front.

He heard her deep intake of breath, and before she could say or react, he put his mouth close to her ear. "There you are, sweetheart. I've been looking for you."

She turned in his arms and smiled. "I was wondering when you were going to show up." Then she shocked the shit out of him when she got up on her tiptoes and kissed his cheek before she whispered in his ear, "God, I owe you one for your impeccable timing. I can't get a break from Tweedle Dee, Tweedle Dumb, and their friends."

He smiled and put his arms around her waist, hugging her to him, and damn if she didn't fit perfectly. He received glares from the two guys who obviously were trying to tag-team A.G. She definitely needed a keeper, he thought.

Grasping her hand, he gave it a slight tug and led her toward the table where Stitch was sitting watching. He had a slight smirk on his face, and Stitch knew what was going through his friend's mind. Yes, he had acted like a jealous caveman.

Anna Grace grabbed her tennis bag, which Skittles took from her, and went willingly with him.

"Are you okay?" He asked as he pulled another stool over to their table for her.

"Yeah. I'm good. They seemed innocent. They were just watching me play. Plus, I have Maggie and Regina who look after me." She took another sip of her drink.

Skittles eyed her over. "Do you come here often?" He found himself asking as Maggie dropped off two beers for them, and Stitch and Skittles picked them up and guzzled about half the bottle in one swallow.

"Every so often. It's close to my place, and it's the only place in the area with a pinball machine."

Skittles' expression soften. Now he remembered—she did like playing pinball. He remembered anywhere they went; if there was a pinball machine, she had to play it.

"So, what happened with tennis this evening?"

She pointed toward the outside. "It's raining. You can't play tennis in the rain. It started right after the first lesson ended."

"You didn't think to call me?"

Her eyes widened with his question, and she cleared her throat. "I figured you would've made other plans since I had already told you I had the lessons."

Damn. She had an answer for everything. He watched her closely. Something was wrong as she started to zone out, then shook her head as if trying to gather her bearings. She grinned, and Stitch must've seen it too because he glanced over and gave him a concerned look.

"Anna Grace, are you okay?"

Anna Grace was trying to concentrate on the conversation with Skittles, but her head felt fuzzy. Suddenly she didn't feel too well. Skittles said something to her, and she just stared at him. *Damn, when did he grow a second head?* She asked herself. Then she grinned as a naughty thought drifted through her normally innocent mind. *Hmmm…double the pleasure.* No. She reprimanded herself. She couldn't think those kinds of things. He was taken.

"A.G., are you okay?" Skittles asked her, and she shook her head, trying to clear the fog that seemed to take over her brain. Why couldn't she focus?

"Anna Grace…" She heard someone say. She looked from Skittles to Stitch. Both of them kept going in and out of focus. She saw their mouths moving, but she couldn't really understand what either was saying.

Something was wrong. She didn't feel right. She tried to stand, but when she went to take a step, her foot felt as if it was made a lead. Thank goodness Skittles had already been reaching for her when she started to teeter. Her chin clipped the edge of the table before he could catch her.

Skittles knew something wasn't right with Anna Grace a few minutes after she had sat down.

"Shit! Here hold this against her chin," Stitch said, handing Skittles some napkins. Stitch came around the table and looked at her chin. "She may need stitches. How much has she had to drink?"

The bartender came over with a ziplock bag filled with ice. "Here, put this on her chin," she said, handing Skittles the bag. "What happened?" She questioned as she met Skittles' eyes, and Skittles could tell right away that the woman cared for A.G.

104

"Do you know how much she's had to drink tonight?"

Maggie furrowed her eyebrows and gave him a strange look. "Club soda. That's all she drinks."

"What?"

"Grace doesn't drink alcohol. She only drinks club soda when she's here."

"You're sure?"

"Positive."

Skittles pulled the ice bag away from her skin and was happy to see that the bleeding had subsided. He then eyed the group of guys who had been swarming A.G. when he and Stitch had arrived.

Maggie turned and looked in the same direction. They both looked at each other as realization hit.

"Shit, you think someone slipped something in her drink?" She asked.

Stitch looked at her eyes, and Skittles could see that her pupils were dilated. She tried to talk, but her words came out slurred.

"Takes me home whif youuuu."

"Shit. Let's get her out of here," Skittles ordered and lifted her in his arms and cradled her against his chest. As he was walking out the door, he felt eyes on him. When he glanced in the direction of the bar, there was a man in a dead stare with him as he spoke with someone on his cell phone. As much as he wanted to go over and have a word with the guy, he knew A.G. needed help right now.

He called to Stitch over his shoulder. "While I get her settled in the truck, can you ask Maggie if she has cameras? If someone slipped her something, I want to know who the fucker was because he's a dead man."

Skittles laid Anna Grace down in the backseat of his truck. She was still trying to talk, but she wasn't making any sense.

Stitch came out, and Skittles threw him the truck keys as he hopped in the back with A.G.

"Maggie already called her partner Regina and had her going back through the tapes. If someone slipped something in her drink, Maggie was confident it would be on the video."

Skittles nodded his head as he brushed Anna Grace's hair from her face. Her eyes were closed.

"Where are we taking her?" Stitch asked.

Skittles checked her pulse. It was strong and steady. He knew some date-rape drugs could cause low blood pressure, especially if alcohol was involved. Which, in Anna Grace's case, it wasn't.

"Let's head to her apartment since it's right down the road." Stitch raised an eyebrow at him but started the truck and pulled out of the parking lot.

The closer they got to her apartment; the angrier Skittles became. What if he and Stitch hadn't decided to go to that bar tonight? She could've fallen victim to a serious crime. His anger intensified when Stitch pulled the truck up to her apartment complex. Not that he would say it to her face, but it was a shithole. In fact, it was right up there with some of the shithole places he'd been deployed to. Even Stitch was glaring at the building in disgust.

He got Anna Grace out of the truck. She was standing with his assistance while he looked through her purse to get her keys. Stitch grabbed her tennis bag.

"Wow, Noah, you've got so many muscles," she said slowly as if she were concentrating on annunciating her words. She rubbed her hands up and down his chest, and he had to bite the inside of his cheek.

"Come on, A.G., let's get you inside."

"You're gonna come home with me?"

"Yep."

"Ten years, and I finally get Noah Young all to myself," she shouted, and he ushered her faster toward her building.

She stopped suddenly and put her hand to her head. "I don't feel so good."

She barely finished her sentence when she bent over and puked in the bush next to the stairs."

"Shit!" Skittles held her hair away from her face as she threw up two more times. Hopefully, she would throw up whatever the hell was in her system.

When she was finished, she collapsed into Skittles arms. He lifted her and carried her up the flight of stairs.

"Holy shit," Stitch muttered as he got his first glimpse into Anna Grace's apartment, and Skittles could tell he wasn't impressed at all—big shocker there.

He carried her over to the sofa and laid her down. Stitch went into the kitchen to get some paper towels. When he came back, he started cleaning up the blood from her chin and wiped the rest of her face. He determined that she didn't need stitches. He found a first-aid kit in her bathroom and used two butterfly band aids to close up the small gash, but he warned Skittles she would probably have a bruise.

Skittles ran a hand through his hair. He was still trying to get a grasp on what happened. All he kept thinking was that she could've been raped and even killed. He felt sick to his stomach.

"You okay, man?" Stitch asked, taking a seat by Anna Grace's feet.

He looked down at Anna Grace and gently stroked her hair. She was out cold and snoring. "I don't want to think about what could've happened to her if we hadn't been there tonight."

"I know. It's fucking scary and sickening what people do to prey on the unsuspecting."

That was an understatement. He kept telling himself that all that mattered was that he was there, and that he could protect Anna Grace from becoming a victim.

The way she laid on her side, he noticed a long scar starting at the top of her shoulder, ending midway down her shoulder blade. He touched it and traced the white line with his finger. It was an old scar, but he didn't remember her having a scar there.

"I'm going to stay here with her. You can take my truck, and we'll figure out something tomorrow," he told Stitch as he pulled his keys from his pocket, but Stitch waved him off. "I called Frost. He's on his way over now to get me."

Skittles nodded his head. "Thanks again."

Stitch gave him an annoyed look. "Dude, you don't have to thank me. I'm just as pissed as you are. Hopefully, Maggie and Regina find out who did this." Stitch looked around the apartment. "I also don't like her living arrangements. When are you planning on changing that?" Stitch asked and raised his eyebrow in question.

"If I knew it wouldn't piss her off, I'd pack up everything she owns right now, throw it in my truck along with her, and she'd wake up tomorrow morning at my place where she'd stay."

"You don't think she'd want that?"

Skittles shrugged his shoulders. "I'm not sure what she wants. I'm trying to be patient, but my patience is running thin, especially now with what happened."

"Have you talked to her about how you feel?"

"No. Like I just said, I don't want to rush her. Plus, she's still holding back. It's like pulling teeth getting her to open up more about the last ten years of her life. Well, not so much her college days and afterward. It's more along with the two to three years prior."

"I get it. But did you ever think maybe she's waiting to see if you're going to really stick around before she spills her heart to you? Maybe if you tell her upfront how you feel about her, that might give her the push she's looking for."

"You're probably right. I just need to get through tonight. This fucking scared the shit out of me."

"I get it. It scared me too, and she isn't even mine."

Skittles looked at Stitch. "You're lucky. Mia's an amazing woman."

Stitch offered a small smile. "Anna Grace is amazing too. And you could have what we have. What all of us have."

Skittles knew Stitch was right. He could have what the others had—love. He'd make it a point to talk to A.G. either tomorrow or the next day. It all depended on how she felt when she woke up.

Anna Grace was having the most amazing dream. She was wrapped in a blanket of warmth. She snuggled closer to the heater and wondered since when her heater felt and smelt so good.

Her delightful feeling and scent had her inquisitive mind wanting to know. She blinked her eyes open, and the first thing she saw was Noah's face. He grinned. *Hot damn! Now, this is a way to be woken up.* Was she still caught amid her dream?

"Hey, you." He said in that deep, raspy voice.

Her arms felt heavy, but she moved them and placed her hands on his face. She squished his cheeks together and pushed on his nose. *Okay, he felt real.* She heard him chuckle.

"How are you feeling?"

"I feel like I have a hangover, but that's impossible because I don't drink." She went to roll over, but her head started to throb. She placed her hand on her forehead. "What happened to me last night?"

He looked at her very seriously. "What do you remember?" He asked.

She started to think, and even that was a painful feat, but she dug into her memory. "I was at Maggie's playing pinball. There were a bunch of people around."

"Men," Skittles said the word in a harsh tone, and she snapped her head back at him.

"What?"

"Men. It wasn't just a group of people. It was a group of men swarming you."

She went to ask him how he knew, but then she remembered the savior who rescued her from a couple of their advances.

"You showed up." She said, but that was all she could recall. After that, things were fuzzy—really fuzzy.

He nodded his head slowly. "I did. And it was a good thing I showed up because there's no telling where you'd be right now or what condition you'd be in." He looked fierce, and his nostrils flared as if he was trying to contain his anger. He was on edge.

What in the hell had happened?

109

"I don't remember. What happened?"

"Somebody at the bar slipped something in your drink."

She sat up slightly and looked into his eyes. "What?"

"One minute, you were talking with Stitch and me at the table, and the next, you had zoned out completely, and it went downhill from there."

He reached out and brushed his thumb across her chin. His touch was gentle, and it felt good. "It hasn't bruised too bad," he said.

She touched her chin and felt the band-aides. "What happened?"

"You lost your balance and clipped your chin on the edge of the table. I tried to get to you in time, but I was a second too late." She saw the remorse in his eyes.

"Do you know who did it? Who drugged me?" Her thoughts went to the guys who were watching her play pinball.

He shook his head. "No. But Maggie confirmed that it wasn't any of the guys who were at the machine with you. The cameras had a clear shot of that area, and nobody touched your drink while it was on the table. Maggie believes it was done when she poured your drink and set it on the bar while she went into the back to get more lemons. The bar was so crowded that there were a lot of blind spots, and your drink was one of them."

She was shocked that someone would do that to her. Okay, well, not totally shocked at the act, but that it happened there—at Maggie's. Maggie's was a place she felt safe at, but not anymore.

She felt the need to go and get cleaned up. She started to get up from the couch, and he moved out of the way.

"You stayed here all night?" She asked as she stood, and he helped her by putting a hand on her elbow until she was steady on her feet.

"I did. I was worried," he said to her, his body towering above hers as he stood behind her.

She felt his finger run along her shoulder and down her back. She knew he was tracing the scar she had there.

"Where'd you get this scar on your shoulder? I don't remember you having one there."

She looked over her shoulder at him. She didn't want to start her day with a trip down *Nightmare Lane,* so she tried to play it off and started toward her bedroom.

"Like you know every detail about my body."

"Trust me. I would've remembered a scar like this." He stepped toward her and again ran his finger down the faded silvery line, and it sent tremors through her traitorous body. They held each other's gaze, and something flashed within his eyes. Did he feel the pull between them too? The intensity that burned in his eyes put a spell on her, and she was about to tell him about the night two men had almost raped her. But then he dropped his hand and looked away, breaking that connection.

She could've slapped herself. *Of course he didn't feel it, silly. Remember, he has a woman, and it isn't you.* That inner voice of hers that she liked to call the devil sometimes told her.

She turned around, and he stood there with his hands on his hips. His hair was all messy, and the whiskers along his cheeks and jaw were dark and sexy. God, he looked amazing.

"What can I say? The streets are a dangerous place for anyone," she found herself saying.

"What?" He squinted his eyes at her.

"Nothing," she mumbled, rolling her eyes, and began to walk away.

"Don't do that," he snapped at her.

"Do what?"

"Cut the shit A.G." He shouted. "Where the fuck did that scar come from? And don't fucking lie to me."

She turned fully to face him. "You really want to know?" She blasted back at him, and he cocked an eyebrow in response to her question.

"I got this one night while I was scrounging the streets for food." He dropped his arms to his side, and it was the look in his eyes that told her he understood. But he wanted to hear it, so he was going to get an ear full. "Yeah. Now you're starting to get it? I was in an alley digging through the dumpsters that I knew usually had decent leftovers."

111

He took a step towards her, and she recognized his expression. She'd seen it before in others. She didn't want his pity.

"No! You wanted to know, so you are going to damn well listen." She felt the need to cry, and she hated to cry. She especially didn't like feeling vulnerable in front of him.

Her voice softened as she remembered that cold winter day in St. Louis. "I wasn't paying attention. I knew better than to let my guard down. I was grabbed from behind by a man who had tried hitting on me earlier." She wasn't about to tell him that the guy was a pimp and wanted her to work for him.

"A.G.," Skittles said, and she shook her head.

"I'll spare you the details. But thankfully, I had a friend looking out for me, and he found me in time. However, during the scuffle, I was cut, and it resulted in this." She pointed to the scar. She was so angry right now that her body shook. All of this was behind her and bringing up some of the darkest days of her life was wreaking havoc on her.

She turned away from him and tried to hide her embarrassment from him. He now knew a sliver of the torture she'd been through, but strong arms folded around her as she was pulled into Skittles' chest.

"I don't want to talk about it anymore," she whispered as she tried to keep the tears at bay.

"Okay, sweetie." He whispered to her.

Suddenly an annoying shrill of a ringtone sounded, and Skittles cursed.

CHAPTER ELEVEN

Anna Grace was sitting at the front counter at the shelter, sipping her protein shake as she glanced over a travel booklet on the Philippines that she had picked up at the bookstore the day before.

She surprised herself when she decided a few days ago that she was actually going to go through with the trip and take Senator DeSmith up on his offer to be part of the group that would bring the first lot of dogs back to the United States under his new bill.

Although the more she read, the more apprehensive she started to feel. Maybe she should've asked for *all* the details before she committed. The region they were heading to, Zamboanga, was listed in the top ten places to avoid when traveling to the Philippines.

The only person who she had told so far was Mia. Needless to say, Mia wasn't thrilled, but she supported the reasons why Anna Grace decided to go. Her only regret was that she hadn't been able to speak with Skittles about it. She truly had intended to discuss it with him, but he had to leave her apartment abruptly when he received a call from work. He had explained quickly that those types of calls usually meant that the team was being called up and would most likely be shipping out.

It turned out that was the case when Skittles called an hour or two later. However, she had been in the shower and missed the call. All she got was his voicemail confirming that he was, in fact, leaving and that when he had the chance he'd try connecting with her.

She worried about him. She always had worried about him knowing he wanted to join the military. That was why she always went to the far end of the airbase and watched the jets take off and land. It was her way of sort of connecting with him. She hated that he left before they could work things out. She hated confrontations, and she definitely didn't like having one with Skittles.

Mia had warned her that Skittles had planned on convincing her not to make the trip. But without valid reasons why she shouldn't, she couldn't in good conscience not help those animals.

The chime on the door rang, and she lifted her head. A guy dressed in a suit stood there looking around the place like he was afraid that something might jump out and bite him. She closed up the book and stood.

"Hi. Can I help you?" She asked, and when he turned to face her, she realized it was Steve from Senator DeSmith's office. She had only spoken with him over the phone, but she'd seen him at the charity event last week, so she knew what he looked like. He was tall, wore black wire-rimmed glasses, and his brown hair was graying. Well, what was left of it.

"Yes. I'm Steve Johnson, Senator DeSmith's Chief of Staff. I'm assuming you're Grace Montgomery."

She smiled, though it never reached her eyes. This guy gave off a bad vibe. But maybe that was just because he worked for an asshole.

"Hi. Yes. I'm Grace. It's nice to meet you." She reached her hand across the counter and shook his hand. He wasn't a very confident man judging from his limp handshake.

"I know you're working, so I won't take up a lot of your time. I wanted to come by and deliver your itinerary and your passport."

He handed over a catalog envelope to her, and she opened it and looked through.

"As you can imagine, Senator DeSmith is a busy man, and the schedule, as you will see, is booked solid with engagements while in the Philippines. Because of the timing and what the schedule consists of before or after, there are some events where you will have to tag along. But don't worry, you don't have to participate."

She sighed in relief. She wasn't there to help the Senator with his Foreign Policy agenda or to help his campaign. She was there for one reason only—the dogs.

"If you have any questions between now and Thursday morning, call or email me."

She looked up from scanning over the itinerary and gave him a soft smile. "Just skimming over this, it looks like you've covered it all."

He gave her a weak smile. "Then I guess we'll see you Thursday morning at the airport."

"Guess so." She smiled back, and he turned and walked out the door. The man had no personality or social skills. It was a wonder how he survived in the job he had.

Moments later, Mia walked through the door that separated the shelter from the clinic. She smiled.

"Who was that who just left in the fancy, Lexus sports car?" Mia asked as she walked closer to the counter.

Anna Grace held up the envelope. "That was the Senator's Chief of Staff. He was dropping off some stuff for me."

Mia walked closer. "So, you're really going to go?"

Anna Grace looked Mia in the eye. "I have to go, Mia. Thirty-one dogs depend on me."

Mia eyed her over. "Those dogs can make it here without you too. I'm worried about you going over there."

Mia's concern touched Anna Grace, and she knew that she wasn't going to convince Mia that it was the right thing because, in all honesty, yes, those dogs could be transported without her help. But she wanted to be a part of it.

"Don't be. It's a quick trip. According to this detailed schedule that Steve just dropped off, we'll only really have two full days on the ground. With the layovers, I'll be home early Monday morning. Nobody will even miss me."

Mia snorted. "We'll all miss you. Just like I'm sure Skittles misses you already."

Yeah, Anna Grace wasn't too sure about that. "Speaking of the guys, have you heard from them?"

Mia shook her head. "Nope. But it comes with the territory."

Anna Grace just nodded. She didn't really know how to respond.

"You're still coming to Bayside for dinner tonight, right?"

115

"Yep. I'll be there."

"Do you need a ride?"

"No. But thank you. I have some errands I need to run beforehand."

"Okay. If you change your mind, just call me."

"I will."

Mia went to turn to head back to the other building but then spun back around.

"Oh! I forgot to tell you. Arianna and Dino set a date for their wedding."

Anna Grace smiled. "Really? When?"

Mia chuckled. "Well, according to Arianna, Dino told her to be ready to walk down the aisle as soon as he gets home."

"I'm guessing they're just going to the courthouse since it takes a while to plan a wedding."

Mia snickered. "You don't know Alex that well yet. All she needs is a date and time, and the bride and groom will have the wedding of their dreams. Trust me. She's hosted all the weddings for the guys on the team, including mine and Stitch's. And, let me tell you, I couldn't have planned it any better. So, it doesn't matter if they give her a month's notice or a day's notice. Alex will come through."

Anna Grace was impressed. She laughed to herself. Alex was like a one-woman show—badass former operative, entrepreneur, and event planner.

"That sounds impressive," Anna Grace replied.

"So, with that, the other ladies and I have planned a little surprise bridal shower for Arianna tonight as well."

"Oh! Well, I'm glad you told me so that I can pick up something for her."

Mia grinned. "It'll be so much fun!"

Anna Grace was sure it would be. For the first time in a long time, she was happy having friends to hang out with and not having to worry about them finding out who she really was.

After telling Mia that she'd see her later, she pulled out the itinerary again and started to look it over thoroughly. Jesus, he wasn't lying when DeSmith said he'd be doing photo ops. There were five scheduled on the itinerary. Whatever floats his boat, just as long as she wasn't included in any of them.

She heard her phone ringing and reached under the counter and grabbed it. It was Xavier. She was supposed to meet him for dinner tomorrow.

"Hello?"

"Hey, Grace."

She cringed, knowing that after tomorrow he'd know her real name.

"Hi, Xavier."

"I'm really sorry to have to do this, but I'm going to need to reschedule our dinner. I didn't realize that Melanie had planned a dinner party with a few of our neighbors.

"That's okay." And it was, as it gave her a little more time to gather her wits and words for when she revealed the secret she'd been carrying around.

"Are you sure? The night at the charity gala, you seemed like whatever you wanted to talk about was important."

"It can wait."

"How about Friday for lunch? I'll actually be over in your neck of the woods, and I can swing by the shelter and pick you up."

"Umm…actually, I'm leaving on Thursday."

"Are you going out of town?" He asked, and she could hear the surprised tone in his voice. Since she'd known Xavier, she'd never gone anywhere.

"Well, do you remember the invitation that I got from Senator DeSmith?"

"I do."

"I've decided to accept it."

He was silent for a moment before he spoke. "You're sure about this?" Again, she could hear the difference in his tone. He wasn't thrilled about her going, just like everyone else.

"I'm positive. I know people don't want me to go, but as I've told them, I feel obligated to go. And not to the Senator; my obligations are for the dogs."

She heard the deep breath he took.

117

"I'm not telling you that you can't go because you're a grown adult." He sighed again. "I'm just worried for your safety. I've heard too many horror stories about foreigners visiting there and the things that have happened to them."

"According to the information I was provided today from the Senator's office, we'll have a security detail the entire time from the moment we land in the Philippines until we board the plane to return home."

She wasn't going to bring up what region of the country they would be in. That would for sure draw objections from everyone.

"Promise me you'll always be aware of your surroundings and that you'll stick close to the security detail at all times."

She smiled at his fatherly words. "I promise. You have my word."

"Well, I guess I'll see you when you return. I'll schedule some time on my calendar for next week for us to get together. Though I'm sure there will be a large fanfare when you arrive home with all the dogs."

She chuckled. "I'm hoping it will be low-key. I'll give you a call to let you know I made it back the moment the plane lands."

"I'm proud of you, Grace. What you're doing is truly commendable."

Her eyes began to burn with tears. She couldn't remember the last time someone told her that they were proud of her.

"I'm trying my best," she told him around the lump in her throat.

"Take care and stay safe."

"I will. I'll talk to you next week."

"Bye, Grace."

"Bye."

She set the phone down on the counter and stared back at the detailed schedule in front of her. She started to second-guess herself. Was she making the right decision? She shook her head. No. No negative thoughts. It was about the thirty-one dogs who were going to have a new life—hopefully, a life full of happiness.

Anna Grace walked up the stairs to Skittles' apartment. She would've taken the elevator if it weren't for her claustrophobia. Alex had given her the key she had to Skittles' apartment. Apparently, Alex was the key-keeper for the team, just in case. However, most of the team had a significant other to keep them in line. Anna Grace wanted to leave her itinerary for Skittles in case he got home before she did. Even though they parted on bad terms, she didn't want him to worry. She also wrote him a note. Earlier, while she was out shopping for some last-minute items she needed to pick up for her trip and a gift for Arianna, she had done some hard thinking. Maybe it was time to open herself up and finally talk to someone about everything she had been through. Who that person would be was another decision she would have to make. To spare the emotions of those around her, she was leaning towards talking to a professional. Knowing that the ladies of Alpha Team have had their own experiences, maybe one could recommend someone. She'd talk to them tonight when she'd see them.

As she made her way down the long hallway, she looked at the numbers on the door until she got to door 409. She inserted the key and turned it but the lock didn't disengage. Alex had told her that sometimes the lock would stick. She tried it again and put a little more oomph when she turned the key, but it still wouldn't budge. She slapped her hand against the door out of frustration.

She'd try one more time, and if it didn't work, she'd just give everything to Alex to give to Skittles.

As she tried to insert the key again, a voice behind her spoke. "Can I help you with something?"

Anna Grace spun around, caught off guard by the woman behind her.

She looked her over, and as she got a really good look, her eyes widened as she realized it was the woman she'd seen Skittles with the night of the charity event—his girlfriend. *Just great!*

Anna Grace stepped to the side. "No. I'm just dropping something off for a friend." She glanced at Skittle's door, and the woman followed her line of sight.

The woman looked her over, and then it was like she suddenly realized who Anna Grace was, and her lips formed into a feral smile.

"You know he's only keeping close to you because he feels sorry for you."

"Excuse me?" Anna Grace questioned.

The woman let out an annoying high-pitched cackle before shooting daggers Anna Grace's way.

"I know all about you and your poor pitiful life. You're nothing but a homeless street rat. Don't think for one minute I can't see through you and what your real intentions are with Skittles."

Anna Grace felt like she'd been punched in the gut. Had Skittles told this vile woman her history?

"How did you plan on getting into his apartment? He doesn't just hand out random keys to people."

"A friend of his gave me a key," Anna Grace replied but then wondered why she was even still talking to this woman.

"Well, I can take that and make sure he gets it." The woman started to reach for the envelope in Anna Grace's hand, but Anna Grace quickly pulled her hand back.

Who in the hell did this woman think she was?

"That's okay. I'll give it to one of his friends to give to him."

The woman crossed her arms and appeared as if she would attack her again, but Anna Grace didn't want a confrontation. So, she beat her to the punch.

"Look, I don't know you, but I do know that you and Skittles are an item." Anna Grace noticed how the woman's eyes grew large with that comment, but she ignored it and continued to say what she had to say. "But that doesn't mean that he can't have friends."

The woman smirked as she pursed her lips before giving Anna Grace the once over again.

"Well, at least you've admitted it. I honestly can't see what he sees in you anyway. Oh, but Skittles always had a soft heart for charity cases."

Anna Grace was so angry that she wanted to cry, but she refused to cry in front of this awful, toxic woman. She wouldn't give her the benefit of knowing she had hurt her. *Shrug it off,* she told herself. They are only words.

She was more upset, hurt, and felt betrayed that Skittles had outed her past to strangers. That was what hurt the most.

She looked at the woman and blinked back her tears. "If you're done making yourself feel more empowered by demeaning someone else, I'm going leave."

With that parting shot, Anna Grace walked back down the hallway until she got to the stairwell. Once she was inside and nobody was around, she let the first tear slip out of her eye. Skittles had crossed a line that she didn't know if she could ever forgive him.

Monique couldn't stop the wicked smile from crossing her face as she watched Grace sulk as she walked away. Thanks to Steve, Senator DeSmith's Chief of Staff and her boss, she had gotten some inside information on the woman who seemed to have snagged Skittles' undivided attention.

She hadn't planned for Grace to see her and Skittles at the charity event, but knowing she had was even better. Maybe now she'd leave Skittles alone.

With Grace scheduled to accompany the Senator to the Philippines, she silently hoped she'd get lost there and never return.

She wasn't quite sure what Steve was up to in regards to Grace Montgomery, but it if got her away from Skittles, she was all for it.

Skittles didn't belong with someone of Grace's nature. He should have a strong woman by his side—a capable woman who had a strong career path. That woman was her. Skittles was her man, and she wasn't going to let anyone get in the way of that.

After her encounter with Skittles' girlfriend, Anna Grace wasn't really feeling up to having dinner with everyone, but she'd suck it up and go through with it.

She walked into Bayside and found Alex sitting at a table talking with Autumn, Frost's wife. Autumn, with her fiery red hair, was glowing as she rubbed her growing belly. Anna Grace felt a pang to her own belly. She always dreamt of having a baby of her own one day, but with the way her screwed up life was, that didn't appear to be in the cards for her.

Autumn saw her first and waved. Alex then turned around and smiled. "Hey. You made it."

Anna Grace plastered a smile on her face. "I wouldn't miss it."

"Come sit down. The others are around here somewhere."

Anna Grace placed the gift she had brought for Arianna on the table with the other gifts then took the open seat next to Alex.

"Autumn and I were just discussing baby names," Alex said and smiled at Autumn.

"Any takers?" Anna Grace asked as a waitress came over and took her drink order. Again, club soda with lemon.

Autumn's smile reached her eyes. Frost and I have decided to let Cody, our son, pick the name. We don't know what we're having, so we told him to pick a boy's name and a girl's name.

"That is so cool. I'm sure that made Cody feel extra special and included in the birth process."

Autumn nodded her head. "Thankfully, Cody's a great kid and has been asking a lot of questions and helping out with everything. One night, Frost and I were picking out the furniture for the nursery, and I guess Frost had left the page up on the computer. Cody apparently saw it and ended up calling Stitch and told him that he wanted to buy it for his new baby brother or sister."

"Did he?" Anna Grace asked.

"He did. Stitch and Mia paid for it with their credit card, and they took Cody to the bank. He withdrew the cash from his savings account and paid Stitch back. Then Stitch took him to pick it up and then helped Cody set it all up in the nursery. Frost and I were blown away by it."

"Wow! What a great kid."

"Yeah. He is. He doesn't know it, but Frost put the money back in his savings account." Autumn grinned, and Anna Grace wished she had family like them.

"So, did you drop off what you needed to at Skittles' place?" Alex asked, changing the subject.

"Umm...not exactly."

Alex lifted her eyebrow, and Anna Grace began telling her about how the key got stuck and then her unfortunate run-in with Skittles' girlfriend.

"Wait. Did you say his girlfriend?" Alex asked, clearly looking baffled.

"Yeah. I think she's his neighbor too. At least she walked out of the apartment next to his." Anna Grace described what the woman looked like.

Alex glanced over at Autumn, and Autumn looked confused as well but then shrugged her shoulders. Anna Grace looked between Alex and Autumn.

"What? Why are you two looking at each other like that?"

"If you are talking about Monique, I don't think that's his girlfriend."

"She said they were dating. Plus, I saw them kissing at your charity event the other night."

Alex's eyes widened, and her expression took on a disgusted look.

"You're sure that you saw the two of them together?" Alex asked again.

"Positive. That's sort of why I left so suddenly."

"Hmmm...I think you may need to talk with Skittles," Alex stated, but she also seemed a little upset.

"Well, that will have to wait until next week or whenever he gets back. Unless he gets home tomorrow."

"Why is that?"

"I guess Mia didn't tell you."

"Tell us what?" Autumn chimed in.

"That I accepted Senator DeSmith's offer to go to the Philippines with him."

"You did?!" Alex exclaimed, and Anna Grace nodded her head. She held up her hand when she saw the questions in Alex's eyes.

"I know Mia and Xavier have already given me the lecture of why I shouldn't, but I'll tell you guys what I told them. I can't in good conscience not help those dogs."

"I get it, but the Philippines?"

"I know. Not the best place in the world, but we'll have a security detail with us the entire time. Actually, that was what I wanted to drop off at Skittles' apartment." She handed Alex the envelope. "If the guys get home before I get back, can you please give that to Skittles? It's my itinerary. I don't want him to think I just ran off. Especially since our last conversation wasn't good." Anna Grace explained what went down.

"Yeah. Ace said he hadn't seen Skittles that pissed off in a long time. I can't believe someone slipped you a roofie. Were the owners able to find anything on the video?"

"No. There were so many people at the bar that the camera wasn't at the right angle to get a clear shot of where my glass was sitting when Maggie went to the back to grab the lemons."

"That's scary, but I'm glad that Skittles and Stitch happened to be there."

"Me too," she whispered, knowing damn well what would've happened.

Moments later, Juliette, Tenley's mom, arrived with Derek. Anna Grace was surprised to see him there, considering the team was out on a mission. Alex must've read her mind because she leaned over and explained that when the guys aren't literally "active," Derek doesn't have to be at the base.

The rest of the ladies joined the group, and everyone was having a good time, Anna Grace included. She realized she needed the company. As everyone got up to fix their plate from the small buffet set up, Derek approached Anna Grace and asked to speak with her. At first, she was a little taken back because what on earth would he have to talk to her about. She was a nobody to him.

As they walked over to the other side of the restaurant where it was less crowded, she noticed that Derek held a bag in his hand. When he reached into the bag and pulled out a fancy-looking phone and handed it to her, she looked at him as if he had two heads.

"What's that?" She asked.

"That is your new phone," he replied with a hint of amusement.

Her mouth gaped open. She always dreamed of having a phone like that, but she couldn't afford one.

"That's not mine."

"It is now. I'm giving it to you because I want to make sure you have a way to communicate with us back here while on your trip."

When she went to ask him how he knew, he just grinned. "One thing that you'll learn about me is that nothing ever happens without me knowing. Especially when it comes to my team and those close to them."

"I don't know what to say." She admitted and was still shocked.

"Just promise me you'll keep it on at all times and make sure it is charged. The battery charge in that phone lasts approximately two days if you don't have a lot of apps open."

Anna Grace felt as if Derek was talking in some sort of code or giving her an advanced warning with the way he was explaining the battery. Either way, she assured him that she'd keep it charged and powered on. He also told her that he programmed everyone's number in it.

She was taken back by his generosity and kindness. He even hugged her, and that almost made her cry.

She spent the rest of the evening laughing, listening to stories, and just enjoying her new friends. No matter what happened between her and Skittles, she would never allow her newfound friendships to disappear.

CHAPTER TWELVE

Anna Grace stepped out of the Zamboanga International Airport and was hit by a wall of heat and thick humidity. It was so bad that her hair probably grew, but instead of longer, it grew outward. She pulled out her ballcap from her backpack and put it on. That should tame the hair until they arrived at their destination near the beach. According to the itinerary, the hotel was only a ten to fifteen-minute drive. After they checked in, got settled and cleaned up, they would depart to a city just north of where they were to meet with the organization holding the dogs.

Steve joined her on the sidewalk. She eyed him through her sunglasses. There was just something off with the guy. He acted strange sometimes, and she had even caught him staring at her during the flight. It was a little creepy.

"This is our ride," Steve said, pointing to the white van that was pulled up in front of them. Steve waved his arm in the air, and the driver lifted his hand in acknowledgment.

As soon as the van came to a stop, Steve slid open the back door and gestured for her to get in. A part of her wanted to turn around and march right back into the airport to the ticket counter and ask when the next flight back to the states was leaving.

Steve cleared his throat as if he was getting annoyed with her, and she looked over at him. He raised his eyebrows and nodded his head toward the door as if telling her to get moving. She didn't know what the big hurry was since the Senator was still inside with his security detail. But so that he wouldn't get his panties in a twist, she picked her bag up and climbed in. She went to take one of the seats in the third row but again, he barked at her telling her that the back was his seat and for her to take a seat in the first row. She wanted to roll her eyes, but she didn't say a word or try to argue. This guy was a royal pain in the ass, and she was already regretting coming. In the back of her mind, she kept telling herself that she was here for the dogs and the dogs only.

She got situated into her assigned seat. She was sweating badly. Apparently, the cars in the area didn't have the luxury of air conditioning. She wiped the droplets of sweat from her forehead as she stared out the window. She called up to the driver.

"Do these windows open?"

Without looking at her, he said, "Window broke."

A motorcycle pulled up next to the van. Seconds later, a second one pulled up behind the first one. She looked closely and noticed both men had a badge pinned to their polo shirts. She wondered if they were the police. If they were, it didn't give her any sense of security. They both approached Steve as Steve met them near the front of the van. They looked like they had just rolled out of bed and threw on the first thing they saw. The smaller of the two kept peering through the windshield at her in a weird sort of way. Instead of worrying about it, she focused on the cars as they drove by.

She wished she had someone there that she knew. The first person who popped into her head was Noah—or Skittles, as she was getting accustomed to. She wondered where he was and how he was doing. Knowing he was a SEAL made her nervous for his safety.

Then she thought about that evil witch who lived next door to Skittles. Anna Grace knew she was going to have to face the reality that Skittles had moved on. She'd let him help her clear her name, and then she'd move on too. As much as it would kill her, especially now that she had found him, it would devastate her to see him with another woman. But if he was happy that was all that mattered. She'd survived this long under her new identity, and she'd continue that life—alone like she was now.

Steve climbed into the van, drawing her back to the current events on hand. Now all they were waiting for was Senator DeSmith.

Moments later, the Senator emerged from the airport with his security detail that consisted of two men. He looked to be in a heated discussion, and at one point, DeSmith had his finger in the one guy's face and looked to be chastising him. She looked away, feeling uncomfortable for staring. She had been shocked that the security detail was local and not the government. She didn't know how all of that worked.

A few minutes later, DeSmith got into the van taking a seat in the middle row. He didn't say anything to anyone, but Anna Grace could tell whatever conversation took place hadn't gone over well. She wondered where the security detail went because they were nowhere in sight. She was under the impression that the detail would stick with them. She suddenly felt uneasy. She placed her hand on the waistband of her yoga pants. She didn't have pockets but wanted to make sure that her phone stayed in her possession at all times, so she tucked it into her waistband.

The driver slammed the door, startling her, and she jumped. When she glanced over her shoulder, Steve was staring at her with that creepy smirk on his face. He had very cold and emotionless eyes. She hated to be reminded of her past, but Steve actually reminded her of some of the men back in Mexico who worked for Senor Castillo. Then she decided the less interaction she had with him, the better.

The driver hopped in and put the van in gear, and stepped on the gas. She noticed that the two police motorcycles stayed with them—one on each side.

As they drove out of the city and toward the resort area, she laid her head against the window.

She hadn't been paying much attention until the van made an abrupt turn down an alleyway. There were tall buildings on each side of the vehicle. She guessed that this wasn't where they were staying. She had seen pictures of the hotel. She tried to remain calm, but when she glanced back at the Senator and Steve, both of them appeared to be confused by the change in direction. Her heart rate increased, and she took a few deep breaths.

It was Steve who spoke to the driver.

"Excuse me. This isn't the way to the hotel."

When the driver didn't answer, Anna Grace began to feel extremely nervous.

Maybe the guy hadn't heard him, so she repeated what Steve said, and she too received the same—silence.

Suddenly, another van similar to the one they were riding in pulled out of a hidden driveway and blocked the road. The driver slammed on the brakes to avoid broadsiding the other van, and she face-planted into the back of the passenger seat.

Anna Grace felt her heart race. Jesus, she wasn't even in the country for an hour, and already she had almost been injured. The driver blew the horn. When the van in front of them didn't move, the driver put their vehicle in reverse and started to back up when another car pulled in behind them. They were trapped.

When she peeked around the front seat to look out the windshield, she felt all the blood drain from her face as she watched two men jump out of the van and point military-style guns at their van. They began to yell at the driver. They spoke Filipino, so she couldn't understand anything they were saying.

She quickly glanced over her shoulder at the Senator and Steve. Both of them appeared to be rattled, and that just made her uneasiness grow.

It all happened so quickly that Anna Grace didn't have time to react. Shots were fired into the windshield, striking the driver. She screamed and fell to the floorboard as the driver slumped over the steering wheel. She covered her head as she tried to hide behind the passenger seat.

Where were the police who had been escorting them? She had been so into her own mind during the drive that she didn't even realize when they had dropped off. Her body shook with fear.

Suddenly the van door flew open, and she found herself staring down the barrel of a long gun. But she had her answer in regards to the police—they were part of the ambush. Another guy appeared, holding a gun identical to that of the other guy.

They started yelling, and she was so frightened that she continued to lie on the floor shaking. She didn't even want to look at them. She couldn't see the Senator or Steve, but she assumed they were just as scared.

She cried out when one of the guys hit her in the shoulder with the gun. He yelled at her again. This time she looked up at him. If his expression was a telling sign, their situation wasn't good. The coldness in his dark eyes made her even more afraid. He wouldn't stop yelling, so she finally looked over and got a good look at DeSmith. His eyes were wide, and he appeared to be in shock.

"I don't know what he wants," she told him as tears poured from her eyes.

Senator DeSmith reached over the back of the seat and squeezed her shoulder. The guy turned the gun on the Senator.

"Calm down, Grace. Just cooperate, and they won't harm you. He wants you to move to the other side, behind the driver's seat."

She looked at the guy, and when the Senator sat back in his seat, the guy pointed the gun back at her. She slowly scooted toward the window, being careful not to make any abrupt movement. She swallowed hard, knowing now she would have no escape route unless she busted the window. Once her body was pressed against the side of the van, both men jumped inside. One took the vacant seat next to Steve in the third row, and the one who'd been torturing her by waving the gun in her face moved in next to her and slammed the door. The sound was deafening. They were trapped with no way out.

Another guy appeared and pulled the dead driver out of the van before hopping into the driver's seat and throwing the van into drive. The van that was blocking them began to move, and her van driver stepped on the gas. She looked out the window and couldn't believe they just left the guy's dead body in the middle of the road. That didn't give her much confidence in what they would do to her.

"What is this all about?" The Senator asked calmly but was silenced by the guy behind him.

"Don't speak!"

Anna Grace watched out the window as the town started to disappear until they were on a tiny two-lane road in a desolate area.

No matter how hard she tried, she couldn't get her body to stop trembling. She was beyond the point of being scared—she was terrified. She had escaped captivity before, but these men seemed ruthless and killed on the spot. They most likely wouldn't care what happened to her. She was a nobody, and the odds of her walking away from this were slim to none. Now

Senator DeSmith, on the other hand—was a different story. The bad guys had leverage with him, and they appeared to know who he was. The question now was what would their demands be, and would it include her?

As the van made its way around a sharp bend, they followed the narrow road parallel to the water. There was a small cluster of buildings just ahead, and as the van pulled up in front, it came to a stop. She looked out the window and saw a dock with several small motorboats.

A few men emerged from one of the structures, carrying their own military-style weapons.

Moments later, Anna Grace, Steve, and the Senator were pulled from the van and escorted towards the dock. There were three boats lined up, and she then understood they were taking them to another island. Or worse, they were going to dump them out in the water.

As they were directed into the boats, the bad guys separated her from Steve and the Senator. She was placed into a boat by herself with three other men. The driver of the boat pointed to the floor for her to sit. It was disgusting—coated in grime and what looked like blood. She kept her eyes on Steve and Senator DeSmith as they were escorted to another boat and told to take seats. Before she could take a seat, someone approached her from behind and tried to cover her eyes with a blindfold, but she resisted. She didn't like the dark. She was relentless, unwilling to give up fighting for her life. If she was going to die, she would die knowing she tried everything in her will to survive. She used one of the moves she had learned while at college in a self-defense class. It was a simple move, but most of the time, an effective move. He shouted as her knee made contact with his groin. He released her, and she started to run towards the road. She didn't know where she was going, but she didn't care. Her legs and arms pumped as her tennis shoes pounded on the dirt road. Just as she cleared the road and ran into an open field toward trees, she was tackled to the ground. She continued to fight. Her arms and legs were flailing all over the place. Suddenly she was lifted off the ground and hoisted into the air. The guy holding her around the waist squeezed so hard she thought he'd break her ribs. Her fight with him only lasted mere seconds before she was pulled backward and hit in the head

131

with a blunt object. As she slumped to the ground, she caught a glimpse of Steve and the Senator still standing there, staring at her. Her eyes began to close, and before she knew it, everything around her faded to black.

"What in the hell did you do that for?" The Senator shouted at the guy who had hit Anna Grace in the head.

The guy didn't take his comment well because DeSmith was met with a gun shoved into his face, and he quickly raised his hands and backed off. Even though he had set this little operation in motion, it still had the potential to go in the opposite direction. But they needed to remember that if they wanted to get paid and secure their cache of weapons, they needed to learn to follow his orders.

Steve stepped forward and calmed the situation.

"Look, we all need to relax. Our plan is working perfectly. Let's get her onto the boat and get out of here before someone comes along and outs us."

Ramil, the guy in charge, stepped forward and looked at Steve.

"You are right. Word is already starting to spread about the Senator's abduction. We need to move now so we can get things in place for the next phase. Your government isn't going to sit long without taking action."

He motioned to one of the other guys to grab the girl and take her back to the boat. At least now, she wouldn't be a hindrance. But he needed her gone for good, and he didn't care how.

When Sue Ellen perished in the fiery car crash that claimed her life, DeSmith wasn't sure what to do with a baby. That baby was supposed to meet the same fate as her mother, but because a good Samaritan had come along, the baby was pulled from the wreckage in time before it had exploded.

When he was contacted by the police and informed about the accident, he acted dumbfounded when the authorities told him that a baby had been rescued, though he was seething on the inside. He had driven down and picked up the baby. He paid a pretty penny to make sure the details of the baby stayed out of the news. The first order of business had been taking a paternity test. He had been relieved when he was told that he wasn't the father. But what in the hell was he supposed to do with a fucking baby? He made a few calls, and in a matter of days, a lobbyist friend of his and his wife, who was a software developer, agreed to adopt the baby in exchange for a hefty sum, including a brand new Potomac mansion. His problem had been solved. Just as long as the Silvers kept their mouth shut.

The problem was that the Silvers knew they had the upper hand, and out of the blue years later, they started making new demands. They wanted more money and threatened to reveal the truth about Anna Grace. DeSmith wasn't going to be controlled nor blackmailed. So, with the help of a few trusted acquaintances, he had the Silvers killed and precious Anna Grace removed from the picture.

The house that her parents were killed in still sat abandoned in the luxurious subdivision. When DeSmith had initially bought the house for the Silvers, he had bought it under his law firm's name, including the deed. Shortly after the death of the Silver, DeSmith's law firm tried to sell the house, but a shocking discovery was made. The Silvers had somehow managed to one-up him and had filed a new deed with their names listed. So legally, he couldn't touch the house—which at one point was a seven-million-dollar home. It was revealed that the Silvers had willed the home and all of the assets to Anna Grace. And with her current status as missing, that meant the house still belonged to her. The home and other assets were held in a trust by another law firm. All of the taxes, insurance, and other fees to maintain the home were deducted from the trust.

The people he sent to take care of the Silvers had made sure to go through the desks and paperwork and remove any incriminating evidence they could find on him. DeSmith sometimes regretted not just killing her like her parents. It would've saved him a lot of money, time, and stress.

DeSmith looked at Steve. "Ramil's right. We need to move quickly. You and I both know there are FBI, CIA, and U.S. military in the country. And I can guarantee you the government already has them looking for us."

"What about Anna Grace? What are you planning on doing with her?" Steve asked, and DeSmith knew that Steve wanted to make sure she would no longer be a thorn in their side.

133

Ramil gave Steve a stern look. "Don't worry about the girl. She'll be taken care of per our agreement."

Steve nodded his head, but DeSmith could see the worry in his tight expression. If this plan didn't go off as expected, many people could be facing federal charges, including him.

DeSmith smiled. Steve had planned the entire operation. All the Senator had to do was activate his tracking device, and those in government positions who were involved in the little scheme knew how to run with the story and ensure whoever the government sent in to find them knew where to look.

They had their stories rehearsed down to every detail as they explained that they did all they could to help poor Grace, but because she wouldn't cooperate, she was taken by another group and hadn't been heard from since.

Grace Montgomery would just be another forgotten name over time.

CHAPTER THIRTEEN

"Excuse me, Commander. Could I speak with you for a minute?" Skittles asked Derek just before they prepared to enter Bayside. The team had arrived stateside a few hours ago and were now meeting everyone for dinner.

Derek turned toward Skittles. "Sure. What's up?" Derek asked as the two stepped aside so the others could go ahead of them.

"It's Anna Grace."

Derek squinted his eyes. "What about her?"

"Well, it's more about her parents' deaths. Do you know anyone who could get access to her parents' murder investigation file at the FBI?"

Derek tossed his head side to side. "It's possible. What's this all about?"

Skittles rubbed the back of his neck. "The file is sealed, and I'm curious as to why."

Derek eyed him. "Do I even want to know how you know that the file is sealed?"

Skittles felt the heat in his cheeks. Everyone on the team, including Derek, knew of his computer capabilities.

"No, sir. It's best that you don't know," Skittles responded, and Derek's lips twitched in amusement.

"Give me a few days, and I'll make some calls."

"Thank you."

Derek cocked his head to the side, and Skittles noticed something cross his eyes. "Have you spoken with any of the ladies yet?"

Skittles shook his head but then smiled, knowing that in just a few moments, he'd get to see Anna Grace. He felt bad for ending their conversation the way he had. But he didn't have an option. When the base called, he went. They had a lot to discuss.

Derek slapped him on the back. "After you do, come back and see me." Then he walked inside and left Skittles standing on the sidewalk. He hated when the Commander said shit like that. He pulled open the door and made his way inside.

He looked around and didn't see her. He was sure that Mia or one of the others surely would've let her know they were home. He had tried to call her, but it went straight to voicemail.

He walked up to the bar where Arianna was welcoming Dino home. As Dino took Arianna into his arms and kissed her, Skittles watched in awe. That right there was what he wanted with Anna Grace. Once Dino released Arianna and she walked back behind the bar, Skittles moved closer.

"Hey, Arianna. Is Anna Grace here?"

"Nope," she snapped at him then turned away as if dismissing him. He stared after her, wondering what in the hell was up with the attitude. Dino was standing beside him.

"What in the hell was that all about?" Dino asked, taking a seat at the bar as he reached for his beer. She didn't even ask Skittles if he wanted a beer—which she knew he did because he always ordered one.

Skittles shook his head. "I have no fucking clue. All I did was ask her if Anna Grace was here. I didn't see her, and I tried calling her, but the call went straight to voicemail.

Dino looked toward his fiancé, who was waiting on another customer at the far end of the bar.

"Give me a minute," he said and got up, then went behind the bar and pulled Arianna aside.

Skittles watched as the two spoke, and every now and then, he noticed that Arianna would look his way. Something was going on. A minute or two later, both Dino and Arianna walked back over. Arianna's expression looked completely different than it did just a few minutes ago.

She pulled a frozen mug from the cooler, poured him a beer, and slid it across the bar.

"Tell Skittles what you just told me," Dino said to Arianna.

She bowed her head and took a deep breath. When she looked back up, her expression was one full of guilt. "First, let me apologize for speaking to

136

you the way I did." Her gaze wandered over to Dino. "Apparently, I didn't have all the facts."

"Okay, apology accepted. But what don't you have all the facts about?"

"Anna Grace."

At the mention of her name, he straightened up. "What about her? Is she in trouble?"

"No," she rushed to say. "She isn't in trouble, but you should know that she had a confrontation with Monique outside of your apartment the other day, and it didn't end well. Monique said a few nasty things to her, including some personal jabs. Anna Grace thinks you betrayed her trust. About what I don't know, because she wouldn't say. She also informed Anna Grace that you and she were dating, and that she needed to go away.

Skittles shook his head, not comprehending a damn thing that Arianna had said. He was still stuck on the fact that she had been by his apartment. And what did Arianna mean about him betraying Anna Grace's trust? That was something he'd never do. Monique had crossed a line and he needed to put his foot down.

"Do you know why Anna Grace was at my apartment?" He asked, and Arianna hesitated to answer but then spoke. "She was dropping something off for you. She was at your door when Monique walked up, and then things got ugly. Whatever Anna Grace had for you, she ended up giving it to Alex." She nibbled her bottom lip, something all women seemed to do when they were either nervous or hiding something.

He scrunched his eyebrows together. What would she need to drop by his place? He looked back at Arianna. "Is that all?"

"You should talk to Alex."

Dino gave him a serious look. "What are you going to do?"

Skittles looked across the room and saw Alex talking to Ace. "I'm going to find out what Anna Grace left me and find out what the fuck is going on." He grabbed his beer off the bar and walked toward the table where the others were.

As soon as he arrived at the table, he noticed the evil daggers all the women threw his way when they saw him. Knowing why, he quickly cleared up any confusion of what they may have thought happened and assured them that nothing was going on with Monique and that he wanted Anna Grace. It was the first time he'd admitted out loud in front of the others that he wanted her. He never wanted to be on the wrong side of the women who sat before him, but it was nice to see they all had Anna Grace's back.

He looked at Alex. "Arianna said A.G. left something with you for me."

Her eyes widened at first, but she quickly looked away, picked up her purse, and pulled an envelope out. But before she handed it to him, she looked him in the eye. "You need to talk to her and make it clear what your intentions are with her."

He gave Alex a soft smile. "I know, and I will as soon as I see her."

Alex let go of the envelope. "She didn't want you to worry, so she left you her itinerary."

Skittles furrowed his eyebrows. "Her itinerary?"

"She left yesterday for the Philippines with Senator DeSmith," Alex informed him as she winced a tad, knowing how he would react.

He closed his eyes. *Son of a bitch!*

"I thought she was leaning more towards not going."

Tenley bit her lip then said, "I think that was before she thought you and Monique were an item."

Mia spoke up. "I tried to persuade her not to go. In fact, we all did, but she insisted she was obligated to go. And that if she could save even one dog, it would be worth the trip."

He went to comment but was interrupted by the high-pitched voice behind him.

"Skittles!"

He spun around and glared at Monique as she waltzed across the restaurant in her designer pantsuit and sky-high heels. *Fucking bitch!*

She rushed over and practically threw herself at him. "When I heard that you might be back in town, I drove down to see if it was true."

She tried to loop her arms around his neck to hug him, but he gently pushed her off and away from him. He didn't want her to touch him. In fact,

138

he wanted nothing from her except her gone and out of his life for good. God, she sounded so fake it was sickening.

He stared down at her like he would his worst enemy. This woman was nothing but a bully who thrived on picking on others.

"Cut the crap, Monique. And while you're at it, why don't you explain what in the hell you said to An…Grace the other day at my apartment?" Shit, he almost had said her real name. God, he couldn't wait until he could use that name all the time.

Monique dramatically rolled her eyes. Cue the Oscar nomination.

She placed her hands on his chest. "Don't sound so testy, sweetheart. I did you a favor and got rid of the trash standing between us."

He pushed her hands away. "I'm not your sweetheart—never was and never will be. All you were to me was a fuck that I honestly don't even remember."

He heard the gasps come from the table behind and knew it was several of the ladies. "Now, answer my question. Tell me exactly what you said to Grace."

"Why are you defending her? She's a street rat. You do know that she was homeless, right?" She bit back, and boy, had she made a mistake.

Tenley jumped up out of her seat, and before Potter could stop her, she was up in Monique's face.

"How dare you speak about our friend that way? You don't even know her, let alone what her circumstances might have been at the time. That is if what you claim is even true. And you know what? Who cares! Grace is more of a woman than you'll ever be. Real women don't go around bashing other women to help their egos. Real women rise by lifting others up. If you can't be nice, then just get the hell out of here because we certainly don't need people like you around."

One by one, Alex, Autumn, Bailey, Arianna, and Mia stood behind Tenley, facing Monique. It was Alex who spoke. "We all stand behind Grace, and like Tenley said, if you don't like it, then don't let the door hit you in the ass on the way out."

139

Skittles stood back in awe and wished Anna Grace could've been there to witness the powerful bond of these amazing women. He even saw the pride in all the guys' expressions, including Diego, who didn't even have a girlfriend.

He turned to face Monique, who had smartly taken a few steps back.

"If you know what's good for you, don't ever go near Grace again."

She jerked back in shock. "Are you threatening me?"

He gave her a deadpan look. "I don't make threats, sweetheart. That's a promise."

With a huff, she threw her purse over her shoulder, spun around, and stomped out the door. *Good fucking riddance.*

When he turned back toward the table, everyone was staring at him. The ladies were all grinning, and Alex looked up at him. "Should I start looking at available dates for my backyard to host your wedding?"

Skittles chuckled and shook his head. It had become a team tradition for those who had left their bachelorhood to get married at Ace and Alex's house.

He took a seat next to her. "Let's not jump ahead."

She just grinned, and her eyes sparkled. Skittles knew she was already planning his and Anna Grace's wedding in that little but brilliant mind of hers. Alex was a pure gem and highly respected in the entire SEAL community. And not only because of her foundation. That helped, but it was her previous years within NSA, and then going into the private sector and what she accomplished mainly during the mission in Afghanistan where the team had initially met her. At the same time, they worked side-by-side to hunt down a terrorist. She had been kidnapped, beaten, shot, and nearly raped, but she lived. And it was because of her courage, bravery, and will to survive.

Suddenly, the music coming through the speakers was silenced, followed by Paul's shrill whistle telling everyone to quiet down just as a breaking news bulletin interrupted the sports games that were being aired on the large TV screens throughout the room.

140

A news anchor appeared on screen along with a headshot of Senator Stan DeSmith:

"We apologize for the interruption, but we have breaking news to report from the Philippines. Sources have confirmed that United States Senator Stan DeSmith, along with two other staff members, were abducted at gunpoint earlier today in the city of Zamboanga during what witnesses say was a traffic stop. According to the Senator's press secretary, the Senator and his party were in the country supporting a new bill on the Senator's agenda regarding international animal cruelty. This trip was in coordination with a local rescue shelter in the Virginia Beach area and a local animal rights group in the Philippines that would see the rescue and safety of about thirty-one dogs.

Again, United States Senator Stan DeSmith and two staff members were abducted earlier today in the Philippines and are still considered missing. This is a developing story, and when we have any additional information to share, we'll cut into the scheduled programming."

As the screen faded back into the sports games, the group at the table were left in shock because each one of them knew Anna Grace was one of the two staff members abducted.

Skittles suddenly felt like he wanted to throw up. As if right on cue, each team member's cell phone rang in a familiar tone. They were being called in, and they had a good idea where they were headed.

CHAPTER FOURTEEN

The team gathered in the secured briefing room in their building. Due to the nature of the situation involving a United States Senator, they were joined in attendance with several agencies within the Intelligence Community, including Mr. Donahue, the Director of National Intelligence.

"So, what are we dealing with?" Commander Connors asked Mr. Donahue to kick off the session.

"At approximately o-eight-hundred hours, Philippine time, the van carrying Senator DeSmith, Steve Johnson—the Senator's Chief of Staff—and a female, was detoured into an alley shortly after they departed their hotel. Intel is coming in with witnesses saying the van was blocked by two other vehicles before being ambushed. The driver of the Senator's van was found deceased in the road."

"Excuse me, Sir." Ace interrupted, and Mr. Donahue looked in his direction.

"Yes."

"Grace Montgomery," Ace said, and Mr. Donahue raised his eyebrow in question. "The female traveling with the Senator. Her name is Grace Montgomery. You put a name with the other two, so I think it's important that everyone in this room knows exactly who is involved in this situation. I believe that everyone's life is just as important as the Senator's, and I want to make sure that she isn't overlooked just because she doesn't hold an official job."

Skittles noticed the slight smirks on the other guy's faces as Ace made the arrogant guy a bit uncomfortable. It was blatant that they were only worried about the Senator's safety and nobody else. That pissed Skittles off, knowing Anna Grace's life was in extreme danger.

With an annoyed sigh and a slight attitude from being called out, Mr. Donahue turned to Ace. "Of course, Ms. Montgomery is just as important as everyone involved. She is a citizen of the United States and an innocent in this unfortunate situation."

Ace glanced over at Skittles and winked, which drew a slight smile to Skittles' lips. He was glad that Ace spoke up because he hated it when these high-up government officials always focused on the popular kids while the less fortunate ones were hung out to dry. He would bet his life that if their team wasn't involved in the mission, these people wouldn't give two shits about Anna Grace. As long as the Senator and his asshole Chief of Staff were rescued, that was all that mattered.

A map appeared on the large screen in front of the room. As soon as Skittles saw the red circle, which he perceived to be the location where the group could be, his stomach almost revolted. According to the Department of State, the Zamboanga Peninsula was one of the worst places for travelers to venture to. That area, along with others in the southern portion of the country, was considered extremely dangerous. The terrorist group Moro Islamic Liberation Front (MILF) was known to control the area and was blamed for violent incidents and kidnappings. Other labeled terrorist organizations had spun off from MILF that included Abu Sayyaf Group and Jema'ah Islamiyah. They, too, were considered to be just as dangerous, and were to be avoided at all costs.

Another picture appeared. This time it was an aerial shot. Once the photo was enlarged, they were now looking at a cluster of run-down buildings that sat directly on the water. In the picture was a dock attached to the property.

"After the group was abducted, it is believed they were driven to this location where they were then moved to a boat and transported across the Basilan Strait to Isabela City."

Upon hearing that, Skittles' stomach churned even more. Basilan Island was littered with terrorists.

"What intelligence are you using to provide this information?" Stitch asked.

"Thanks to the tracking device that the Senator had in his possession, we were able to pick up the signal here." Mr. Donahue flipped to another photo and pointed to a large building on the water.

"How populated is that specific area?" Potter asked.

"It's not. Being that it's on the water, years ago, it was used as a shipping port, but as terrorist organizations moved in, the crime took over the city, and eventually, the citizens who lived and worked there fled. With nobody living or working there, the town slowly died. However, our intelligence says the area is still under the control of certain organizations, including MILF. They still occupy some of the structures when it is warranted. It's a perfect place to hide someone they don't want to be found, such as Senator DeSmith."

Skittles swallowed hard.

"What about the Senator's security detail? We were informed that the Senator was traveling with one," Frost asked next. The team knew that little tidbit thanks to the itinerary that Anna Grace had left for Skittles.

Skittles noticed the guy swallowed hard and hesitated just a fraction before he answered Frost's question. Those actions right there sent alarms blaring.

"The Senator went against the recommendation to seek assistance from the U.S. Marshall's office. Instead, he personally hired a local security company that he had used in the past. That detail was in a separate vehicle. From what we've gathered, the Senator requested the security personnel to travel in another vehicle. When the van driver was forced to turn into the alley, the security detail lost them."

Skittles wasn't buying this story. And judging from the rest of the team's expressions, they thought so too. Something fishy was going on. What government official traveling to a country and region with known terrorist ties, doesn't take along an official security detail?

The lead female FBI agent in the room spoke. "We have a team on the ground now in Zamboanga. They are in contact with the detail who the Senator contracted with. Another team is en route to the resort where the Senator and his party were staying. The local authorities are providing all resources that are needed and available."

"What about the Philippine government? How are they responding to the situation? Do we foresee any issues in my team infiltrating their country in this operation?" Commander Connors asked.

Donahue nodded his head. "They are aware and have pledged any assistance and resources needed to recover the Senator—and his party." The guy glared at Ace as he said party to insinuate that he covered everyone.

Skittles then realized something important that hadn't been spoken about or asked.

"What about motive?"

"I'm sorry, what did you just ask?" Mr. Donahue asked, turning towards Skittles. Skittles knew the jerk had heard him, but he'd play the game.

"I asked about the motive. Has there been any sort of communication or demands from the kidnappers?"

Mr. Donahue pushed his glasses up the bridge of his nose. "No. We haven't been contacted yet. As I said, we don't even know who we're dealing with."

Skittles glanced over at Ace and could read his expression. He was just as perplexed. Usually, when a high-profile individual such as the Senator, in this case, is abducted, the group or organization behind it doesn't wait too long to claim responsibility and start making demands.

Mr. Donahue looked around the room. "We are going to need all hands on deck for this mission." He then turned to Derek. "Commander, I'll leave the mission logistics in your hands. Whatever resources you and your team need are at your disposal."

Derek nodded his head, but Skittles noticed that the Commander wasn't as vocal as he normally was during their mission briefings. Something was on his mind.

Once everyone left the room, the team quickly got to planning for the mission. When an operation was being planned by the SEALs, emotions and ranks were left at the door. With the high-profile types of missions, they were engaged in, there was little room for games or politics amongst team members. When it came to putting together the best overall plan to succeed, every team member had a voice regardless of their rank, title or tenure.

The team was working on a tight schedule. The plane was scheduled to depart at zero hundred hours, not leaving them with a lot of time. Still, as with any other mission, they laid out all of the steps in the planning process.

In a little over two hours, the team had devised a strategic rescue operation, along with several contingency plans should the original plan go FUBAR.

Before the team headed to their gear lockers to pack up all the equipment needed to complete the mission, Derek gathered everyone around the table.

He pulled out his laptop and connected it to the screen at the front of the room. With a push of a few buttons, a map appeared on the screen. Seconds later, a blinking red dot could be seen.

"What's that?" Ace asked, and Skittles thought it looked like a beacon of some sort.

Derek looked at the team. "That is Anna Grace's tracking device."

The entire room went completely silent. Skittles looked closely where the blinking dot was on the map. He turned toward Derek.

"I don't understand."

Derek grinned. "Come on, guys. You know damn well that I wouldn't let one of our own go off on some bullshit trip without some sort of device planted to her ass."

Potter, of all people, smiled. "You do have a soft spot for your girls."

"Damn straight, I do." He looked at Skittles. "When I found out that Anna Grace was going to go on that trip, and knowing that she didn't have any sort of communication device, I bought her a phone and had one of Tink's guys install a chip that I could use to track her whereabouts."

For the first time since Skittles watched that breaking news bulletin, he felt that there was some hope.

"Nobody else knows about this?" Ace asked, pointing the dot.

Derek shook his head. "They don't need to know. The signal is a little weak, and I don't know how long the battery will last. But at least right now, we know that phone is in that location."

"That's where the Senator's tracker was, right?" Diego asked, and Derek nodded his head.

Derek then looked at Skittles. His facial expression was all business. "Skittles, I know this mission is close to you. It's close to home for all of us. I need you to be honest with me and tell me now if you think there's any chance of you going into this mission wearing your feelings on your sleeve. I need your head in the game."

Skittles felt his heart pounding. Even though this mission involved the woman he loved, he'd never put his teammates' lives in jeopardy by thinking with his dick instead of his head.

He licked his lips and looked around at all the guys. Each one of them, except for Diego, had faced a similar dilemma when their women encountered trouble. He would treat this mission no different than all those before. The second this mission began; his emotions were turned off.

"You have my word, commander. My head is on straight. We complete this mission as a team like we always do."

Derek glanced at Ace, and Ace nodded his head.

"Okay, then. Let's get you guys over to the hanger. And Skittles?"

"Yes, Sir?"

"Bring our girl home." Derek grinned, and Skittles smiled. "Yes, Sir."

Ace was pulling some of his gear from his gear locker when his phone vibrated. He picked it up and smiled, seeing it was Alex.

"Hey, sweetheart." He greeted her.

"Hey, you. I know you normally call right before you head out but not knowing when that might be, I wanted to give you a call and let you know that I wouldn't be available when you did call."

He scrunched his eyebrows together and stopped what he was doing.

"Why wouldn't you be?" He questioned.

"Well, Tink just invited me to go on a trip with him."

"What kind of trip?" He asked cautiously. With Tink owning his own security company known for its under-the-radar missions to places that the government preferred to stay out of, Ace could only wonder where they were going and the nature of the trip.

Alex laughed. "Not the kind of trip you're thinking of. Tink has an associate he is looking to contract with, and he agreed to fly out and meet with him. He asked me if I wanted to tag along."

Ace breathed a sigh of relief. Alex kept him on his toes when it came to her abilities. She could tackle any sort of project with ease, including military-style missions that she had retired from.

"That's cool," he said casually, and she laughed again.

"You are so full of shit. I know exactly what was going through your mind."

He chuckled and rubbed his hand along his jaw. "Okay. You got me. Anyway, where are you two headed?"

"Australia!" She yelled so loud that Ace had to pull the phone away from his ear.

"Australia, huh?" He replied, then thought, what were the odds of them being in the same time zone on the other side of the world, just in separate countries.

"Believe it or not, that is one country I haven't been to, and it's number one on my list to visit. The guy Joe lives in Perth."

He smiled. "Well, I'm happy you have the chance to. Is it just you and Tink, and when do you leave?"

"Yep. Just him and I and...well...we're on the plane right now. The plane is scheduled to depart in a few minutes."

His eyebrows shot upward. "You're leaving now?" His voice was raised just a tad, and the other guys looked in his direction. He held his finger up, letting them know he'd clue them in when he was finished.

"Yeah. He called right after you guys were summoned to the base. Are you sure you're fine with it?"

"Why wouldn't I be? You know I don't care. Plus, you'll be with Tink."

"I know. I just don't like springing things on you like this, especially when you're getting ready to head out."

"It's fine, Alex. Who's watching Zuma?" Ace grinned, thinking about their chocolate lab. He was a badass dog even though he was a momma's boy.

"Arianna said she'd watch him. You know how much he and Nigel get along."

Nigel was Arianna and Dino's dog, who had become best friends with Zuma.

"Perfect."

"Well, I won't keep you. Be safe, and I love you. Tell the others they better come back in one piece or I'll kick their asses."

He snorted a laugh. "I'll do my best, and I'll be sure to pass the message along to the others." He paused a moment and closed his eyes. She was the light of his life and soul to his heart. "I love you too, Alex."

"Okay, before you make me cry, I'm going to hang up."

He smiled. "Alright, babe. Love you, and I'll see you when we both get back."

"Love you too. Bye."

Ace disconnected and hung his head. That was the worst part about having someone here at home—the goodbyes. They sucked and it never got easier. In fact, it only got worse.

Potter walked over. "Everything okay?"

Ace grinned. "Yeah. Apparently, Alex is taking a trip of her own." He then explained about Tink's business dealing there.

"Shit, I'd rather be going to Australia. I haven't been there in a while. Not since we did those joint exercises with our Aussie buddies."

"That was a good time. Those guys are awesome and a great group of men to serve with."

Potter nodded, then glanced over toward where Skittles was standing next to Diego and Dino, talking to them.

"Do you think he'll be okay?"

Ace looked over. "Yeah. I do. He's one of us. We've all been in this type of situation—where one of our own is in trouble. But as a team, we've conquered each mission."

"You're right. I just can't believe it. That poor girl. Everything she's been through already and then to have this happen."

"Yeah. It's terrible. And, we don't even know everything she went through. Even Skittles doesn't know it all."

"That has to be tearing him up. But I understand where she's coming from too. It's hard to open up."

"That it is." Ace gave Potter a side glance, then smirked. "Although I do believe that it was you who got a certain somebody to open up a little bit back in Afghanistan."

Potter smiled. "I remember that conversation."

"That conversation was a turning point in Alex's life."

"And look where she is now. Though she'd be a lot happier if she was Mrs. Chambers," Potter teased, taking a shot at Ace and Alex's wedding fiascos.

Ace gave Potter a half-smile. "In due time. Patience."

"Yeah, yeah. I've heard that before," Potter joked.

Ace laughed and slapped Potter on the back as they headed out. Ace couldn't stop smiling because soon, the joke was going to be on everyone after they found out what he'd been up to.

CHAPTER FIFTEEN

Senator DeSmith paced the room. He was getting antsy and just wanted this trip to be over with. The building they were in was filthy, hot, and littered with rodents the size of full-grown cats.

As he paced the length of the room, he rehearsed his script that he'd recite to his rescuers when they came for him. According to Steve, who was the mastermind behind this devious plan, rescue operations were already underway. He wondered which Special Forces Unit had been selected to lead the rescue operation—SEALs or Delta Force. Both units consisted of highly trained soldiers, whose stealth gave them the ability to slip in and out of places undetected. In his situation, his money was on the SEALs, considering the water access they had. He inwardly laughed. Maybe he should up the stakes and offer Ramil a little extra if they engaged with the soldiers. Perhaps another time, he thought to himself. This plan had to be executed perfectly.

Steve entered the room, and he, too, wiped the sweat from his forehead. "Ramil wants to see you."

"Where is he?"

"Downstairs."

"Downstairs? Do you mean there's a basement to this shithole? DeSmith countered but then followed Steve through several rooms until they came to a brick wall.

He looked at Steve, and Steve smirked as he pressed on a specific part of the wall, and suddenly a hidden door was revealed as it opened inward. *Fucking genius*, he thought.

He and Steve descended the stairs, and the further down they got, the colder it got. By the time they reached the bottom, DeSmith felt like he was inside a refrigerator.

He looked around. The space wasn't lit well, and the hallways split off into two directions. Steve guided him toward the left. "You don't want to go to the right," Steve told DeSmith.

"I don't?"

"No. That side is a stash for people Ramil and his crew don't want to be found—if you know what I mean. Plus, I think they also harvest and sell organs through this place."

DeSmith swallowed hard. He knew exactly what Steve was referring to. No wonder it was so cold down here. It was like a morgue.

As they came to another fork in the hall, they went right, and the hall opened into a larger space. It looked like a space for storage. It was wall to wall and floor to ceiling with boxes. They moved a little further into the room, and DeSmith spotted Ramil. He was standing next to what looked like a large pet carrier that someone would use to transport a dog on an airplane. But as he approached, he realized that there was a person inside. He couldn't stop the evil smile that formed on his face when he saw who it was.

Anna Grace lay completely still, making sure she didn't dare move a muscle. She was even afraid to breathe out of fear the guy who'd been loitering would realize she was awake. Her head throbbed, but that was expected, considering someone had whacked her on it. But the most challenging part was trying to control the shivers that wracked her body. She was freezing, and she wondered where they were.

She wasn't sure how long she'd been in there. The last thing she remembered was trying to fight the big dude. She had almost reached the tree line when she was pulled back into the enemy's grasp.

She had no room to stretch out, so she remained curled into a tight ball. Doing so had kept her a little warmer. When she first woke up, she had started to panic, being that it was dark and she was locked in a confined space. Her anxiety had skyrocketed, but she talked herself off the ledge.

The cage reminded her more of a kennel used to transport dogs. A padlock secured the door. She tried to locate her cell phone, but it was gone. Either they had found it on her, or she lost it while she had been fighting that guy.

She heard more footsteps approaching.

"She's still here?" The voice sounded a little muffled.

"We have a buyer, but they can't do the exchange for another three, possibly four days." The voice sounded like the Ramil guy, and she wondered who he was talking to.

"I don't give a shit what happens to the bitch as long as she is never heard from again," a second voice said, and she froze. She may not be able to see or move, but she could certainly hear. It sounded like Steve Johnson—the Senator's Chief of Staff. Was he talking about her?

"Wait a minute. You assured me that she'd be gone by the time the calvary showed up to get me out of here."

She fought the gasp that wanted to come out of her mouth as she took in Senator DeSmith's words. He was there.

"I can't help it if the buyer is delayed," Ramil responded, and that had set off DeSmith.

"Goddammit! I don't need any more fuck-ups or the chance of this girl resurfacing. The only reason she wasn't killed along with her fucking so-called parents was that I still had half of a heart because she was a child."

Anna Grace covered her mouth with the one hand she had use of as tears formed in her eyes. Had Senator DeSmith just admitted that he was responsible for her parents' murders? *Oh, God!*

All three men started to argue. Their voices echoed in the room. They were all trying to speak over each other.

"You need to remember that I can halt that shipment of weapons with one phone call," Senator DeSmith said.

Ramil fired back. "Don't fucking threaten me, old man. I can end you just like you want her gone. You are the one who needs the reminder. You're on my fucking turf now."

Senator DeSmith was involved in illegal arms sales? She couldn't let on that she was awake because if they realized she had just heard everything they said, they wouldn't wait for a buyer to come for her. They would kill her on the spot.

"Look, don't you worry about the fucking girl. I can guarantee that you'll never hear a peep from her again. She's going somewhere special." The malicious tone in Ramil's voice sent shivers down her spine.

153

"Fine. Half of the money has been wired to the account. The rest will be moved once I have confirmation that she's been taken care of."

"Will she be staying down here until the buyer arrives?" Steve asked.

Ramil nodded. "Yes. I can assure you that nobody knows about this place who isn't supposed to know. That door is impossible to see unless you know it's there. I'll make sure it's secured before I leave."

"Fine," Senator DeSmith said on a sigh.

"Senator, let's move back upstairs. We need to go over our stories, so they are consistent when we're questioned," Steve said.

"I'm going to finish down here, then I'll be up and will secure the door at that time."

"Where will you and your men be?" DeSmith asked Ramil.

"Far enough away, so we're not seen. It's already been over twenty-four hours, and I assume help is on the way. We'll give it a day or two before we return."

"Will she be okay for that long?"

Ramil peered down at the crate and grinned wickedly. "What does it matter to you? You want her gone."

Through the small slats in the crate, Anna Grace saw a shadow close in on her, and she quickly shut her eyes and hoped whoever it was would think she was still sleeping. She laid motionless. One of her hands had been pulled through an opening within the cage's metal bars and secured to a metal pipe sticking out of the floor. The person held her hand against the floor, and she felt a prick-like bee sting on the top of her hand. She peeked one eye open and saw the guy had jabbed her with a needle. It wasn't just any needle; he was putting in an IV line. She wasn't fond of needles and didn't like giving blood or having to get IVs. She had tiny veins, and it normally required the person doing it to use a small butterfly needle. She flinched ever so slightly as he fished around for the vein. She heard him curse a few times before he said "sa wakas," meaning finally in Filipino. He stood, then she heard a beeping sound but couldn't see that high up to watch what he was doing.

She watched his feet as they moved away from her. Suddenly the room was plunged into darkness, sending a bolt of fear into her. Once she heard no sign of anyone, she let her tears fall. She felt as if she was in the middle of a twisted nightmare with no means of waking up from it. There was no way she could go back to being under the stronghold of someone. She'd rather die before she had to experience that torture again. Her eyelids started to become heavy, and she wondered if this would be the last time she saw life. She didn't know what they had given her.

As her eyelids slowly closed, an image of Skittles appeared in her mind. At least she would succumb to the darkness with a bright vision. But her subconscious couldn't stop repeating—*Senator DeSmith was a murderer!*

CHAPTER SIXTEEN

The team crept closer to the shoreline near the mouth of a river just south of Kumalarang Beach. The area was unpopulated, and that proved to be a benefit for the mission. It was dark, and the moonlight guided the team to maneuver through the calm waters and obstacles that breached the water's surface. As Diego steered the Zodiac toward their landing point, all eyes were trained on the lush tropical terrain surrounding the welcoming coastline. Not only were they on guard for enemy combatants, but the area was also known to be home to saltwater crocodiles—a dangerous predator to humans, as well as many different species of snakes.

Once on land, Diego, Frost, and Potter secured the Zodiac in a small clearing hidden by large rocks. Using night-vision goggles, the team fanned out in pairs of two as they prepared to hike up the riverbed to their location point. The team was working in tandem with a small unit of Marines who were already assisting the Philippine government in their fight to combat terrorism.

If their mission went according to plan, once the Senator and others were secured, the team would move all hostages to an extraction location positioned approximately one and a quarter-mile due north. The Marine detachment would be waiting with a vehicle to take the group to Menzi Airfield. From there, the group would be flown to the U.S. military base in Okinawa.

As they faded into the tropical landscape, the team descended into a small rundown neighborhood. Following the GPS coordinates and tracking the beacon from the Senator's device, the team surrounded the perimeter of the building thought to be where the Senator, Steve, and Anna Grace were being held.

Skittles had kept his cool, knowing more harm could be done if he didn't. But that wasn't to say that Anna Grace hadn't been on his mind. Frost was in charge of monitoring and tracking Anna Grace's cell phone signal while Ace had the Senator's signal. However, the Senator's signal was a hell of a lot stronger than Anna Grace's. There were periods where her signal would disappear. When it did that, it scared the hell out of him.

Once the perimeter was cleared, the team split into two units. One team led by Ace would breach the front entrance while the second, led by Potter, would infiltrate the back entrance. Irish and Dino were in an overwatch monitoring the ground and surrounding area.

The silence in the air gave an eerie vibe. Every once in a while, the sound of gravel crunching under their feet could be heard. Even though SEALs were trained to walk lightly, there were times where it was just impossible. Skittles could feel the adrenaline flow within his body as they moved in closer to the dilapidated building.

The drone flying above using thermal imaging indicated only two heat signatures inside.

Derek's voice came over the comms unit. "Alpha One, two heat signatures registered from the second floor in a room on the south side. Both appear stationary near the west wall."

"Copy that," Ace replied calmly.

As they were given the order to move in, the first team breached the front and went immediately up the stairs to the second floor. The second team breached the back entrance and spanned out, sweeping the main floor.

As each passing minute went by, Skittles felt his anxiousness increase. It didn't matter how many times he tried to talk himself down; he couldn't help it.

Skittles and Potter were in the process of clearing the back of the main floor when word came over the comms unit that the Senator had been found. However, nothing was said about Anna Grace's status.

Frost looked over at Skittles. "A.G.'s signal is still indicating it's coming from this building."

Minutes later, Ace, Stitch, and Diego descended the stairs with a weary and exhausted-looking Senator DeSmith and his Chief of Staff.

"Grace?" Potter questioned, and Ace sent a quick look Skittles' way, but even with the face covering that Ace wore, Skittles could tell from his eyes that he held a grim expression and that the answer wasn't good.

157

"We don't know what happened to her," the Senator blurted out. "Steve and I were ordered to get out here, but they kept Grace in the van. We haven't seen or heard from her since."

"Who are they?" Frost barked out, appearing just as agitated as Skittles was.

The Senator appeared rattled. "Abu Sayyaf militants."

"I overheard a group of them talking yesterday, and one of them said that the main guy who stayed in the van with Grace was a commander in the organization," Steve voiced. He, too, looked as if he'd seen better days.

Fuck! Skittles muttered under his breath. Abu Sayyaf was considered violent and were solely responsible for the worst terrorist attack in the Philippines. If they had Anna Grace, Skittles knew the chances of finding her dead or alive were slim to none.

"What is the location of her signal?" Ace asked Frost, but before Frost could answer, DeSmith interrupted.

"Signal? What signal?" The Senator questioned in a harsh tone, drawing glares from some of the guys.

"Ms. Montgomery was equipped with a tracking device," Ace stated.

DeSmith's eyes grew large. "She was? Why wasn't I aware of this?" He turned and shot daggers at his Chief of Staff. "Did you know about that?"

Steve's face had suddenly taken on a sickly look, and Skittles wondered what had triggered that sudden panicked reaction, not to mention the Senator's outburst. Big deal if she had a phone.

Steve cleared his throat and seemed to gain a little bit of composure, though he still looked a little unsure. "No. I was not aware she had a phone. When I asked her before the trip, she told me that she didn't have a phone. Or, let me clarify—a cell phone that she'd be bringing with her."

Skittles kept an eye on DeSmith. His face started to turn red, and it wasn't from the temperature inside.

"Who gives a fuck right now." He turned toward Ace. "Shouldn't you be escorting me to safety instead of standing here blabbering about some no-name girl who's probably lying dead in a ditch by now?"

Skittles saw red. Who the fuck did this asshole think he was? Even Steve seemed shocked at the Senator's outburst. Skittles had taken one step toward DeSmith before Diego stopped him by pulling on his ruck. It was a good thing because he would show the Senator firsthand what it was like to be lying in a ditch.

Irish's whispered voice could be heard over the comms. "Dick!"

DeSmith must've realized that he had inserted his foot in his mouth because he apologized, but Potter held his hand up.

"Senator, with all due respect, just shut the fuck up."

Skittles bit back his smile just like the others were doing.

Suddenly, Irish's voice broke over the comms. "Y'all might want to save the chit chat for later because I see headlights in the distance."

"Shit!" Ace stated out loud before he hit his comms unit.

"Command, this is Alpha One. We have the package and COS in our possession. Female still unaccounted for."

"Copy, Alpha One. Proceed to the extraction point. MEU is awaiting your arrival."

Ace glanced around at everyone. Had command just told them not to pursue A.G.'s whereabouts?

"Command, please repeat the order," Ace asked.

"Alpha One. Your orders are to proceed to the extraction point. MEU is standing by for transport."

As the message was relayed, Skittles saw the disappointment in each team member's eyes. Again, politics won out.

"Alpha One to Alpha Four. Are we clear to exit?"

"If you move your asses now, you should hit the tree line without being detected."

"Copy that."

Ace looked at the Senator. "Well, what are you waiting for? Get a move on it."

Skittles exited the building taking up the rear with Potter. As they moved through the darkness, an approaching vehicle could be heard. Part of him wanted to stay behind and see if Anna Grace was in it. But doing his job was

159

first and foremost, and he stuck with the team. But a piece of his heart broke with every step he took further from the building.

As they approached the extraction point, they handed off the Senator to the waiting MEU without so much of a goodbye. Skittles hoped to God that he never had to deal with that prick again. If he did, there was no telling what he may do to him—government official or not. For now, though, he'd make damn sure that he did his part to ensure Senator DeSmith never held another public service position again.

As Ace was gathering the team and preparing to hike back to the beach to retrieve their Zodiac, another MEU vehicle pulled up next to them, and the window rolled down. "Lt. Commander Chambers?" The soldier questioned the group, and Ace stepped forward.

"I'm Lt. Commander Chambers."

"Sir, I have Commander Connors on the line for you." He passed Ace a phone through the window.

Skittles could only hear one side of the conversation.

"Sir?" Ace answered.

"Thank you, Sir."

Ace smirked. "Yes, Sir. We're all well aware that Senator DeSmith is an asshole."

Ace's smirk was short-lived as his eyebrows drew inward, and a serious expression covered his face.

"We are?"

"Okay."

Ace glanced at Skittles as he continued listening to Derek.

"Yes, Sir."

"Understood."

"As soon as we're settled, we'll make the call."

Ace disconnected the line and handed the phone back to the Marine.

"What was that about?" Potter asked.

"It seems we're sticking around a little while longer. Derek got Command to give us some extra time to have another look around for Anna

Grace. It seems Command isn't thrilled with the Senator's behavior, nor the circumstances surrounding this incident."

"That's great news," Dino exclaimed, and Skittles agreed.

"It is. However, we're somewhat on our own."

"Somewhat?" Stitch questioned.

Ace grinned and glanced toward the two Marines in the vehicle. "If we run into trouble, the MEU is our backup."

"Are we going back there now?" Dino asked, and Skittles was right there with him. He was ready.

"Not just yet. Derek wants to talk to us. These fellas are taking us to our quarters for the evening. According to Derek, we have visitors waiting."

"I don't like visitors," Potter said in his usual broody tone.

"Potter, you just don't like people in general," Irish teased, and everyone chuckled.

As they all started to pile into the oversized Jeep, Ace snickered and pointed to the side of the Jeep. It was an imprint that read, "Property of United States Navy." Skittles chuckled along with Ace getting the joke.

"What's so funny?" The Marine asked, and Ace pointed to the words.

"I guess that saying is true about a Marine." When the kid looked confused, Ace laughed. "M-A-R-I-N-E. My Ass Rides In Navy Equipment."

The Marines laughed along. Every branch of the military had its own funny acronym.

As they pulled out on the road and headed toward the beach, Skittles felt a little bit of hope build inside him, knowing they weren't giving up on finding her. He didn't know why, but his gut told him she was nearby. He wouldn't stop looking for her until he found her.

He felt a hand squeeze his shoulder. When he looked over his shoulder, Ace was staring at him. "She's out there, man. We're gonna find her. We always bring our women home."

Skittles nodded his head and took a deep breath.

Fifteen minutes later, the team stood in front of a beachfront bungalow.

"Are you sure this is the right place?" Irish asked the driver.

The guy looked at his GPS, then back to Irish. "Yep."

Skittles looked at Ace, who shrugged his shoulders. "I'm not going to say no to spending the night here." He started for the front door, and everyone followed.

Skittles scanned the area. There were a few other bungalows, but they were much further away down the beach.

"Did Derek give you any information on who our visitors might be?" Stitch asked.

"Nope."

There were lights on inside the bungalow. Ace knocked on the door. They all had their hands on their pistols. It didn't matter if Derek had told them to expect visitors. Until they actually saw who the visitors were, anyone was considered a possible enemy.

When the door opened, and Tink and Alex stood there with smiles on their faces, Skittles wasn't sure what to think.

"Hey, guys!" Alex greeted them in a cheery tone.

"Alex? What in the hell are you doing here?" Ace asked his fiancé, looking shocked to his core. It was pretty funny.

With her hands on her hips, she narrowed her eyes. "Nice to see you too." She started to walk away, but Ace snagged her around the waist, pulled her back, and kissed her. It left Skittles feeling like he should look away.

Tink started to laugh. "Come on in, guys."

Once Ace released Alex and moved out of the doorway, the rest of the team filed in. Everyone put their gear down, then Alex had to hug each one of them. When she got to Skittles, she gave him an extra squeeze.

"We're going to find her," she told him, and he tried to stay positive for Anna Grace's sake.

"I hope so."

"So, what brings you two out here?" Frost asked as he took a seat on the couch.

"Derek had a hunch."

"A hunch?"

Tink nodded his head, then looked at Skittles.

162

"Derek had a feeling something wasn't right. That's why he gave Anna Grace the phone to take with her."

"Speaking of that phone. What was with Senator DeSmith's reaction when he found out about it?" Diego asked.

"Yeah. He seemed pretty pissed off finding out she had a phone." Ace reiterated then explained to Tink and Alex about the senator's outburst.

Now that the adrenalin from the mission had worn off, Skittles started to replay the entire mission back in his head, and he kept coming back to one question that kept wracking his brain. His frustration must've shown because Ace asked, "Skittles...something bothering you?"

"Did that seem a little too easy to you guys?"

"You mean like it was staged," Ace shot back.

"Maybe." He ran his hand through his hair. "I mean, Senator DeSmith and Steve both admitted that Abu Sayyaf was behind the abduction. We're all very well aware of Abu Sayyaf and how well put together their organization is. Why would they leave two hostages, let alone a high-profile United States Senator and his chief of staff unguarded? They had to have known that someone would be coming for them. Not only that, but keep in mind that there were no demands, nothing. What was their motive? People like Abu Sayyaf do shit for a reason. Even the senator's words seemed as if they were scripted and rehearsed.

"He has a point. They both had an answer for everything," Stitch said.

"Except for Anna Grace," Frost stated and looked at Skittles.

"She's still there," Skittles stated confidently. "I just know it."

"We swept the entire building. Every fucking nook and cranny. She wasn't there," Ace replied, appearing frustrated just like they all were.

"Neither was her phone, but that signal still says that the phone is there—somewhere. At one point, I was literally standing on the blinking dot," Frost told them.

Tink stepped forward. "Look, you guys have been given the green light to have another look. I have an idea how we can keep an eye on things until tomorrow when we all go back in."

Skittles' head snapped to the left where Tink was standing. "What's that?"

Tink smirked. "I didn't come empty-handed. The only downside is that this extension to the mission is considered off the books, meaning—"

"We're on our own," Ace finished.

"Yep. Derek had a gut feeling, and he called me early this morning, and thankfully, Alex and I were only six hours away by plane."

"What about your business deal?" Ace asked.

Tink shrugged his shoulders. "Business can wait. Anna Grace's life can't."

"Just wait until you see some of the toys Tink brought along," Alex exclaimed, and Ace rolled his eyes.

Tink grinned. "It was a good thing I had brought along a few items to show the client, including a couple of drones. Derek says to wait until tomorrow evening, but to monitor the area to see if anyone comes or goes."

Skittles nodded his head then looked at everyone, appearing confident because he was. He just wished they didn't have to wait another day.

A little while later, Skittles found himself in the kitchen staring at the device tracking A.G.'s phone. Watching the red blinking dot was torture. Several times he swore he saw the dot move, but maybe it was just his eyes playing tricks on him.

He set the device down and ran his hands down his face. He was frustrated, sad, but most of all, he was pissed off. Pissed that someone had taken something that belonged to him.

"Hey. Whatcha up too?"

Skittles grinned and looked up at Alex standing there in the doorway. He then glanced at the device. She gave him a soft smile then took the seat across from him at the table.

"Staring at the damn thing will only drive you crazy. Tink and Ace are talking with Derek trying to figure out logistics and contingency plans. Without having access to certain equipment, I think we'll have to improvise when it comes to our strategy."

Skittles grinned. "Isn't that what we're trained to do—improvise, adapt and overcome?"

"Are you quoting the unofficial slogan of the Marines?" She teased, and Skittles shrugged his shoulders.

"It's a great quote."

Stitch popped his head in, "Hey. Tink got the drone working. You guys want to come out and watch its inaugural flight?"

Alex grinned. "Watch? Hell, I've been dying to pilot that thing."

Skittles stood, and so did Alex as they followed Stitch outside. The rest of the team were already out on the beach.

Stitch called over to Tink. "Alex wants to pilot it."

Ace swung his head toward Alex. "Since when do you know how to pilot a drone, let alone one sophisticated as this?"

Skittles bit back his laugh when her cheeks turned pink.

"Hey. Just because I no longer go out on crazy missions doesn't mean I can't keep my skills sharpened or learn new things."

Ace playfully pointed at her, and she laughed. But the laughter was brought to a halt when Tink pointed out something he saw.

"Shit!"

"What is it?" Ace asked, and everyone gathered around as Tink squatted down so everyone could see the screen.

Skittles looked closer. "Is that a kid?" He asked. It was hard to tell because of the darkness. But in Skittles opinion, it sure as hell resembled a kid.

"Sure as hell looks like it," Tink replied.

"Did he just come from the building where the senator was?" Diego asked.

"Yeah. Look. Now he's going into the structure across the street."

"The drones used earlier during the Senator's rescue didn't detect any heat signatures of any kind in any of the surrounding buildings. Where in the hell did this kid come from?" Irish questioned as they watched him disappear into the brick building.

"My question is, where are his parents? Christ, he can't be more than six or seven years old," Frost stated, appearing upset. They all had soft spots for children. More so now that some of the guys had kids of their own."

Alex looked at the group. "Well, there's only one way to find out."

Ace gave her a sideways look, but Skittles knew that Ace valued any insight that Alex had. She was a brilliant operative.

"What are you thinking?"

She looked at her watch. "It's two in the morning now. The sun won't rise until sometime between five-thirty and six. That gives us three, maybe three and a half hours to go check things out now."

Ace glanced over at Tink. "I'm fine with it if you are. We can keep one person back to pilot the drone, that way we'll have eyes in the sky and can be alerted to any incoming company."

"I'm okay with it, but let's give Derek a call. Which one of you is going to operate the drone?"

All eyes zeroed in on Alex. She started shaking her head. "No. Not me. I'm going with you guys."

"Alex…" Ace stated, but Alex wasn't relenting.

"No. Hear me out before you judge me."

Ace softened his expression and interjected. "I'm not judging you, Alex. Hell. Every man here knows you're more than capable of handling yourself on a mission."

"Then let me finish what I was going to say. If that is a child, how do you think they'll react when nine big ass men come beating down their door?" She looked each team member in the eye. "Don't you think they'd be a little more comfortable with a female who was less combative and intimidating?"

Stitch looked at Ace. "She's got a point. I mean, we all love kids, but sometimes, during missions, we can come across as unapproachable."

"I agree with Stitch," Skittles seconded it, and everyone else nodded in agreement.

"Fuck…" Ace muttered under his breath, and a few chuckles could be heard.

166

Tink smirked. "Well then, who gets drone duty?"

"I'll do it," Diego volunteered. "I took some training just recently."

Tink nodded his head.

"Okay. Let's get our shit together and draft a plan pronto since we're on a short schedule."

CHAPTER SEVENTEEN

Anna Grace wondered where her little angel ran off to. He was such a sweet boy. She kept falling in and out of consciousness. The little boy visited her when none of the mean men were around. Maybe he was the child of one of them. That was hard to imagine, though, because this boy was kind. With her one arm immobile, she couldn't move much. Not that she was allotted much room anyway. He had found her a little bit of water and held the bottle up to the cage while she took a few sips. He also offered her a few pieces of his strawberry Potchi candy, and he sat with her until the IV machine pumped more sedatives into her, and she fell asleep. She had wondered if she had dreamt it, but when she found a few pieces of candy next to her in the cage, she knew it had been real.

He never spoke and seemed timid, but something about him made her smile. Maybe it was just youthful innocence, or maybe her subconscious thinking that this was the last good thing she would see.

Her body started to tremble again. At this point, she wasn't sure if she was just cold or if it was the drugs they were filling her with. She wondered where everyone went. With all of the time she spent asleep, she wasn't sure how long she had even been locked up. She felt the urge to cry, but she refused to. She wasn't going to spend whatever time she had left alive wallowing in her misfortune. Yeah, it sucked, but she had learned years ago that crying never made it better. She wasn't going to let the evil people responsible for her current situation feel empowered by seeing her tears. Instead, she would just lay there and think about all the good things she had been offered in her life.

The IV machine beeped again, which meant it was releasing more poison into her system that would make her sleepy and disoriented. As the liquid drugs flowed through her veins, she closed her eyes. Instead of the happy dreams she was looking forward to, she was met by a horrific nightmare that left her questioning the type of person she really was.

❦

It was like déjà vu as the team moved with stealth through the thick vegetation towards their target location. Diego, who was back at the beach bungalow, gave them updates as they moved closer. Lightning streaked across the black sky. The rumble of thunder followed it. A severe storm was approaching the island, and a flood warning had been issued. Tink had been in contact with the two pilots, and they had informed him that the small airstrip where his plane was had shut down all operations until the storm passed. That put a wrench in their extraction strategy.

Irish and Dino had gone ahead of the rest of the team and took positions in overwatch to support the team should they encounter any enemy combatants.

As they neared the tree line that would lead them to an open clearing, Ace held his hand up, signaling everyone to stop. He spoke into his communications device.

"Diego, how are we looking?"

"All good at the moment."

"Copy that. Irish and Dino, state your positions and how things look from your vantage point."

Irish was the first to respond. "I'm just across from the structure on the water. Found a nice, tall, sturdy tree with the perfect branch to hang out on. I've got a gorgeous view."

Skittles shook his head at their crazy sniper. Irish was a damn good marksman, but he was also their comedian as well.

"Irish. I'd be careful up in that tree. I hear that a tree is a Wagler Pit Viper's favorite place to hang out," Alex stated with amusement in her tone. Wagler Pit Vipers were just one of many venomous snakes known to roam the islands of the Philippines.

"Really, Alex? You know I hate fucking snakes," Irish responded, and the whispered snickers over the comms were hysterical. Alex loved fucking with the guys anytime she got the chance to.

"Unlike the snake wrangler, my position is north of the structure that the boy was seen going into. I'm in the block building on the second floor, the last window to your right," Dino said.

"Do either of you see anything out of the ordinary?" Ace followed up with.

"Negative." Both voices stated.

"All right. Let's move in."

Skittles moved in tandem with the team. He was fourth in line behind Alex. She was the only one without night vision, and only because there wasn't another pair. Ace led the way along the perimeter of the building where the boy was last seen. Potter, Frost, and Stitch broke off and went around the back to look for another entry point. Ace, Tink, Alex, and Skittles made their way to the front.

Using the barrel of his rifle, Ace pushed the broken door open. He and Tink entered first. Skittles covered from the rear.

"We just entered the front," Ace communicated to the others near the back."

"We've located a woman and young boy back here near the back exit," Potter's voice echoed through the comms.

As they entered the room, Skittles saw the woman crouching in a corner shielding what he assumed to be the young boy."

"Please don't hurt us. We mean no harm," she spoke in a soft whisper and surprisingly very good English.

"You speak English?" Tink asked as he stepped toward the frightened woman. Frost has a small light directed toward them.

"Yes."

"Why are you here?"

"I have no other place to go. Men are looking for my son and me."

"Why?"

"Because I escaped from them."

"How long have you been living here?"

"A year or so."

Skittles felt his gut clench. This was no way to live, especially with a child.

Tink knelt down next to the pair. The woman was timid and turned her face away from Tink. She was obviously scared and shaken up. Tink glanced over his shoulder at Alex and motioned for her to give it a try.

Alex stepped closer and knelt next to Tink. She placed her hand gently on the woman's back in a comforting way.

"My name is Alex, and this big guy next to me is Tink. We're not here to harm you or your son."

The woman raised her head and looked at Alex with wide eyes. "You're a woman."

Alex smiled. "I am." She waved her hand around the room, gesturing toward the other guys. "These guys are my friends, and they won't harm you either. We're the good guys."

"You weren't with them earlier," the woman said, and Skittles' eyebrows shot upward.

"You saw them?" Alex questioned.

"You got the two men out, but not the girl."

Skittles' breath caught in his throat. They had seen A.G. He wanted to ask so many questions, but he willed himself to stay silent and let Alex take the lead.

"You saw her? The woman with the men?" Alex asked, and the woman nodded.

"Yes, although a man had carried her over his shoulder. She looked to be asleep."

"Have you been watching the building the entire time?"

"Yes, when you're on the run and hiding like I am, you keep your eyes open. The group who took the men and woman are bad people."

"Abu Sayyaf?"

"Abu Sayyaf? No. They're not members of Abu Sayyaf. They call themselves the Viper Squad." She looked Alex in the eyes. "You have to get the girl out. She is not well."

Skittles' heart rate started to increase.

"What do you mean she isn't well? Have you seen her?" Alex continued to ask.

171

The woman looked down at the little boy wrapped in her arms. He kept quiet but stared at all of the guys.

"I have not, but my son has. He said she's in the basement."

Skittles looked at Ace, who appeared just as perplexed.

"Ma'am," Ace greeted the woman. She looked up. "Are you sure there's a basement? We didn't see a door that led to a basement, nor did the plans we were provided indicate a basement in that dwelling.

"Maybe you were given old plans. This entire neighborhood has been abandoned for years. The Viper Squad are the only ones who occupy it."

She looked back at her son. "Christian likes to explore and told me about the basement. It is not a good place to be."

Alex smiled then looked at the little boy who looked scared to death. "Christian is a beautiful name for a handsome little guy."

The woman managed a small smile. "Thank you. My name is Mary Beth."

"It's nice to meet you, Mary Beth."

Alex then went around the room and introduced everyone to help put the woman and boy at ease.

"Mary Beth. How often do the members of the squad come here?"

"It varies. But normally, when they bring an outsider here, those people never leave."

Skittles swore under his breath.

"That's why I was surprised to see you get the two men out. That never happens."

"Mary Beth. Do you think Christian can show us where the basement is?"

The woman looked down at the boy, and he nodded his head before he looked at Alex.

"I shared my candy with her," he whispered in the cutest little boy voice.

"That was very nice of you, Christian."

"She sleeps a lot," Christian told Alex, and Skittles wondered what he meant by that.

"Well, if she isn't feeling good, then she is probably tired."

"The bad men make her sleep."

"She is our friend, and we would really like to help her. Do you think you could help us?"

The little boy looked up at the guys. "I want to be like you when I grow up. I want to help people," he said, and Skittles thought his heart would melt. He knelt down next to Alex, looked the little boy in the eye, and held out his hand.

"Hey, little man. My name is Skittles, and I'd love to have you on my team. When we go on missions, we always make sure that we have a buddy. Would you be my buddy?"

The little boy grinned and nodded his head, and it brought a smile to Skittles' face.

He took Skittles' hand, and Skittles helped him stand. Tink helped Mary Beth to her feet and stood next to her. Mary Beth was an attractive woman. She stood a bit taller than Alex, who was five-three. She had long brown wavy hair that reached her lower back and big brown eyes. If Skittles had to guess, he would say she was in her late thirties or early forties.

"Mary Beth, are you okay if Tink and I stay with you?" Alex asked, and the woman looked up at Tink, and he gave her a soft smile and a wink.

"I'll be fine," She replied and hugged Christian before she cupped his small cheek. "You be a brave boy and help these nice people find their friend."

"I will, momma," he told her, then walked over and took Skittles' hand. He looked way up at him. "I'm ready, Skittles," he said, and Skittles and a few others laughed.

"Alright, buddy. Let's go find our friend."

Even though Christian told them that none of the bad guys were in the building, the team wasn't taking any chances. They did a complete sweep of the building again on the second floor and the main floor.

Christian led them to a brick wall, and Skittles wasn't sure what to think. Skittles glanced over at Ace, and Ace shrugged his shoulders as if saying he didn't know.

173

They were running out of time. They only had about an hour and a half left of darkness before the sun started to rise. The ferocious storm was making its way through the island, and it was a doozy. The wind was blowing so strong that, at times, Skittles thought the entire building was going to come down.

Christian pressed his hand against the left side of the wall. He moved it around until he found what he was looking for. He motioned for Skittles to go to where he was standing, and Skittles obliged. Christian then took Skittles' hand and placed it against the wall.

"Press right there," the boy instructed, and Skittles did what he said and pressed the spot. There was a clicking noise, and then a crease in the wall appeared. Skittles moved the boy behind him, and Ace and Frost each stepped forward as Skittles pushed the hidden door inward. A set of stairs came into view.

Ace radioed to those not with them that they were heading down the stairs.

Skittles led the way down the stairs with his weapon raised. He was met with cold chilled air, and he was in full gear. Christ, it was like a refrigerator down here. He looked at Christian for direction, and he pointed to the left but then said, "You don't want to go the other way."

As Skittles made the turn, he saw four body bags stacked against the wall and could tell by their shape that they weren't empty.

"What the fuck?" Skittles mumbled under his breath.

"This place is like a fucking morgue," Frost stated.

"More like a dumping ground to cover up murders," Potter followed up on both of their statements.

The further they went; the more disgusted Skittles became. As they rounded another corner, something in the distance caught his eye. Suddenly, Christian took off in the same direction.

"Shit!" Skittles exclaimed and ran after him.

Once he caught up with the boy, he found Christian kneeling next to what looked like a large dog crate. He signaled to the rest of the team, and they quickly made their way over. As he slowly approached the crate, he saw Christian holding the person's hand inside it.

"She's sleeping again," Christian told him. Skittles knelt next to the crate, and that was when he saw the blonde hair. Seeing Anna Grace curled into a little ball inside and the IV stuck in the top of the hand that Christian was holding made him want to throw up. He stuck his fingers through an opening in the cage, brushing back the platinum locks covering the woman's face. She didn't move a muscle at his touch. She looked dead, but then her body twitched, and she moaned.

He was already picking the lock and had the cage opened when others realized who was in the cage. Skittles removed his glove and felt her pulse. Christ, she was cold as a popsicle. There was no way she could have survived much longer in this temperature.

Frost cut the zip ties around her ankles while Potter pulled out an emergency blanket to cover her and get her body temperature up.

"Her muscles are going to be tight and sore from being in one position for so long," Stitch told him as he removed the IV from her hand and wrapped her hand in gauze.

"Okay, stretch her legs out slowly," Stitch said.

Once her legs were hanging out of the cage, they worked in tandem to slide her out. She still hadn't moved an inch, and Skittles was worried. Once she was out, Stitch did a quick workup on her. Aside from sleeping and being cold, her vitals looked okay.

"It looks like they were pumping her with sedatives, probably to keep her complacent until they were ready to do whatever they had planned for her," Stitch grimly said, and Skittles agreed. She was out cold, but at least she was breathing normally. She was a little pale, but hopefully, once they got her warmed up, her coloring would return.

"Is she okay to move?" Skittles asked as he anxiously waited to hold her in his arms.

"Yeah, let's just get her wrapped in the blanket."

"Good, because I don't like being pinned down here," Ace stated. None of them were comfortable with being cornered with no exit.

Skittles didn't need to be told twice as he bent down, lifted her into his arms, and held her close to his body. Any heat he could infuse into her was good. As they made their way back up the stairs and through the house, Ace had radioed Tink, letting him know their location.

Once Irish gave the signal that all was clear, they ran to the tree line and made it through the thick brush to the waiting vehicles. Tink was in one of the vehicles with Mary Beth, and Alex was in the driver's seat of the second.

Skittles slid into the backseat of the jeep with Anna Grace. Christian and Stitch followed. Christian sat in Stitch's lap while the rest of the team piled into the other vehicle.

"Alex is picking up Irish and Dino. We'll meet them back at the house," Tink told them before stepping on the gas. It was pouring rain, and streaks of lightning continued to flash across the sky. It was a hellacious storm, but that didn't matter because he had what he had come for—Anna Grace was safe in his arms.

It wasn't until they were down the road that Skittles let out the breath he had been holding since the moment his eyes laid sight on that fucking cage.

He looked down at the bruises along her skin and could only imagine the torment she had been put through before being thrown in a fucking cage like an animal. He felt himself shaking, and it must've shown because Stitch squeezed his shoulder.

"Hey man, we got her."

He was afraid to speak with all the emotion he was feeling, so he just nodded his head, knowing that Stitch was right—and he wasn't letting her out of his sight.

Anna Grace felt the warmth spread through her body. Someone called her name, but she still couldn't shake the blackness blocking her vision. She saw a tad bit of light, and she tried desperately to reach for it, but all too soon, she felt the pull back to the abyss.

"Noah?" She mumbled and tried blinking her eyes open, but it was hard. She felt so tired.

"Hey, sweetheart." Noah's voice sounded in her ears.

"Am I dreaming?"

"No, baby, I'm right here."

"I'm so cold," she whispered as she tried to burrow herself further into the warmth around her.

She heard more mumbling before she saw darkness again.

Skittles pulled the covers up over Anna Grace before he walked out to the living room. He cracked the door to the bedroom where Anna Grace was sleeping. He then took a seat on the couch next to Irish, where he could see into the bedroom and keep an eye on Anna Grace.

"Is she still asleep?" Alex asked, still looking concerned.

"Yeah. She's still out cold."

"Well, not knowing what they were injecting her with, it could be a while until she wakes," Stitch answered, looking pissed off.

Skittles looked out the window. The storm was beginning to clear out, and he could see the first signs of the sun starting to rise over the ocean. Hopefully, the airport would restart operations soon, and they could get the hell off the island.

"Where's Tink?" Skittles asked as he looked around the quaint little bungalow.

"He's in the other bedroom with Mary Beth and Christian. I think we're going to have two extra passengers on the way home," Alex told him then turned her laptop around so he could see the screen. It was a newspaper article from fourteen years ago about a family of seven who were in the Philippines doing humanitarian work after a major typhoon had struck the area. The entire family had gone missing in the middle of the night. Weeks later, all but one of their bodies were found in a remote area. All six had been murdered. Skittles looked up at Alex.

"Is Mary Beth the missing family member?"

Alex appeared somber and nodded her head. "She was twenty-two—the youngest of her siblings. She said that a group of masked men broke into the home where they stayed and ordered everyone into two trucks except for her. She was put into another vehicle by herself then driven to a large estate owned by a cartel leader. He had seen them out working the day before, and apparently, Mary Beth's dad confronted some of Vedasto's men and, I guess, gave them a hard time. Vedasto didn't take that well and ordered them killed. All except for Mary Beth. He had his eye on her and wanted her for himself. You can fill in the blanks about what happened over time."

Skittles ran his hand down his face. "That's awful. How did she escape? Does she have any family left in the states?"

"She said that both her parents were only children. That was why her parents had five kids. Her grandparents on her mom's side were alive at the time of their trip, but she isn't sure if they are still alive. She and Christian have been on their own for four years now. They traveled by boat down to this island. She doesn't have any papers that she can travel with, so she was limited to where she could go."

Skittles went to respond when suddenly a blood-curdling scream came from Anna Grace's room. Everyone leaped from their seats. Skittles was the first one to the bedroom. As he pushed the door open, Anna Grace was thrashing her arms and kicking her legs as she screamed, "Please stop! Don't do this!"

Skittles reached the bed and tried talking to her to get her to wake up, but the nightmare had a firm hold on her. He placed his knee on the bed, leaning over, and touched her shoulder. She smacked his hand away and screamed again. Tears were now leaking out of her eyes. She rolled toward the edge of the bed, and before she could hurt herself, Skittles reached out and wrapped her in his arms. She continued to fight him and the nightmare. He lost his balance and fell onto the floor. He took the brunt of the fall.

"Anna Grace!" He shouted to pull her from the nightmare.

Suddenly, her eyes popped open. She looked deep into his eyes then sucked in a deep gasp. "I killed them!" She exclaimed before she buried her face in his shirt. Her body shook violently as she sobbed uncontrollably.

He looked at the others, and he could tell by their expressions that they were just as shaken as he was by what they just witnessed.

He ran his hand down the back of her head as he held her close. All the while, he wondered who she killed. Had it just been part of the nightmare? Or had she really killed someone?

He felt her stir in his arms, and when he looked down, her violet eyes peered up at him. Her black lashes appeared thick because of the wetness.

"I need to use the bathroom," she said as she hiccupped.

He stood with her in his arms and walked her to the bathroom before he set her down. He didn't want to let her go, but he knew she wouldn't appreciate him standing guard while she did her business.

He took her face in his hands and looked into her eyes. "Are you okay by yourself?" He asked, and she nodded her head.

Anna Grace stood in the middle of the bathroom and watched as Skittles closed the door behind him. As soon as she was alone, she leaned against the vanity and hung her head. Immediately, she felt the wetness hit her cheeks. She took a few breaths to try and calm herself down.

When she woke up in Skittles' arms, she wondered if her nightmare was playing a cruel trick on her, and then when she woke up for real, she'd be back in that cage in the cold room. But the scent of him and the feel of his strong arms holding her made her realize that her nightmare no longer enthralled her and that she was indeed safe.

Recalling her nightmare, she looked down at her hands. They were the hands that had blood on them—the blood of three men who she took the lives of. She wasn't sure what had triggered her memory, but she now remembered her final night at Senor Castillo's estate—her seventeenth birthday.

She wasn't going to let them take her and make her their wife. She tried convincing herself that she did what she had to do. But if she heard Senator DeSmith correctly, it was him that had put her in that position to begin with. He was responsible for her parents' deaths, meaning he was responsible for the two and a half years she spent in hell.

She covered her mouth as she felt the bile from her stomach begin to rise, then turned around where the toilet was and threw up. She continued to throw up everything her body could dispel. She cried and heaved again until her stomach and sides started to hurt. Slowly she laid her body on the cool tiled floor. Nothing made sense to her. Why?

Alex's heart broke for Skittles as she watched him walk outside with Frost and Diego to get some fresh air. She understood what he was going through because she'd witnessed the same emotions that the other team members experienced when their women were put in a dangerous and unfortunate situation—including herself.

She knew from experience that Anna Grace needed someone to talk to. Maybe she'd open up to her. She walked to the bathroom door and what she heard frightened her. She listened to the cries, then the heaving sound. Something was wrong. She tried the knob, but the door was locked. She knocked again but got no answer, except for the horrific wrenching sound.

Shit! She called over Ace and Irish.

"What's wrong?" Ace asked.

"It's Anna Grace. She sounds like she's sick, and she won't answer the door."

Ace tried knocking, "A.G. honey, open the door."

When another sickly sound came from under the door, Ace cursed. "Stand back."

Skittles appeared with the others, and they asked what was going on, and Alex explained. When Ace broke down the door, Alex wanted to cry at the sight in front of her.

She pushed past Ace and dropped to the floor, where Anna Grace lay curled into a fetal position next to the toilet. She was pale, sweating, and trembling. She brushed her hair back from her face.

"I killed them," she said to Alex under a shuddered breath.

That was the second time she had said that, and Alex wondered who "they" were.

"Who did you kill?" Alex calmly asked Anna Grace as she held her and tried to comfort her the best she could.

"The men who wanted to make me theirs. It was all Senator DeSmith's fault," she choked out.

Alex looked up at Skittles, and Alex recognized the fierce look on his face and the fire that burned in his eyes. It was the look that every man she knew got when someone messed with what was theirs.

"Let me help her get cleaned up and talk to her, and then I'll bring her out," Alex said, holding Skittles' gaze.

She thought that Skittles would argue with her, but he nodded his head; but not before he lowered himself to the floor and kissed Anna Grace's forehead.

"I'll be right outside. Let Alex help you," he told her softly, and Alex had to reel in her emotions. She could see how much Skittles cared for Anna Grace—possibly loved.

"I'm sorry," Anna Grace whispered back to him, and Alex almost lost it as she remembered her own battle with PTSD when she came back from Afghanistan and the battle that she had with herself over killing five people while she had been held in captivity.

"Oh, baby, there is nothing for you to be sorry about," Skittles said to Anna Grace as he ran his knuckles down her cheek. "Come on. A nice hot shower will help. Then we'll talk, okay?"

Alex stood back and let Skittles help Anna Grace up. Once A.G. was on her feet, Skittles hugged her tight and glanced over her head at Alex.

"I'll be right outside if you need anything," he told her, and Alex nodded her head.

Once all of the guys left the bathroom, and it was just Alex and Anna Grace, Alex made sure that she was steady on her feet before she turned and got the shower started. Knowing that Anna Grace had no clothes or toiletries, she'd loan her some of hers.

Anna Grace stood under the spray of the shower, letting the water flow over her skin. Her body still felt numb despite the warmth of the water. She had to pinch herself a few times just to make sure that she was fully awake and not dreaming.

She felt dirty, and it wasn't because of all that had happened to her in the last forty-eight hours or so. She looked down at her hands that still shook from her anxiety. She was tainted in death. She had shot and killed three men, and she wasn't sure how she felt about it. A side of her believed they deserved what they got. But another side of her wondered if that made her a murderer as well.

"Anna Grace, you doing okay?" Alex called out, interrupting Anna Grace's wandering mind.

"Yes. Finishing up," she answered, then turned around and tilted her head back to rinse the shampoo out of her hair. Turning back toward the spray, she let the water hit her face for a few seconds before reaching for the handle and shutting the water off. She stood there for a few seconds until Alex flung a towel over the shower rod.

"Here ya go. I also left you some clothes on the vanity. I'm going to step out so you can change."

Before Alex could take two steps, Anna Grace blurted out, "No! Please don't go. I'll just change here in the shower." She wasn't ready to be alone. Then she wondered if she would ever be. At least not until Senator DeSmith and his no-good Chief of Staff were behind bars and paid for the crimes they committed.

"I'm still here, A.G. I'm going to hand you the clothes."

Anna Grace took the sweatpants and long-sleeved t-shirt and quickly pulled them on. It had felt weird not wearing underwear or a bra, but she wasn't going to complain. She was at least clean, and that made her feel a tad bit better. When she pulled the shower curtain back, Alex was standing there with a worried expression.

"Feel better?" Alex asked her, and Anna Grace nodded because she felt hundred times better on the outside, but on the inside, she wasn't quite sure.

"Can I ask you something, and if you can't tell me, I'll understand."

"What's the question?"

"I don't even really know how to word this, but you mentioned that you used to go on secret missions for the government." Anna Grace wrung her fingers together. "Have you ever killed anyone?"

Alex's facial expression softened.

"Where's this coming from, A.G.?"

"I'm struggling with an internal battle, and I can't get it under control."

"You mentioned you killed them. Can you tell me who it was that you killed?"

"My captors down in Mexico. It was the last night I was there. All these years, I couldn't remember my last night down there, and now I know why. I guess my subconscious blocked it. I'm afraid of what people will think of me knowing that I took someone's life."

Alex understood exactly how Anna Grace felt, because she experienced the same when she had returned home from Afghanistan.

"Oh, A.G., nobody will think badly of you for acting in self-defense. Remember the night we went dress shopping?" Anna Grace nodded her head. "Remember when I told you that something really bad had happened to me?" Anna Grace nodded again. "All of us ladies in this unit have had their fair share of trouble. Myself included."

"Like what?"

"Well, in my case, I used to work for a private black ops firm. Long story short, the mission I was on is where I met the guys. We were working together to hunt someone down. Toward the end of the mission, I was double-crossed by someone who I thought was on our side, and ultimately, I was abducted in a not-so-nice part of the world. I was injured badly and didn't think I was going to survive. But then I told myself that I had too much to live for. I had to kill five of my captors to make it out alive. The guys and another team who you'll meet sooner or later found me. I remembered once I was rescued and made it home. I was afraid how Ace and the others would see me. I, too, wasn't sure what to make of having to kill someone until Ace explained it to me, and he was right. It was either them or me, and I chose me. Did I like having to do it? No! But I had to." Alex smiled. "Even with both my physical and mental scars, I know Ace still loves me."

Alex looked at Anna Grace and saw the fear. "Are you afraid of what Skittles will think?"

Anna Grace's snapped her head up, but then she shrugged her shoulders, looking defeated.

"It doesn't really matter what he thinks."

Alex cocked her head sideways. "Why is that?"

"He moved on. I need to get used to him with his girlfriend."

Damn Monique! Alex thought to herself.

"A.G., I'm not going to speak for Skittles, but I think that the two of you need to sit and have a long talk. There—"

A knock sounded on the door, and Skittles poked his head in.

"All good?" He asked, but Alex grinned because he wasn't looking at her. He was looking directly at Anna Grace.

Anna Grace gave him a soft smile. "Yeah. Alex and I were just about to come out."

Skittles' gaze moved over to Alex, and Alex smirked before raising her eyebrows. Alex glanced over Anna Grace.

"You got this," she told her, then winked.

CHAPTER EIGHTEEN

Anna Grace sat in the chair while everyone else gathered around her. Some stood while others sat. Thankfully, Alex pulled over a chair from the kitchen table and sat next to her. Skittles pulled another chair up and sat on her other side.

She looked around and felt nervous as everyone turned their attention to her. She was introduced to Tink, one of Alex's unofficial uncles and former member of her dad and Derek's SEAL team. She then found out that her little angel—as she called him—was in the other room with his mom. Alex told her that she would explain more about their situation but informed her that they were coming with them.

Focusing on the audience in front of her, she wasn't sure where to begin, so she decided to speak from her heart and what she was feeling right there in the moment—thankful.

"Before you guys start interrogating me, there's something I need to say to each of you." She looked around the room. They were all big, handsome men—men who were trained as warriors to hunt and kill. She swallowed the lump of emotion that was stuck in her throat. "Thank you." She told them. "Thank you for not giving up and thank you for coming back for me." She wiped away a tear before it could fall. "I look back now and think how stupid I was to fall for something like this and put myself in danger. Or worse, I now have dragged you guys into my mess."

Irish was standing behind the sofa with his arms crossed in front of his chest. He came forward and squatted in front of her.

"Sweetie, don't sit here and beat yourself up. An evil power took advantage of your kindness and abilities to help others, which in this case were animals. You didn't know this was going to happen. And don't think for a minute that you've dragged us into your mess. Your mess, as you call it, is what we do—our ultimate goal is to help and assist, and I'm thankful that we're the ones who got the call to help you."

She looked over at Skittles. "He's right, Anna Grace. None of this is your fault, and we're all going to help you through this," Skittles told her.

She had to take a moment to compose herself, or she would've wound up a blubbering mess if she tried to speak. As if knowing she needed it, Stitch handed her a bottle of water, and she took a few sips. Once she felt ready to dive into the situation, she once again glanced at Skittles.

"Are you still really handy with the computer?"

He nodded and squinted his eyes. "Why?"

She took a deep breath. "Because after what I have to tell you, I'm going to need all the help I can get to find out why Senator DeSmith had my parents killed. Why he paid Senor Castillo to take me away. Why he arranged this staged kidnapping and to find out what terrorist organizations he's been selling U.S. weapons to."

She managed to get that all out in one breath, and she waited for a reaction, but none came until Tink finally spoke.

"You care to explain that a little more?" He asked as he crossed his massive arms across his chest. Boy, was Tink a big man. She swallowed hard.

"You're telling us that a U.S. Senator faked his own kidnapping and paid someone off to make you disappear?" Skittles asked her, appearing a bit surprised.

"Yes."

"That's a pretty big accusation," Ace stated as he stood behind Alex.

She looked up at him. "It's not an accusation. I heard him admit that along with everything else I just said." She then glanced Tink's way. "Where is the Senator now?"

"He and his Chief of Staff are already on a plane."

She rolled her eyes. "Figures. Well then, how much time do we have until we leave?"

"About two hours, but then we have roughly a full day of travel between stops and flight time," Tink told her. He looked angry, and she wasn't sure if it was directed at her or if he was upset at the situation as a whole.

Skittles took her hand, and she looked down at their clasped hands before she peered up at him.

"I don't know where to start," she admitted to him, feeling lost in her own mind, and Skittles gave her a gentle smile.

"As Tink said, we've got some time. So, take your time, and we'll go through all your allegations one at a time. But, first, let's start with the comment you made earlier that we're concerned about. You said you killed someone."

She closed her eyes and took a couple of deep breaths. When she opened her eyes, she glanced at Alex, who gave her an encouraging smile.

"I actually owe Alex a thank you for making me realize that what I did was okay. I never intended to take another person's life. But Alex was right when she told me that I did what I had to do because it was either my life or theirs."

She took another deep breath then exhaled before she began. "It was the night of my seventeenth birthday. Senor Castillo had arranged a huge party for the celebration. I was given a gorgeous gown to wear. For the whole day, until I was supposed to be introduced to the party guests, I was sequestered in my room.

Jorge and Fernando were Castillo's sons. They were ruthless individuals who would do anything to get what they wanted and that included me. They, along with Senor Castillo, had come to my room that evening when it was time. Well, at least I thought it was time."

She pulled her hand from Skittles' grasp and stood up. She walked over to the window that faced the beach and water and wrapped her arms around her midsection.

"Come to find out the celebration really wasn't for me, but instead for Jorge and Fernando. I was being gifted to them from Senor Castillo."

Behind her, she heard a few mumbles and low curses from the guys. She glanced over her shoulder at them.

"It wasn't a birthday party after all. It was actually a wedding. It all started to make sense."

She looked at Skittles with tears in her eyes, but she refused to let them fall. "I know I told you that I wasn't raped, but that didn't stop them from making me watch things and make disgusting comments toward me."

She told them about the awful scenes she was forced to watch play out, and how Jorge and Fernando would make women perform sexual acts on them. She had been expected to learn from it. They were cruel and abusive. She had witnessed them beat a woman so severely that she died from her injuries the next day.

"When the three men showed up at my door, I realized what was going to happen. I knew what my fate was going to be."

She looked right at Skittles.

"I would've rather died than be subjected to the physical and mental abuse they would've put me through." She took a deep breath. "Senor Castillo explained how I was going to belong to his sons. I remember pleading with him, but instead, I got a backhand to my face to shut me up. Soon after, he left the room, leaving me in the care of his sons."

"They didn't waste any time, as they pounced on me. They said they wanted to claim what was theirs before marrying me. I noticed they both were armed with guns. I knew that would be my only opportunity, and if I died trying to protect myself, so be it. At least I'd be at peace."

"A.G.," Skittles said and tried to reach for her. But she shook her head and took a step back. She needed to do this—to get it all out. This was what had been haunting her subconscious.

"They got me onto the bed. Both of them started to remove their clothes. Jorge placed his gun on the bed next to where I was lying. I couldn't see what Fernando was doing because Jorge climbed on top of me. As he started to pull at my dress, I began to resist. I knew better than to let someone touch me without my consent."

"They became angry and started to hit me all over, trying to beat me into submission, but that just made me fight even harder. I remember how much pain I was in when I managed to use my legs and feet to push Jorge off me. That was the moment I realized the gun was just lying there within my reach. I didn't even think as I grabbed for it. As soon as I had it in my hand, I

188

pointed it and pulled the trigger. I didn't release the gun until I emptied all the bullets."

She felt herself start to tremble, remembering what she saw next. She looked at Skittles, hoping that Alex was right and that he wouldn't think any less of her.

"I killed all three of them. I don't remember when Castillo came back into the room, but he was there, lying on the floor next to his sons. The next thing I knew, Dr. Hernandez arrived and told me that she'd take care of me but that we had to move quickly. I was in a daze. I was beaten up and in so much pain that she had to help dress me. I had a broken nose, broken ribs, and a concussion."

Holding Skittles' gaze, she said, "You pretty much know the rest about how I got back to the states."

Skittles wanted to speak, but he couldn't. He was filled with so much emotion and anger. Not at Anna Grace, but at the cowards who prey on helpless women and children. It was sickening. He swallowed hard and was trying his darndest to keep his emotions in check. What she went through was something he never wished on anyone. He was glad to hear that the three individuals responsible for most of her misery were dead and could never touch another person again.

Ignoring Anna Grace's stubbornness, he felt she needed a hug, or maybe it was him that needed the connection with her to tamp down his anger. He stood up, walked to where she stood by the window, and pulled her close. Her cheek rested against his chest. He whispered to her, "I'm sorry. Nobody will ever lay another hand on you again. I promise you that."

She tilted her head back and looked up at him.

"How can you promise something like that when it's obvious I have a target on my back? As soon as I get back home and Senator DeSmith finds out I was rescued, he'll just find another way to get rid of me. I don't think I'll ever be safe as long as he's in the position of power. I just don't understand why, but I plan on finding out."

"We're all here to help you."

She shook her head. "No—"

Skittles interrupted her before she could continue on her stubborn streak. "You just accused a senator of several offenses, and we can't ethically ignore those. Plus, the guy is the biggest dickhead, and all of us in this room would love nothing more than to take him down."

"You can't. He knows people. I don't want you guys to get into any trouble, or worse, get hurt because of me."

"Oh, don't worry. We know people too. People that would be willing to hear what you have to say—including us. So, why don't you start from the beginning," Tink commented.

She looked back up at Skittles, and he slid his hand down her arm, took her hand, and guided her back over to her seat. Once she was seated, Skittles scooted his chair closer to her.

"Let's start with what you overheard—unless there's something else, he did or said before that."

"No. The Senator and Steve pretty much stayed quiet during the ride until our van was ambushed. We had just left the airport and were on our way to the hotel."

"Whoa! Hold up," Tink interrupted. "What do you mean, you had just left the airport?"

She gave Tink an odd look. "Exactly what I said. We were about ten or fifteen minutes from the airport when we were detoured into an alley."

"So, you were never physically at your hotel?" Tink pressed, and Skittles knew why. The FBI had recovered the group's belongings from the hotel they were supposed to be staying at. Her admission just opened up the situation even more.

"No," she said, shaking her head.

"Anna Grace, the FBI recovered your bag along with the Senator's and Steve's from the hotel."

She stared wide-eyed at him. "That's impossible. My bag was in the van with me. When we pulled up to the marina and were forced to get out, my bag was still inside the van."

190

Anna Grace covered her mouth. "The security detail. There were two people who the Senator was talking to when he came out of the airport. Steve told me it was the security detail that Senator DeSmith hired. They weren't with us, which I thought was weird. They also weren't around when we were detoured."

With his hands on his hips, Tink shook his head in disgust. "The son of a bitch had it all planned out. I'd bet my life savings that the security detail was in on the whole scheme. They were most likely nearby, and once the kidnappers had Anna Grace and the other two on the boat, they swooped in and picked up the bags and took them back to the hotel to make it look like everyone had checked in."

"I tried to run away once I got out of the van. There was a grouping of trees, and thick brush was in my reach, but one of Ramil's men caught up to me."

"Ramil? Who was that?" Ace asked.

"Ramil is the leader—the one in charge." She turned back toward the rest of the group. "I tried to fight them off, but I was soon outnumbered and overpowered. When I wouldn't listen to their demands, one of them hit me in the head. The next thing I remember when I woke up was being in that damn dog crate. I don't even know how long I was in there. The little boy—he came to see me. He shared his candy and gave me some water."

"His name is Christian, and you'll get to meet him in a little bit. He's the one who led us to you. We knew your phone was still inside the building somewhere, but we couldn't locate it," Skittles told her, and she looked at him.

"How did you know my phone was there?"

Skittles grinned. "Derek installed a tracking device on it before he gave it to you."

She smiled. "Well, I'm going to have to thank him for that when I see him."

Tink cleared his throat. "You said you heard Senator DeSmith admit to killing your parents?"

She lowered her eyes. "Yes." Again, even though she and her parents weren't close, their deaths still saddened her.

"They didn't know I was awake. Ramil mentioned that they had a buyer for me, but the guy who was supposed to pick me up was delayed, and it could've been another two or three days before he arrived."

"Thank god for that," she heard Skittles mutter under his breath next to her.

"It was Steve who said that they didn't care what happened to me as long as I was never heard from again. But the senator wasn't happy. He was under the impression that I would've been gone by the time you guys or whoever was coming arrived to rescue him and Steve."

"Fucking asshole." She looked up and thought that comment came from Dino.

"Anyway, DeSmith and Ramil got into a heated argument, and that was when the senator told Ramil that he needed to remember he could halt the shipment of weapons with one phone call."

Tink stared at her for a moment, and when he didn't say anything, she wondered if he believed her. But then he finally spoke.

"Anna Grace, would you be willing to state everything that you just said to federal investigators?"

She would have shied away from that idea any other time, but knowing what she knew now—no, there was no hesitation. She would talk to whoever the hell she needed to in order to reclaim her life and make sure that Senator DeSmith couldn't harm another person.

"Absolutely."

Skittles was so angry that he could spit nails. A fucking United States Senator had not only committed murder and kidnapping, but he also committed treason. A man who stood before Congress when he was elected into office and vowed to support and defend the Constitution of the United States against all enemies. It was sick and disgusting.

He looked toward the front door that Anna Grace disappeared through. She said that she wanted to get some fresh air. He could still see her through the window as she walked out onto the beach with Alex. He turned back towards the guys.

"That is some fucked up shit," he said, stating his disgust with the situation.

"I agree one hundred percent. I think we need to come up with a plan to keep Anna Grace hidden until the feds can complete their investigation." Ace said as he sat in the chair that Alex had been sitting in.

Tink nodded his head. "Derek is already working on it."

"How?" Skittles asked.

Tink smirked. "He heard everything. I had him on speakerphone so he could hear. He also is reviewing the FBI files from Anna Grace's parents' murder investigation."

Skittles didn't hide his surprise. "He was able to get them?"

"Yep. Arianna and her dad still have some trustworthy connections."

"And...did Derek say anything?"

"Nothing in detail, but he did say that it is an interesting read. I agree with Ace—Anna Grace should stay hidden. In fact, I wouldn't even let on that she has been found. We'll use this to our advantage. If she has no family, then nobody will be advocating for the authorities to continue searching for her. And if what she says is true, which I believe her, we have a huge fucking problem on our hands. Let's start packing up since we'll be leaving in about thirty minutes."

Skittles stood along with the others. He knew every single one of them would have his and Anna Grace's back. If he had to hide her, he knew exactly where she'd be safe and comfortable. He told the others that he was going out to talk to Anna Grace, and then walked out the front door.

CHAPTER NINETEEN

Anna Grace stepped onto the beach and let the sand squish between her toes. Now that the storm had cleared out, the sun was shining with minimal cloud coverage. It was a gorgeous day, but she was ready to go home. She was ready to face her past, and the individuals who had brought her pain and suffering for the last ten years would pay.

With Alex off taking a phone call, Anna Grace was so deep inside her head that she hadn't even heard someone come up behind her until she heard Skittles' voice.

"A.G."

She spun around and appeared frightened, which she was. Her nerves were at an all-time high. With her hand against her chest, she stared up into his light brown eyes.

"You scared me," she told him, and he appeared guilty.

"I'm sorry."

She shook her head. "Don't be. I imagine that I'll be skittish for quite some time."

He reached out and took her hand. "We've got about thirty minutes before we leave. Let's walk down the beach."

They walked hand-in-hand while Skittles explained that Derek was working on a plan and how they wanted to keep her rescue quiet.

They came to an area at the end of the beach that was secluded by large rocks, and Skittles pulled her behind a set of them. When he looked down into her eyes, she could tell he was angry. She just hoped it wasn't directed toward her. She realized what she had done—agreeing to go with the senator when her gut and everyone else warned her not to.

"You're angry," she told him.

He cupped her cheeks and looked deep into her eyes. "You belong to me."

She tried to shake her head, but he held her still.

"When I realized that it was you lying in that cage, I became enraged." He sat back and ran his fingers through his hair. "Jesus, I thought you were dead. You were still and so cold. I was so scared, A.G."

She took his hands in hers, and she smiled up at him. "You saved me. You didn't give up, and I'm right here." She told him.

She could see that he was breathing heavily as he continued to search her eyes as if looking for an answer to something. She opened her mouth to ask him what was wrong, and he lifted his pointer finger to her lips.

"I can't take it anymore," he told her before he swooped down and kissed her.

She closed her eyes the moment she felt his warm, wet lips touch hers. He kissed her tenderly as he held her face between his palms. Suddenly her enjoyment was interrupted with the image of his neighbor—his girlfriend. She pulled away abruptly and covered her mouth with her hand.

Sensing her pulling away, he asked, "What's wrong?"

She shook her head. "You're confusing me. Why did you just do that?"

"What? Kiss you?"

She nodded her head.

"Because I wanted to, and I was in the position that I could."

"You have a girlfriend. The woman who lives next door to you; I saw you with her the night of Alex's charity event. She also told me that you two were dating."

He grinned and pulled her back in front of him, holding her around the waist. "We're going to get one thing straight right now. There is nothing between Monique and me. She lied to you, A.G. Although I won't lie. One night a few months ago, I don't remember something that may have happened between her and me. She took advantage of my inebriated state. But that's in the past.

He pressed his forehead against hers. "I only want you. I always have. I wanted to kiss you because I'm attracted to you. Now, if you don't want me to, then you need to tell me right now because the way I see it, once we get back home, things between you and I are going to change."

195

Her heart felt like it had grown double its size. "I've always wanted you too," she smiled and laughed. "Even when everyone told me you were too old for me and that you wouldn't want to date a freshman."

He grinned. "I was just waiting for the right time."

Suddenly, Skittles turned serious as he pressed his finger against his ear. "Shit!"

Could he ever get a chance to just enjoy a romantic moment with Anna Grace without something going haywire?

Ace's voice came over Skittles' earpiece. "If you two have kissed and made up, may I suggest you both get your asses moving. We've got company moving in. Irish is heading your way. The rest of us are taking the vehicles. Tink's group is heading to the plane. There's a market about two hundred yards from your location. Do you think you guys can make it there, and we'll pick you up?"

"Shit!" Skittles exclaimed. He looked at Anna Grace as he replied. "On our way." He then looked down at Anna Grace and cupped her cheek. He didn't want to freak her out any more than she already was. "That was Ace. He thinks your friend Ramil may have found our location."

Her eyes widened, and her mouth opened, but no words came out. He saw the fear, and he quickly explained the plan.

"How did they find us?" She finally asked.

"I don't know, but we can't stay here. Are you still a fast runner?" She nodded. "Good, because we need to book it." He pulled her along, and when she looked over her shoulder, she locked gazes with the man.

"Noah, he sees us."

Skittles took a quick glance back and cursed under his breath as he picked up the pace. Suddenly, a gunshot rang out from behind them. The bullet whizzed by them, hitting the building to the left of them.

Ace was barking in his ear. "Were those gunshots?"

"Yep. Where in the hell is Irish? I've got one on our tail."

"I see you," Irish said. "I'm two blocks up behind the green building on your right. Take your next left, and that side road will take you into the market. I've got two guys I'm eyeing right now, making sure they aren't with our buddies. They both are carrying."

"Shit. A lot of people carry guns around here."

"Yeah. Well, I'm not taking any chances. So, everyone is suspicious to me at the moment."

He had a point.

"What do we do?" Anna Grace asked as she kept up with his pace.

"We keep running and hope we lose him."

They weaved their way through the market, zig-zagging in between the vendor carts. He saw an archway between two buildings and ducked in. They continued until they came to an end and had to choose left or right.

Anna Grace squeezed his hand, and as he looked down he saw fear in her eyes. "Where to now? I think we missed the road we were supposed to take to meet Ace."

He rubbed her neck. "It's fine, A.G. We always have contingency plans." He offered her a smile and winked, and that made her smile.

He nodded his head, signaling for them to go right. He knew that they would be close to the main road if he could get to the next block over. As they jogged along, he spotted a bar, and they ducked into it. It was dark and pretty empty, maybe with two or three customers. He glanced around, looking for another way out, and spotted a door behind the bar. He glanced down at Anna Grace. "Play along and act sick."

She gave him a quick nod as they approached the bartender.

"Excuse me, Sir....my girlfriend isn't feeling well. Our hotel is just behind this place, and I was wondering if you wouldn't mind if we used the back exit so she doesn't have to be in the heat longer than she needs to be."

The bartender gave A.G. a quick look, and when Skittles looked down, he couldn't believe his eyes. She actually looked as if she would pass out. *How in the hell?*

He didn't have time for questions and looked at the guy, and he motioned them around the bar. He gave the guy a fifty-dollar bill before he scooped Anna Grace up and ran out of the door.

The problem with his plan was that the guy following them was still looking for them. Skittles didn't see the guy until it was too late, but Anna Grace did, and as the guy lunged at them, Anna Grace pushed Skittles out of the way, and she took a hit from the guy and fell to the ground. That was when Skittles saw the knife in the guy's hand. Skittles kicked the knife out of the guy's hand using some serious combat moves before throwing a couple of punches at his face. He didn't stop until the guy fell to the ground and didn't move.

He heard someone running behind him, and when he turned, he saw it was Irish and blew out a sigh of relief.

"Shit! Are you guys, okay?" Irish asked as he bent down and searched the guy's pockets for any sort of identification.

Skittles nodded then reached for Anna Grace to help her up. He noticed she was slow to get to her feet. He brushed her blonde hair from her face, and he noticed she stood there looking white as a ghost. She appeared to be in shock. Maybe she was.

"A.G., are you okay?" He asked her, taking her hand.

"I don't know," she whispered.

What in the hell kind of answer was that? His patience was growing thin with this entire situation.

"We need to go," Irish stated. "Ace is waiting for us two blocks down. He said the coast looks clear."

Skittles started to walk, and as he guided Anna Grace to go in front of him, she fell into his side as if losing her balance, and he caught her.

"A.G.?" He questioned, and she looked up at him. All he saw was pain and agony in her violet eyes.

Anna Grace looked down at her hand that she had pressed against her side. Then she pulled her hand away, and Skittles saw all the blood.

"I think he stabbed me."

"Oh fuck!" He steadied her as she pressed further against him. He noticed her breathing become rapid, and she took one last look at him right before her eyes rolled back in her head.

Hearing the panic in Skittles' voice, Irish turned back toward him just as he lifted Anna Grace's limp body into his arms.

"What the fuck happened?" Irish questioned, then saw the blood on her clothing and hand.

"He must've stabbed her when she pushed me out of the way. Fuck!"

Skittles was in a panic. He spoke into his mic as he carried Anna Grace the two blocks to the meet-up point. "Ace, is Stitch with you?"

"No, he's with Tink at the plane. What's up?"

"A.G. is wounded. We're heading your way now."

"SITREP." He heard Ace's voice boom in his ear.

"Stab wound to her left side. She passed out."

He heard someone mumble a curse then Ace's voice came over the ear piece. "Do you think she needs a hospital, or can she fly?"

Skittles rolled his eyes in frustration. "I honestly don't know. I haven't had a chance to look at it. The three of us are about two minutes out."

"Roger. We'll access when you get here."

Two minutes and thirty-four seconds, they made it to the Jeep. Diego moved to the front passenger seat, and Alex sat on his lap to make room for Skittles, Irish, and Anna Grace. Once they were safely inside the Jeep and on their way to the airstrip, Skittles laid Anna Grace out over his and Irish's laps. He cursed when he lifted her shirt and saw all the blood. It looked to be more of a slice than a stab wound. But he wasn't sure how deep the cut was. Alex handed him a towel, and he placed pressure on it. It was all they could do until they arrived at the plane.

A long twelve minutes passed until they were all on the aircraft, and Stitch was looking over Anna Grace. Skittles stood there as he thought back to what he could've done to protect her. He blamed himself. He was supposed to keep her safe, not the other way around. She had suffered enough already. He ran his hands through his hair.

"I think she's okay to travel. It looks like the blade tore through the flesh and maybe some muscle. Her pulse and blood pressure are stable at the moment." He looked at Tink. "Are you able to get hold of Derek and ask if he could put a call into the base in Guam? It's about a three-and-a-half-hour flight from here. But I'd rather have one of our doctors look her over before we begin the long trek over the Pacific. I can apply some butterfly band-aides for now."

Tink nodded before disappearing into the small office he had in the rear of the plane.

Moments later, everyone got situated in their seats as the plane started to taxi out. Skittles sat on the couch where Anna Grace lay. Her head rested in his lap as he ran his fingers through her silky hair.

She started to stir, and her eyes slowly began to open. She stared up at him and started to move and cringe, but he held her still.

"Don't move unless you have to. We don't want your wound to open back up until we can get you to a doctor."

"What doctor?"

"We're making a detour to the Naval Base in Guam to have someone look at your injury."

She continued to stare at him, and he wondered what was going through her mind.

"He was going to stab you," she said.

"Why did you put yourself between him and me? Why?"

When her eyes filled with tears and started leaking, he felt like a jerk. He didn't want to see her cry. He wiped the tears from her cheeks.

"Please, tell me why you did it?"

She lifted her arm and pointed toward the rest of the team sitting all around them.

"I did it because of them," she told him, but he didn't understand.

"Explain," he replied.

She closed her eyes and took a deep breath before looking back at him. "I did it because you're all a family, and if something happened to you or one of them, I couldn't live with myself. You guys are here because of me. I am a job for you. You have a family back home who would be devastated if something happened to you." Another tear fell from her eye. "I don't."

"Jesus Christ, she is a perfect fit." Skittles heard one of the guys say. He missed the rest of the statement because he was too focused on what Anna Grace had said. She was clearly mistaken.

He ran his knuckles down her cheek. "Baby, you've seemed to have gotten the wrong message somewhere, but what you just said is untrue. You do have people who would care if something happened to you." He pointed to his team and Alex as they all nodded as if knowing what he would say. "Every single one of those people right there would care. The others back home would care. And most of all, I would care, because whether you believe me or not, I love you. I lost you once, but I don't intend to lose you again."

CHAPTER TWENTY

Derek lifted his cup of coffee to his lips and took a sip of the piping hot liquid. Now that he knew the team was on their way home with Anna Grace, he could relax a wee bit.

In his hand, he held a copy of the FBI case file relating to the murders of Anna Grace's parents. That was thanks to Arianna and her dad Paul who still had some reliable connections in the Bureau.

He wasn't even halfway through the second page of the eighteen-page file, and already there were red flags. In his opinion, the investigation was done half-assed. Two adults, brutally murdered in their mega-mansion; their fourteen-year-old daughter was missing; however, traces of her blood were also found at the murder scene, but she's their only named suspect? That made no sense whatsoever.

He pulled his laptop onto his lap, and in the search field, he typed in Anna Grace Silver. He was surprised at the lack of results that came back. For a high-profile crime in a prestigious community, it sure lacked media coverage. From the few articles he could find, it seemed it was Skittles' family who kept putting Anna Grace's face out in the news and actively searching for her.

Another interesting fact was that the entire house had been cleaned immediately following the "investigation." But even more interesting was who requested the cleaning service—Aaron Merlin, the lead agent on the case. The same agent who died a mysterious death just months after the investigation was placed in an inactive status.

Derek stared at the computer screen, and many ideas and thoughts circled his mind. One being, what had happened to the house? Potomac was a wealthy area. What happened to all of their assets as well? Curious, he pulled up the county tax collector and typed in the name Silver. Nothing came back with Dennis Silver or Sandra Silver, so he typed in the address, and he got a result—SES Trust was listed as the owner. He looked further and saw that the deed was transferred to the trust four months before Anna Grace's parents' murders. The mystery deepened.

Juliette walked into the room, and he smiled at her. She was the light of his life. He was such a dumbass for not pursuing her years ago. But that was the way the cards fell. He had her now, and he never planned to let her go.

She sat down next to him, and he placed the laptop on the coffee table in front of him.

"You doing, okay?" She asked him, and he grinned. It was a question she always asked him.

"I am now that you're here." He pulled her into his side and kissed the side of her head.

She glanced at the open laptop. "Is that Anna Grace's file?"

"It is," he answered with a sigh.

She turned her head to look at him. "Your response and expression tell me that what you've found isn't good."

"It's not. But not so much for Anna Grace. The investigation isn't adding up." He smiled at her. "But enough work for now. Let's talk about you and me."

She raised her eyebrow at him. "What about us?"

Taking her hand, he looked down into her eyes. She and her daughter, Tenley, shared so many similarities. "What do you say you and I make us official?"

"Official?"

He nodded. "As in, let's get married."

Her eyes began to glisten. "I thought you'd never ask," she teased.

They had talked about it in the past, but they never set a date as neither one wanted to have an actual wedding.

"And how soon are you looking to do this, Commander?"

He took her face between the palms of his hands. "What's your schedule like tomorrow?"

Her eyes grew big, and he grinned, knowing that his suggestion would shock her.

"Tomorrow?" She stammered out.

203

"Yep. What do you say? Remember we already filed for our marriage license a few months ago when I asked you to marry me."

"At the courthouse like we talked about?" She asked, and he nodded. "Don't we need an appointment? And what about the girls, Alex and Tenley? You know they would be upset if we didn't tell them."

He smiled. "I already made an appointment for us, hoping that you would say yes. And as for the girls, think about it. You know they would never let us just have a small courthouse wedding."

She laughed. "You're absolutely right. And I don't want a big wedding." She leaned forward and kissed him. "All I need is you."

As they got comfortable on the couch, Derek started to laugh, and she asked what he was laughing at. "Just thinking what the girls' expressions would be when we tell them."

Juliette chuckled. "Shocked. However, I know those girls. Don't be surprised when they throw some sort of a surprise wedding reception."

He barked out a deep laugh. "Nothing would surprise me with those two."

CHAPTER TWENTY-ONE

Skittles closed the bedroom door and went downstairs to the living room. They had gotten home a couple of hours ago. Anna Grace woke up when they landed, but once they got inside their building on base and in the Commander's office, she had fallen asleep again. He needed to remember that pain medicine was powerful on her.

It had been decided that until they found a place to hide her so the feds could complete their investigation, that they both would stay with Ace and Alex, which was where they were now. Once this shit consuming her was over, they would sit down and discuss buying a home together.

That thought brought a smile to his face. He dreamt of having a wife and eventually adding some little ones to their family for so long. He ran his hand down his face, still in disbelief at times that Anna Grace was sleeping just feet from him. He wasn't a hugely religious person, but there were times in the past when he'd called upon the Lord to help guide him, and Anna Grace had been one of those.

Right now, the important thing was keeping her safe and hidden while the team and their friends did some recon. After discussing where it would be the safest and the most comfortable for Anna Grace to relax and recover, it was decided that she'd stay at his parents' house. He'd be staying with her. He didn't want her out of his sight—not until this shitstorm blew over and those responsible were found and charged. Anna Grace had suffered too much for too long, and she deserved justice.

He held his cell phone in his hand, preparing to make the call to his parents and tell them the good news. His mom especially was going to flip out. She loved A.G just as much as he did. A smile spread across his face. Yep, he loved her, and he vowed to give her the world.

He pulled his mom's number up and pressed the call button. It started to ring and then she answered.

"Noah!"

"Hey, mom."

"It's been a few weeks." She got quiet for a moment. "You aren't hurt, are you?" He could hear the nervousness in her voice. She always worried about him.

"Everything is good. Are you busy?"

"Never too busy to talk to my favorite son."

He grinned. "I'm your only son."

"True. But you're going to have a little competition, considering I'm going to have a son-in-law soon."

What the fuck!

"Say that again," he asked his mom, and she chuckled.

"I said I'm going to have a son-in-law soon. And, you're going to have a brother-in-law."

He smiled. "For real? Nicole and Julian?"

"Yes!" She squealed in delight, and Skittles had to pull the phone away from his ear to she didn't rupture his eardrum. "Julian proposed last weekend. Nicole tried to call you, but it went to voicemail, and she didn't want to leave that on a message."

"Wow! That's awesome."

"It is. I'm over the moon. He's such a nice man and loves your sister so much."

Skittles couldn't deny that. Julian was a good guy and had a clean record, though he hadn't spent a lot of time around him to get to really know him. But all that mattered was that Nicole was happy and that Julian treated her well.

"I'm happy for them," he told his mom, and he could hear how happy she was. She couldn't wait for grandkids. He felt a slight sensation hit his belly, thinking about little kiddos running around. Maybe a little girl with Anna Grace's platinum blonde hair and a son who resembled both of them. *Jesus, talk about putting the cart before the horse.*

"I'm sorry, honey. I hijacked your call. I'm sure you don't have a lot of time to talk."

"It's all good. I'm actually home right now."

"Oh." He heard the relief in her voice.

206

"Listen, is Dad around? I need to talk to you both."

"He's in the living room tinkering with the new television he bought. Let me get him."

A few moments later, his dad's voice came through the line, and he could tell his mom put him on speakerphone. "Hey, son!"

"How's it going, dad? You prepared to give your little girl away?" He teased his dad, and he heard the sigh come from his dad. Nicole was definitely a daddy's girl—always had been.

"I don't have much choice. Julian's a good guy."

"Yes, he is, and that's all that matters."

Skittles took a deep breath. Here it goes.

"By chance, are you guys planning on being at home for the next few days?"

His mom was the first to speak. "Oh, Noah! Are you coming to visit?" He could hear the hope in her voice.

"I am."

"That makes me so happy," she said, then his dad spoke. "It'll be nice to see you and catch up."

"Umm…for this trip, I need you guys to keep my visit on the down-low. As in nobody can know."

His dad got quiet for a second. "Are you in some kind of trouble?"

He chuckled. "Me, no. But the person coming with me—sort of. It's complicated right now."

"You're bringing someone home with you?" His mom asked.

"Are you both sitting down? Because if you're not, you really should."

"Okay, we're sitting," his dad stated.

"I found A.G., and I'm bringing her home."

There was dead silence. After a few more seconds, he thought he might have gotten disconnected. He looked at the phone, and the line was still showing they were connected.

"Mom…Dad… are you still there?"

He heard the slight sniffle and knew his mom was crying.

"Yeah, son." His dad answered, and Skittles heard the emotion in his dad's voice as well. They both cared so much for Anna Grace, and he was pretty sure he had just given them the shock of their lives.

"Damn, Noah. I don't even know how to follow that up," his dad admitted. "Jesus! Where did you find her? She's with you now?"

"Believe it or not, she's been living the past seven years right here in Virginia Beach. There's a lot more to her story that she and I will explain to you both when we get there. Her whereabouts need to be kept secret. Nobody can know she's there, at least not yet."

"You have our word. What about Nicole? You know your sister is going to be pissed if she finds out and we didn't tell her."

"Have Nicole at the house tomorrow."

"Noah?"

"Yeah, Dad?"

"Answer this. Is she okay?"

"Physically, a little banged up. She's been through a lot in the last ten years, more so in the last few days. Mentally, it's going to take some time for her to heal with what she's been through."

"Sounds pretty bad."

"It's bad, Dad."

"Okay. What time should we expect you?"

"Around one or two?"

"That's perfect. Park in the garage," his dad told him.

"Will do."

"Noah?" His mom asked.

"Yeah, Mom"

"Please tell her that we can't wait to see her."

He smiled but then heard the bedroom door upstairs open. "I will, but I need to run. I'll see you guys tomorrow."

"Love you!" His mom called out.

"Love you too. Bye."

He ended the call and set the phone on the table just as Anna Grace appeared at the bottom of the stairs holding her side, and he feared she might

208

have reinjured her wound in her sleep. The doctor at the base in Guam put in something like fifteen stitches to close the wound. Thankfully, he confirmed that no significant damage had been done. He stood and hurried to her side. She tilted her head back to look up at him. She still looked exhausted, but then a tiny smile hit her lips.

"You, okay?" He asked, and she nodded her head before she leaned against his side, and he put his arm around her.

"Just tired and thirsty."

She had been drinking water like a camel ever since they found her.

"Come sit down for a bit, and I'll get you something to drink. Alex picked up some things, and I think there was some Gatorade. You should drink a little bit of that for electrolytes."

"Whatever you say. I'm just parched."

He got her seated on the couch, went into the kitchen, and pulled out a blue Gatorade from the refrigerator. "Are you hungry?" He asked her, and she scrunched her nose up, and it made him laugh.

"I could eat something light—maybe crackers if you have them. Or something like that."

He looked in the pantry. Alex had everything, including several types of crackers. As he grabbed the boxes, he spotted a few cans of tuna fish and cringed as his stomach revolted. Ever since Irish's daughter, Sienna, fed the entire team canned cat food instead of tuna fish, he hadn't touched the stuff. He still got the chills just thinking about it.

He gathered the crackers and some Gatorade and walked out to the living room. He found Anna Grace cuddled in the corner of the plush couch. He could tell she was in some discomfort judging from the pinched look on her face.

He set everything down on the coffee table before he sat down next to her. She looked over at him, then scooted closer, and he opened his arms and let her lay on him. He ran his fingers through her silky locks.

"You're hurting. I can see it on your face."

She stared up at him. "I won't lie. I'm a little uncomfortable, but I don't want one of those pills that Stitch gave me, or I'll be asleep for the next two days."

He smiled. "But rest will help you heal."

She wrinkled her nose, and he couldn't help but chuckle under his breath. She was freaking adorable.

"Can't I just take some Tylenol or something like that?"

"You can try it, but if you're still in pain, promise me you'll take the pill that the doctor at the base gave you."

She squinted her eyes at him. "Deal."

He grinned, knowing she would do anything not to reveal any sort of pain in front of him.

"You're such a little liar," he teased, and she laughed. But then her facial expression grew serious, and she took his hand in hers.

"All joking aside, I never told you, but thank you for coming to rescue me. You and your team."

He looked down into her eyes.

"You don't have to thank me for being there for you." He cupped her cheeks and pressed his forehead against hers. "I will always come for you. I promise you that."

The warmth of her puffs of breath against his lips as she exhaled was enticing, and he brushed his lips softly over hers. This he could get used to.

A little while later, after Anna Grace had fallen back asleep, Skittles heard the front door open. Ace and Alex appeared, and surprisingly the rest of the team filed in after them. They had gone over to his apartment to get some clothes for him, along with some other items he needed to take with him. After that, they would swing by Anna Grace's apartment and pick up some clothes for her.

They all glanced at the couch where Anna Grace lay sleeping beside him. She didn't know it yet, but he had given her half of a pain pill instead of Tylenol. If she realized it when she woke up, he'd deal with it.

"How's she doing?" Alex asked as she and Ace sat down a massive amount of shopping bags.

He slowly got up from the couch, trying not to wake her. He motioned them toward the kitchen. Dino handed him his duffle bag and computer bag. He looked around, then frowned when he saw they didn't have anything except a small shopping bag that Potter held.

"She was in a little pain when she woke up. Where's her stuff?" He asked.

Ace suddenly appeared angry. "A.G.'s apartment was broken into and ransacked."

Skittles put his hands on his hips. "You're fucking kidding?"

"Wish we were, man," Frost said.

Skittles sat down at the kitchen table. A.G. was going to flip out when he told her.

"Coincidence, or were the intruders looking for something?"

"Considering the sofa and mattress were ripped to shreds, our opinion is whoever it was had been looking for something. We don't know what that could be until you can talk with her and see if she did, in fact, have anything she was hiding. Most of her clothes were also destroyed, and what other little stuff she had was broken.

"Other than the LEGOs, the only thing we found that we thought she'd want are these." Potter handed Skittles the bag he had been holding. When he peered into it, he scrunched his forehead up. It was filled with a bunch of small journals.

He looked back at the guys, and it was Diego who spoke. "We found those in one of the LEGO boxes." Diego's expression changed. Skittles couldn't tell if it was anger or regret. "We weren't sure what they were, but considering they were in a LEGO box, it made us think that she was keeping them hidden there."

"What are they?"

Diego looked at Alex, and Alex answered. "Basically, it's her life from the past ten years. When we realized what they were, we knew she'd want them, so we grabbed all of them along with her LEGOs. Like Ace said, everything else was pretty much destroyed. We stopped by the store and got her new clothes and some other things she might need. That's what's in the bags in the living room."

Seeing the remorseful looks on their faces, Skittles knew whatever they had seen in those journals had upset them. He knew there was much more to her story than what she had told them. He wasn't bashing her for it. He knew it was her way of explaining what had happened without going into detail. But he knew that by writing, people could express their feelings better than talking it out.

"Thank you. I'm sure she'll be thankful you were able to salvage these."

Skittles immediately thought about Ziggy. According to Anna Grace, nothing happened at that apartment complex that he didn't know about. He had to have heard something. If he hadn't, Skittles was pretty sure Ziggy could find out.

"Whoever it was didn't want it to look like a break-in. When they left, they relocked the door."

"She's going to be devastated when I tell her." He looked at Alex. "Thank you for picking up some clothes for her. Just let me know how much everything was, and I'll pay you back."

She waved him off. "You'll do no such thing."

Changing the subject, Ace asked. "What time are you planning on leaving for your parent's house tomorrow?"

"I told my mom we'd be there around one or two. Why?"

"It seems that we're hosting a small celebratory breakfast tomorrow." Ace said, but Skittles noticed how Alex squinted her eyes.

"What in the hell are we celebrating?" Skittles asked.

Ace grinned. "The Commander and Juliet apparently snuck off and got married."

Skittles' eyes about popped out of their sockets. "Seriously?"

"Uh-huh," Potter said dryly.

"That's good news, right?" He asked, looking between Ace, Potter, and Alex.

"Potter and I are dealing with this one," he pointed to Alex, "and Tenley."

212

"Oh."

"Yeah, oh!" Alex said as she took Zuma and walked out back with him.

Ace watched Alex through the French doors. "While they're happy for their parents, they're a wee bit upset at the fact that Derek and Juliet didn't tell them."

Skittles chuckled. "That's Derek for you—spontaneous. I think that's awesome."

"According to Derek, neither he nor Juliet wanted all the attention of a wedding that they knew the girls would have thrown for them." Ace smirked. "Though, I believe that Alex and Tenley are already concocting a plan of some sort. You can count on it that Derek and Juliet will have a party."

"I have no doubt," Skittles replied. "I'm sure that Derek realizes that, too."

"Does anything get by him? Especially if it involves those two?" Potter said.

"True."

Skittles knew firsthand the trouble Alex and Tenley could bring. Though, most of the time, it was considered innocent trouble. He never knew how two people could be almost identical in every aspect and not be related until he met the pair and saw them together.

"A.G. and I will definitely stick around for breakfast. I think she'd also enjoy seeing the other ladies. Especially since she won't have a lot of contact with anyone outside of my family."

"How is she doing? Besides the pain," Stitch asked.

Skittles told them that overall, she seemed okay right now.

"How'd your mom and dad react when you told them?"

"They were ecstatic and can't wait to see her."

"I bet they were."

Ace, who was standing next to Skittles, squeezed his shoulder.

"This'll all work out."

God, he hoped so.

CHAPTER TWENTY-TWO

Anna Grace fidgeted in her seat as Skittles made the turn on Branhum Road. The same road she used to walk down multiple times a day—the same road that would put a smile on her face.

Skittles reached over and placed his hand on her thigh as he glanced at her before looking back at the road.

"Are you okay?"

She stared back out the window, looking at how the community had changed over the last ten years. There were more homes now.

"Yeah, just nervous."

"It'll be fine. In fact, it's going to be great." He gave her a reassuring smile and her eyes teared up.

"I'm nervous of what your parents will think."

"A.G., I told you I've already talked to them and they assured me they are not upset with you. They were excited and can't wait to see you, especially Nicole. On second thought, maybe you should be nervous because you never know how Nicole will react. You may want to prepare yourself for that freight train."

She turned and looked through the windshield as they pulled through the gates into the driveway. She looked at the large brick colonial home in front of her. The same house that when you walked through the doors you knew the home was filled with love, joy and laughter. Tears instantly built in her eyes. There had been a time back in Mexico where she thought she'd never see this place again.

Skittles pulled the truck into the spacious three-car garage, and before he could get the truck in park, Adelle, Marty, and Nicole came flying out the door. Anna Grace couldn't get her door open fast enough as Nicole yanked it open and practically pulled her out of it and into her arms. She heard Skittles telling his sister to be careful, but Anna Grace tuned him out and ignored the slight burn she felt to her side. Soon she was wrapped up in one big family hug and she lost it. She couldn't stop the tears even if she wanted to. Adelle was crying, Nicole was crying, and Marty's eyes were glistening. After a few minutes of hugging, crying, and more hugging, Skittles finally ushered everyone in the house.

As they made their way into the large industrial size kitchen Anna Grace took in the new décor. Adelle loved to cook and she always said that one day she would have the kitchen of her dreams. Well, she definitely got it. The white cabinets and stainless-steel appliances were stunning.

Adelle hurried around the counter and went to the refrigerator. Next thing Anna Grace knew the counters were covered in a spread of food and desserts.

Skittles laughed. "Mom. I told you that you didn't have to make all of this.

She waved him off and looked at Anna Grace. She still had tears in her eyes. "Anna Grace, I made all of your favorites."

Anna Grace smiled. "Thank you, Mrs. Young. But as Noah said, you really didn't have to go through all this trouble."

Adelle rested her elbows on the countertop and stared at Anna Grace. "I still can't believe you're standing here." She shook her head and smiled. "Why don't we all grab some food and then we can talk while we eat."

Anna Grace thought that was a great idea—as did everyone else.

It was late in the evening and Anna Grace was upstairs getting a shower. Skittles could tell she was still exhausted from her traumatic experience, and then mix that in with his overly excited parents and sister and the busy day she had, he was pretty sure she was ready to crash.

Now that he knew everything she had faced, he didn't know how she came out of it with her wits still intact. She was strong-willed, but he knew not only from experience but seeing others who had gone through traumatic experiences as she had, that she'd need a lot of support to get through some dark days ahead mentally.

He heard the front door open. His dad walked out and took a seat in the chair next to him. Neither said a word for a few minutes as they both stared out at the night sky. It was a cool and refreshing evening.

"Has she talked to you in detail about what she went through?" His dad asked. And Skittles knew his parents would worry about her even now that she was home and safe.

Skittles stared out toward the neighbor's house across the street. He really didn't want to be reminded of the horror she was put through.

"I don't want to get into details, but I will say it wasn't good. She was locked in a damn cage in a makeshift morgue when we found her this last time.

"The important thing is that she's safe and with people who love her."

"She was really scared about coming here."

"Why?"

"She was afraid that you and Mom would be upset with her for not coming to you guys. But I sort of get why she didn't. I don't think that until someone is put in the position she was in can judge her on her decision to stay hidden and on the run."

His dad nodded. "I can understand."

Noah laughed. "Believe it or not, she saved my life."

"How so?"

Skittles explained how Anna Grace pushed him out of the way when the guy lunged at him with the knife.

"That explains why she's favoring her side," his dad stated and Skittles nodded.

"She was lucky. It could've been a lot worse." Skittles was quiet for a few seconds before he spoke again. "She's special, Dad."

"That she is, son. And brave."

"I told her that I loved her."

His dad grinned. "I can't tell you how happy that makes me. I've always considered her a part of this family." His dad then got serious. "Have you talked to her about counseling?"

"No, not yet. But I think it would be a good idea since she said that she was willing to talk about her ordeal."

"Noah, you know she is going to have to talk to the police. She is still considered a missing person."

216

He blew a breath out. "I know Dad. I just don't want to overwhelm her right now. She has managed to stay off the grid for seven years. My commander and some of his buddies are working on a few things. That's why we don't want it to get out that she was found. If that happens, things could get nasty and dangerous."

"Like what?" His dad questioned.

He turned and looked his dad in the eye. "Dad, we believe that Senator DeSmith is behind everything that Anna Grace has been through for the last ten years." Skittles explained what they knew and what Anna Grace had overheard.

"Shit!"

"Exactly. And for some reason Senator DeSmith is hellbent on getting rid of her and it's pretty much up to us to figure out why. We've got a little help inside the FBI, but with as many people that the Senator is connected with, it's hard to know who you can trust."

"I just want to keep her safe and have all of this shit be behind her. I want her to have her identity and life back without having to constantly look over her shoulder."

"Well, you two can stay as long as you'd like. I know your mother enjoys your visits."

"Thanks, Dad. I really appreciate it."

"No thanks needed, son. As I said, A.G. is a member of this family and we all protect our own."

Anna Grace slowly climbed up the wooden ladder to the tree house that still stood perched up in the humongous oak tree in the backyard of the Youngs. She and Nicole with the help of Mr. Young and Skittles had built the tree house when they were in the fourth grade. She couldn't believe that Noah's parents had kept it and not tore it down. As she reached the top, she pushed the door open and ducked her head to enter. She shined the flashlight she had around the small but spacious space and she was in awe. The place still looked as it did ten years ago when she'd last saw it. Nothing had changed. There were still pictures of her, and Nicole tacked up on the walls along with posters of various boy bands they used to listen to. But it was the one picture in the gold frame on a small table that stole her attention. She picked it up. It was a picture of her and Skittles' family. She remembered that day. It was taken during Skittles' graduation party; just weeks before her life was turned upside down. She wiped the tear from her eye.

She heard the floor creak and looked toward the door. She was surprised to see Skittles' trying to fit his large body through the small opening.

She set the picture down and sat down with her back against the wall to make room for him.

"I can't believe your parents kept this place."

"Yeah, me neither, but it was a happy place. I think Nicole convinced them to keep it."

She patted the space next to her. "Want to sit?"

He smiled and gracefully lowered himself next to her. She leaned her head against his shoulder.

"What are you doing up here?"

She pursed her lips. "I don't really know. I was standing out on the deck just thinking how wonderful it felt to be back home even though this isn't really my home, and when I looked out and saw the tree house was still intact it was like it called to me."

"I feel so relaxed here."

"What do you mean?"

"The last ten years I've always been looking over my shoulder. Waiting for someone to snatch me and take me away again. But here with you, I feel safe and protected."

He put his finger under her chin, making her look up at him. He cupped her cheeks. "You are safe, and nobody is going to take you away again." Then he leaned forward and pressed his lips against her forehead.

"Thank you, Noah." She whispered to him and he looked down her.

"For what?"

"For never giving up searching for me."

He shook his head as if he was frustrated. "At times I thought I was close but then the trail ran into a dead-end. And all this time you've been right under my nose." He tapped her nose with his finger and she smiled.

"Noah, what happens if the feds come up with nothing on the Senator? Will I ever be safe? Senator DeSmith isn't going to just let this go. Especially when he finds out that I ratted him out."

"I'm not going to let that happen. With your statements alone, there is already too much evidence against him. And I'm pretty sure when Tink's computer guys get into the Senator's server, more dominos will fall."

"You seem so confident."

"Because I am. I'm confident that Senator DeSmith has spent his last days as a free man."

"I hope so."

She looked down at the small white bakery type box that Skittles had brought with him. "What's in the box you got there?"

As he reached for the box, she watched his muscles in his arms flex through the fitted long sleeved t-shirt he wore. Suddenly, she had no need for the blanket she had brought with her because her temperature was reaching its max limit.

As he sat back up, his shoulder rubbed against hers and she couldn't stop herself from leaning into him, and he immediately lifted his arm and let her snuggle close to his side as he draped his arm over her shoulders and held her.

She inhaled and closed her eyes as the scent of his cologne wafted around her. She loved his scent.

"I brought you something," he said from above her and she lifted her head.

"What is it?"

He set the box on his lap then reached inside and pulled out an extra-large cupcake. And it wasn't just any type of cupcake, it was her favorite strawberry shortcake with the whipped topping from the little bakery in town that she used to go to. It was topped with a single candle which Skittles then lit with a lighter.

As the small, orange flame burned between them, their eyes met.

"I never got to really celebrate your birthday with you alone. So, I'm doing it now."

She smiled wide and wondered if he could get any sweeter. Though, with his status as a Navy SEAL, he might not want to be referred to as sweet.

"Go ahead, make a wish, and blow out the candle," he told her.

Keeping her eyes on him she leaned forward, took a tiny breath and blew the candle out.

As the smoke lifted into the air he asked, "Did you even make a wish?"

She grinned as she leaned into him then stopped when her lips were a hair's breath away from his.

"I didn't need to because my wish already came true. I have you."

She pressed her lips against his. She had been proud of herself for being so brazen and making the first move this time. She needed to show him how much she loved and cared for him.

With their lips pressed together, Skittles used one arm to maneuver her onto his lap. Once he got her into the position that he wanted, he deepened the kiss using his tongue to explore her thoroughly.

Needing to breathe, as their lips parted, he sought out her neck and kissed her there before trailing his lips upward to her jaw and peppering her with butterfly kisses until he landed on her lips once more.

"You are everything I have ever wanted," he told her.

She smiled and could feel herself blushing.

"I have something else for you," he said and reached beside him and pulled out a jewelry box.

"I saw you at the farmers market when you were looking at the vendor's tables. I noticed you were very interested in an item at a certain table.

Anna Grace immediately recognized the necklace box from Wanda's vendor table at the farmer's market. She looked from the box, up into Skittles' eyes.

"How did you know?" She asked him as her emotions started to take over. The day she had stumbled upon Wanda's table and had seen that necklace a while ago she had been in total disbelief. What were the odds that

220

she found the one piece of jewelry that had meant the most to her? She had been fortunate when Wanda offered her to pay for it in installments.

"That day I met you at the farmer's market, I spent a few minutes watching you. And, when you stopped at the jewelry counter, I was curious in what you were interested in."

She wiped her eyes. "You should've seen my reaction when I saw it sitting in her jewelry case. I couldn't believe it. My hands were even shaking."

He grinned. "Things happen for a reason."

He removed the necklace from the box and reached up and clasped it around her neck.

She took the heart pendant and wrapped her palm around it.

"Thank you, Noah. You don't know how much this necklace meant to me." She started to choke up as she had a flashback from that ill-fated day. "The person who took me had ripped it off me."

"It belongs with you and you're welcome."

She cupped his cheeks and leaned in and kissed him.

"How do you do it?"

"Do what?"

"Even though you're a bad ass Navy SEAL you're still the guy I fell in love with all those years ago. You make everything seem so simple. You're patient, compassionate, and loving."

She couldn't believe the shade of red that Skittle' cheeks turned.

He cleared his throat. "The SEALs made me stronger both mentally and physically, but I never let it take away who I am inside here." He held a hand over his heart. "My family is my world." He stared at her and she recognized the familiar look in his eyes. It was the same look he had before he kissed her the first time, ten years ago.

He leaned forward as if he was going to kiss her, but before his lips touched hers, he said, "I was serious back in the Philippines, A.G. I want the whole thing with you. I want you forever."

221

She was so aroused it felt as if she was drowning in lust that she completely forgot about her wound until Skittles wrapped his arms tighter around her waist and pulled her closer to him.

"Ow…" She blurted out and pulled back.

"Shit! I forgot." He kissed her forehead then hugged her to him, being extra careful to be gentle. "I'm sorry, so sorry."

She pulled back but kept her arms around his neck. "It's okay. I still forget myself."

He shook his head and Anna Grace saw how her injury upset him. "It's not okay. You should've never been put into that situation in the first place. I don't like to see you hurt."

"Noah. Look at me."

"I would've ended up in that situation no matter what. And, if it wasn't in the Philippines, it would've been somewhere else. I'm lucky that you and your team were persistent and found me."

He just stared into her eyes and she knew that it was time to change the subject.

"Do you know how many times I've been in this treehouse and wished that you would join me up here?"

He scrunched his eyebrows together. "You wanted me to come up to the treehouse with you and do what?" He then grinned. "Wow, A.G. I didn't realize you had such a mind to think dirty thoughts. And here I thought you were such an innocent little girl."

Her eyes got big, then she slapped his shoulder playfully. "Noah Young. You should be ashamed of yourself for thinking of me that way. Back then, I was referring to cuddling."

"Back then? What about right now? I'm here with you now and I'll be honest with you. With you sitting on my lap and in my arms, I know what I want."

She pulled her bottom lip between her teeth. She knew that he wanted her. She was both excited and nervous—excited because holy smokes, Noah Young wanted her. But nervous because she didn't know what to expect. She'd never had sex before. That was the one thing that she'd give Senor

Castillo credit for. He had protected her sexually from his sons and other men. At least until the night of her seventeenth birthday.

Realizing she had zoned out; she moved her gaze back to Skittles. He looked sexy as sin, sitting there with a small grin on his face as if knowing what she was thinking. She wanted him, badly.

"I know what I want too," she told him as she leaned in and kissed him. Soon that simple kiss turned into a breathtaking and life changing event. At least for her.

When Skittles pulled away just slightly, he said, "I don't want to hurt you."

"You won't. I need you. Please." Ignoring the slight chill in the air, she reached under and pulled at the hem of his shirt and lifted it over his head. Her mouth watered at the sight of all his muscles. But then her eyes landed on a few scars as well. As if knowing what she was looking at she directed her eyes to his.

"Those are just battle wounds."

She nodded her head in understanding, though, she wanted to ask him how to he got them. She may not know a lot about the SEALs, but one thing she did know was not to ask questions when it came to their jobs.

Focusing on the task at hand, she reached down to the button on his jeans.

"A.G." He said in warning as she popped the button. She looked up and gave him a coy smile but continued her mission in divesting him of his clothes.

She could feel her body shaking from the anticipation. She stood and pulled off her shirt and sweatpants. She wasn't wearing a bra. When she went to pull her panties down, Skittles stopped her.

"Let me," he ordered and she stood completely still as he gripped the waistband of her panties and slowly slid them down her legs. She was thankful that she had decided to shave her legs and other areas while she was in the shower. She had no idea what this night was going to turn into.

Once she was in her glory like he was, he helped her lower herself back onto his lap.

"Shit!" He whispered.

"What?"

"I don't have a condom. I wasn't expecting for you to seduce me in the treehouse," he teased and she grinned feeling proud of herself.

"I'm on the pill," she told him and he smiled.

"You're sure about this? Because once I seat myself inside of you, you will belong to me fully."

"I only want you."

She grinned then slowly sunk down on his shaft, praying that wouldn't make a mess of things with her inexperience. She noticed the tightness in his face and she became concerned.

"Are you okay?" She asked.

"Yeah. It's just hard to hold back. You feel so damn good."

She didn't want him to hold back on her account. She craved that dominant, bossy, alpha man ego she saw in the Philippines. She wanted to put him out of his misery, so she took a deep breath and slid the rest of the way down until he was fully inside of her. She closed her eyes and breathed through the slight discomfort as he broke through the barrier that once held her innocence. But soon that ache morphed into an amazing feeling that literally brought tears to her eyes.

Tilting her head back with her eyes closed she said, "Amazing."

When she looked back at him, he was staring at her intently, and she knew from his look that he just realized what she had given him.

"Why didn't you tell me you were a virgin?" He asked as he held his palm against her cheek.

"Because I know you. And you would've wanted to wait." The way he smiled told her that she was right. "I didn't want to wait. The moment was right."

He kissed her softly on the lips. "I'm honored to be your first and your only."

"Only you," she whispered then gripped his shoulders and started to rock her hips, praying she was doing it correctly.

She heard him mumble something then the next thing she knew she was being lifted up and placed gently onto her back on the blanket. He covered her with his body before entering her wet heat once again, making her lose her breath, as they both let go and exploded together. It was a beautiful moment and one she would cherish for the rest of her life.

"I love you," he told her.

She felt the tear slip out of her eye and she reached up and cupped his cheek. "I love you too."

He smiled and then rolled to his back and brought her with him. She curled into his side and they stayed just like that until their bodies cooled down and it was too cold to stay in the treehouse.

CHAPTER TWENTY-THREE

The following morning Anna Grace and Nicole helped Adelle prepare breakfast for everyone.

When they were alone in the kitchen, Nicole turned toward Anna Grace. "Were you out in the treehouse last night?" Nicole asked, and Anna Grace immediately felt her cheeks start to blush.

"Yep."

Nicole raised one eyebrow. "And my brother was with you."

"Not at first."

She quickly held her hand up. "Nope. Don't say anything. I don't want to know." She shook her head.

"You don't want to know what?" Skittles asked his sister as he walked into the kitchen. He went right to Anna Grace and surprised her when he kissed her in front of his mom and sister.

"Morning," he said with a sexy smile, and she wanted to melt.

Feeling slightly embarrassed of being kissed in front of an audience, she took a quick glance at Nicole and Adelle, and they were both smiling—Adelle more so. Nicole gave her more of a smirk.

Skittles must've realized her embarrassment because he chuckled, pulled her back into his arms, and held her around her waist.

"I told my parents about us last night," he informed her.

Adelle walked over to them. She was still smiling. "When Noah told Marty and me last night, we were both ecstatic. We've always considered you part of this family. Who knows, maybe we'll be planning a second wedding soon."

"Mom!" Skittles said, and Adelle just laughed and went back to finish cooking the home fries.

As they all sat around the table eating, Anna Grace asked, "Speaking of Tink, how are Mary Beth and Christian?"

Skittles smiled. "They're good. They are staying at Tink's place for now. Although I don't think Tink plans on letting them leave."

"Why?" Anna Grace asked, but then realized what Skittles was saying, and she smiled. "Christian is a sweet boy."

"Who are they?" Nicole asked, and Anna Grace looked to Skittles to make sure it was okay for her to talk about her incident. He gave her a wink and nod.

Both she and Skittles explained how Christian led the team to where she was being held. Skittles then told them a little about Mary Beth. They then talked about Senator DeSmith and his admittance.

"I knew something wasn't right, and I prayed for you every night. What you went through and are going through now just frosts my cookies. I have never been a fan of that Senator DeSmith. He strikes me as a big bully."

"He is a bully," Skittles second.

"More like an asshole." Noah's dad said, reaching for the plate of bacon, and Anna Grace couldn't help but snicker. He wasn't lying.

Skittles enjoyed this time with his family and Anna Grace, but he knew there was something that he and his parents needed to discuss with Anna Grace. It was monumental, and he wasn't sure how she was going to react to the news. It was why he had held off on saying anything to her until his parents could be there, as they knew more of the details than he did.

Once everyone had finished, and they were all just talking, Skittles cleared his throat and looked toward his dad. His dad nodded in understanding and looked at Anna Grace.

"Anna Grace, there's something we need to talk to you about." Marty started the discussion, and Skittles could immediately see the concern on her face. He grasped her hand.

"It's nothing bad. I promise."

She licked her lips nervously, and he gave her hand one more squeeze before his dad began.

"Sweetie, at the time of your parent's tragic passing, they had a will in place. All of their assets, including the house were placed in a trust."

"What does that mean?" She asked.

"Well, you are the sole beneficiary. It all belongs to you. You were only considered a missing person. Without a death certificate, everything has just been sitting there waiting to be claimed."

Skittles eyed her looking for any signs of distress, but all he saw was confusion.

She looked at Marty. "Are you saying that my old house is still my house?"

Marty nodded his head. "It is. Not one thing has been removed from the home. It is all yours to do what you want with it. Well, after we deal with the Senator DeSmith issue and can get you in contact with the lawyer handling the trust."

She looked at Skittles, and he could see the turmoil circling her. For most people, something like this was life-altering.

"I don't want it," she told them and wiped a tear from her eye. He went to hug her, but she shook her head. He knew she was trying hard to be strong. "What are my options?" She asked his dad.

"If you're sure you don't want it, then you can sell it. It is a seller's market right now. You can get top dollar for that home."

She nibbled on her lip. "What do you mean when you said that nothing had been removed from the home?"

"Everything that was there ten years ago is still there. Although there were most likely a few items removed during the FBI's investigation, they would list what those items are. The trust is responsible for the upkeep and making sure everything on the property is operational."

She stood up and started to pace the kitchen. After several tense moments, she turned and looked at Marty.

"I don't want it. Will you help me?" She asked, and Marty offered her a small smile.

"Of course, honey. Whatever you want or need, we'll help wherever we can. However, you do realize that you're going to have to decide what you want to do with everything."

She placed her hand over her stomach. "Oh, wow."

Skittles could see she was becoming overwhelmed with the news, and that was the last thing he wanted for her. He stood, walked over to her, and pulled her into a hug. "There's no time frame for you to make a decision. This was a lot to take in. But know that you don't have to go through this alone. All of us here and our friends back home are there for you."

She pulled away, and he could see the emotion in her eyes. But then she surprised him when a small smile appeared. "I think I'm going to need all the help I can get."

He smiled as he held her cheeks between his hands. "Then help is what you shall receive."

CHAPTER TWENTY-FOUR

Two weeks had passed since Anna Grace returned home, and those days just rolled into the next. It had been a whirlwind of events, but Skittles and his family never left her side.

She had been questioned by the FBI not once but three times. Come to find out, Arianna and her dad still had some contacts in the Bureau, and the agents assigned to the investigation were the complete opposite of what she had been expecting.

The night before her first meeting, she had gotten herself so worked up that she made herself sick. But Skittles made a call to Arianna and let Anna Grace speak with her. Arianna told her that she knew the two agents and that one agent had been her supervisor at one point and assured her that both agents had been briefed on the situation and there was no reason for her to feel nervous.

With her statements to the FBI and some other incriminating evidence that Tink and his team discovered, it looked as if Senator DeSmith's days in office were coming to an end. The agents had assured her that they would let her know once formal charges were filed.

Between Skittles and the team, and Adelle and Marty, she hadn't had to leave the house for anything. All of the meetings with the FBI took place at the Youngs' house. Adelle had even spoken with a friend of hers who was a physician's assistant, and she also came to the house to remove the stitches from her side, which was healing nicely. And lastly, with the okay from the FBI, she met with the lawyer overseeing the trust. From the meeting with the lawyer, she learned that she owned the house and there were stocks left to her. She knew nothing about the stock market, so she was letting Marty handle that for her.

There had been a bit of good news that Tink had provided. One of the men who was killed in the Philippines had been identified as Ramil. At least the world had one less scumbag.

She had been itching to get out of the house, but right now, since she was still advised by the FBI to stay out of sight, there was only one place she could go and not be seen—her old home. She needed to go and just get it over with. These last couple of weeks, being with Skittles and his family affirmed that she was ready to be free of all the negativity she had been subjected to for the last ten years.

She wished that Skittles was there. However, he had received a call from his commander and was summoned back to base. Derek had assured him that it wouldn't take long.

She walked downstairs and found Adelle in the kitchen. When she walked in, Adelle looked up from the cookbook she was reading and smiled.

"Hi, honey."

Anna Grace smiled. "Hi."

"Uh oh. I know that look. What's on your mind?" Adelle asked her.

"I was thinking about how I needed to go over to the house and get it over with."

Adelle stood up straight, looking concerned. "Okay."

Anna Grace twisted her fingers together as her nerves started to take over. "Well, I was wondering if you wouldn't mind coming with me? I don't want to go by myself, and Noah isn't here."

"Of course, I'll go. Do you want to go now?"

"Whenever you have time. You look like you're busy."

"Nonsense. I'm just trying to find a new recipe to try. Let me grab the envelope that the lawyer gave us that has the keys to the house and let Marty know."

Anna Grace slowly entered the front door to the house. Her legs were trembling so bad that she thought they might buckle under her. As if knowing what she was feeling, Adelle took her hand and held it.

Standing in the large foyer, Anna Grace looked around. She was amazed at how everything looked the same as it had ten years ago. As her eyes landed on the hallway that led to the back of the house, she turned toward Adelle.

"I don't think that I'm ready to go to my dad's office. In fact, I don't know if I'll ever be able to step inside there."

"You don't have to, sweetie."

Anna Grace looked around again. She was surprised at the condition of the house.

"What are you thinking about, honey?"

"How clean everything is. I expected dust, filth, and cobwebs."

Adelle smiled. "Marty and I made sure that the estate kept the house up to its pristine condition."

Anna Grace appeared surprised. "Why would you do that?"

Adelle pulled her into a hug. "Because we always knew that one day, you'd find your way back home."

Anna Grace felt a tear slip out of her eye. God. She longed for the day to feel a real motherly hug again. When she pulled away, she caught Adelle wiping her eye.

"Where do you think we should start?" Anna Grace asked.

"Let me ask you this; what do you plan on doing with the house?"

"What do you mean?"

"Do you want to keep it or sell it?"

She definitely didn't want to keep it. "Sell," she stated quickly.

"Well, if you want to sell it, my suggestion is to go room by room and sort through everything. You can decide what you would like to keep and what to sell or donate."

Anna Grace would rather donate everything than hold an estate sale. She'd go through the house and take anything that was personal, then call one of those organizations that would come and pick up everything. But either way, it was going to be a big project. One that she couldn't tackle by herself. And if she wanted to have a quick sale, then she was going to need some reinforcements.

Skittles entered the team's building and went straight to the commander's office. When he got the call early this morning asking him to come to the base, he feared that they were being called out. As much as he loved his job, he really hoped that wasn't the case. At least not yet, with things still in limbo with Anna Grace. He wasn't comfortable leaving her just yet.

Derek's door was closed, so he knocked and was surprised when the door opened and Ace was standing there.

"Hey," Skittles said.

Ace grinned, then opened the door wider to let Skittles enter before shutting it. Derek was sitting at his desk; he smiled and motioned for Skittles to take a seat.

"Thanks for making the drive and coming in this morning."

"It wasn't a problem," Skittles replied.

Ace snorted a laugh. "You're so full of shit. You were probably cursing the whole drive here."

Derek smirked, and Skittles had to agree with Ace. He hadn't wanted to leave Anna Grace.

"How's Anna Grace doing?" Derek asked.

Skittles smiled. "She's good. I actually got a call from my mom a little while ago telling me that they were at A.G.'s old house. A.G. told my mom that she wanted to sell the house, so Mom is helping her sort through everything in the house."

"Does she need help?" Ace asked.

"I don't think she'd turn it down. Her goal is to have everything she wants to keep out of the house by next weekend. All of the furniture and other stuff that she doesn't want she's going to donate."

Ace looked at Derek. "Do we have any orders coming down the pipeline that you know of?"

Derek shook his head. "No. In fact, I just got an updated rotation schedule. You guys look clear for the next two weeks unless something major pops up."

Derek then looked at Skittles. "I think a few days of team building is on the calendar."

Skittles grinned. "I think A.G. would be very grateful."

"We can get there on Wednesday. But I can guarantee that some of the ladies wouldn't mind going up earlier."

"That would be awesome, and I'm sure Anna Grace would be happy to see everyone." Skittles then looked at Derek. "I'm guessing you didn't bring me in just to ask about Anna Grace."

Derek grinned. "Well, what I have to tell you does involve her. But there is also something that we would like to gift her. Knowing now that we all plan on visiting her in a few days, we could've brought it with us. But since you're here now, you can take it with you."

Skittles scrunched his forehead up. "You have something for her?"

Derek glanced over at Ace, and Skittles saw Ace type something on his phone.

"First, let's start with a little bit of positive news. I just received a call from Tink that Senator DeSmith and Steve Johnson had some visitors to their office this morning."

"Visitors?"

"Federal Agents."

"Seriously?"

Derek nodded. "Yep. And it seems like his staff was questioned as well, including your neighbor, Monique Page. And apparently, she wasn't about to go down for any of the Senator's crimes because she had a lot of information to tell the agents about the Senator's life outside of the office. The Senator likes to engage in threats to his staff if they don't keep quiet about certain things. And Monique had come across some information that the Senator wasn't aware of, and she completely backed up Anna Grace's claim about DeSmith selling U.S. weapons to known terrorist organizations. When asked why she didn't go to the authorities, she told the investigators that she feared for her life if she made what she had uncovered public. She also said that Steve questioned her about you."

"Me?" Skittles asked, pointing to himself.

"Yeah. When they saw you and Anna Grace at Alex's charity event, she heard Steve talking about you, and she mentioned that you were her neighbor.

234

"And what type of information did she offer?"

"Not too much because she said she really didn't know anything personal about you, except that you were a SEAL." Derek chuckled. "She didn't even know your real name."

Skittles thanked the lord that he never shared any personal information with her.

"What about Senator DeSmith and Steve? Did the investigators say anything about their meetings?"

"Well, of course, both of them are denying any involvement, and I heard they've both already retained lawyers. So, that tells you something. Tink did tell me that the Feds are also looking back into the accident that took the life of DeSmith's wife."

"Why? Do they think he killed her?"

"I don't know who it was, but according to Tink, when the Federal Agents showed up at the Senator's office in D.C., word spread like fire. Soon afterward, a very good source came forward with some information that raised some eyebrows."

Skittles shook his head. "How does Anna Grace and her parents fit into all of this?"

"They're still looking at that. Tink did say at one time that Anna Grace's dad was a lobbyist. So, they are looking down that avenue."

Skittles ran his hand through his hair. "I have a feeling this is just the tip of the iceberg. God knows what else the Feds will uncover."

"Very true. I never liked the guy, and now that it has been confirmed by multiple sources of what he's been up to, it just makes me dislike him even more. So, there's that. As soon as we know any more, we'll be sure to keep you in the loop. I know this has to be hard on Anna Grace, but I'm glad to hear she's doing well."

"The second thing I called you in for is, well—"

"Sir, how about if we just show him?" Ace said, and Derek nodded.

Skittles watched with curiosity as Ace stood and went to the door. When he opened it, he couldn't see anything other than the rest of the team standing there. But then, when they parted, the only thing left standing in the middle of them was Anna Grace's best canine buddy, Beretta.

Skittles looked at Derek. "What's he doing here?"

"He is going to his new home."

"New home?"

"Anna Grace's home."

Skittles' eyes widened in both shock and surprise. "You mean the military is going to adopt him out? I thought they—"

Derek grinned. "People tend to change their tune when they get a call from the President of the United States."

Skittles knew Derek and Tink knew a lot of people high up in office, but the President was a new one.

Potter walked the gorgeous Belgian Malinois into the room, then handed the leash to Skittles.

"If anyone deserves this dog, it's Anna Grace. If it weren't for her, I don't think he'd be around anymore," Derek stated, and Skittles couldn't agree more. Like Anna Grace had told him before, the two shared a lot in common with each other. And both helped heal each other.

"I don't know what to say. I mean, this is awesome, and she's going to be ecstatic when I show up with him."

"And she should be."

They all spoke for a few minutes, and Ace explained to the guys about Anna Grace needing help to get the house ready to sell, and they were all in. The team had even stopped by the store and had picked up a few necessities the pooch would need. He was definitely going to need to start looking for a house with a yard because Beretta would need the room to run.

As he drove back north to Maryland, he called his dad and gave him a heads up about what he was bringing home for Anna Grace.

CHAPTER TWENTY-FIVE

Senator DeSmith was on a rampage. Word had spread fast through the ranks of the Senate, and he was already being pressured to resign by not just the Senate Minority Leader but by his party. He had already fired many of his staff members who he knew spoke with the authorities. Then of those that were left, half of them resigned. All that he was left with was a handful of loyal staff and Steve. Though Steve's absence today had made him wonder if Steve squealed to the Feds to save his ass.

His life and status as a United States Senator were crumbling by the minute. His lawyer even informed him that with the evidence the Feds had presented against him, there was no possible way to avoid going to prison.

For twenty-five plus years, he'd flown under the radar and had gotten away with his crimes. Why now? What had triggered this investigation? The main charge he was facing was treason for selling U.S. weapons to known terrorist organizations, which carries a sentence of prison or even death. But the list of allegations didn't stop there. They were investigating the alleged kidnapping in the Philippines; also, the murders of Dennis and Sandra Silver, and even the car crash that claimed his wife's life. Someone had to have tipped them off. But who? Knowing this situation could one day come, he had prepared for it. He had transferred enough money to offshore accounts and bought a house in Cuba where he'd be protected from extradition. But before he fled, he wanted to make whoever created this mess pay.

CHAPTER TWENTY-SIX

Anna Grace smiled as Adelle pulled the car into the driveway, and she saw Skittles' truck parked in the garage.

She was tired and couldn't believe the amount of progress that she and Adelle had made in just a few hours they were at the house. The one thing she could credit her parents with was that they weren't people who liked clutter. That in itself made it easier and faster to go through the rooms.

They had completed all but one of the bedrooms upstairs, including her old bedroom. Again, she was going donate most of everything except for some of the items she found in her bedroom that held special memories. Adelle took care of boxing those things for her. She did come across a few file cabinets that contained some paperwork, so she also boxed those up and brought them back to the house to go through later. But the strangest thing she had found was a small lockbox shoved under her bed. She had never seen it before. Seeing as it was locked, she assumed it might hold something important, so she brought that with her too. The problem was that she needed to find the key to open it.

As Adelle turned the car off, she turned toward Anna Grace. "Why don't we leave this stuff in the car for now, and I'll ask the guys to bring it in?"

"Sounds good to me," she replied before exiting the car.

Adelle let her go first into the house, and when she came into the kitchen, something to the right in the middle of the living room moved, catching her attention.

Curious, she moved into the living room, and when she came around the sofa and saw the brown and black Belgian Malinois come into view, she had to cover her mouth to hold in the gasp.

"Beretta?" She said in such a low voice that she almost couldn't hear herself. But when the ears on the pup stood at attention, she knew he had heard her.

"Beretta. Hier!" She said, giving the command in German for come. As the dog lifted off the ground and came running to her with his tail wagging, she dropped to her knees. Beretta was so excited that he knocked her over onto her back and proceeded to lick her to death.

"It looks like someone missed you," Skittles said laughingly as he, Adelle, and Marty all joined her and Beretta.

Anna Grace couldn't contain her laughter as Beretta continued the onslaught of kisses. Finally, Skittles helped her out and called Beretta off her. He then helped her stand, then she fixed her ponytail.

Once she was able to catch her breath, she looked at Skittles.

"What is he doing here?" She asked, still smiling.

"Well, you see; apparently, the military has had a change of heart." She furrowed her eyebrows, not understanding. "He's yours, A.G."

She felt her mouth drop open at the shock of his words. "He's mine? As in I get to keep him for good?"

Skittles smiled. "Yeah. He's all yours. When we get back to town, you'll need to fill out some paperwork, but for now, he can stay with us here."

"I can't believe this!" She exclaimed, and Skittles walked over and hugged her.

"You two deserve to be together," he whispered to her, and she couldn't hold back her tears.

When she pulled away and wiped her eyes, she looked up at Skittles. That man she loved with all her heart.

"What made them change their mind?" She asked.

"It seems a few calls were made on your behalf."

She bent down and scratched Beretta behind the ears. "It doesn't matter as long as he's with me."

During dinner, a little while later, Skittles told her about the team coming to help her out, and Anna Grace felt some relief. She couldn't wait to spend some time with her new friends.

CHAPTER TWENTY-SEVEN

When Wednesday rolled around, Anna Grace couldn't believe the number of people who showed up to help her go through the house. The entire team and their families were there, and the biggest surprise was when Xavier and Melanie showed up later in the afternoon.

Skittles explained that Xavier had been distraught ever since it was announced in the news that she had been abducted. Since they kept her rescue quiet for the time being, Derek and Tink agreed to let Xavier know what was going on.

Later in the evening, after the entire house had been sorted through and items boxed for either donation or for her to keep, everyone headed back over to the Youngs' house for a barbecue. Marty and Adelle, had it catered by the local barbecue pit place just down the street.

Anna Grace had been up in the attic and wanted to take a quick shower before she ate to make sure she didn't have any insulation on her. While she was changing the bedroom, she noticed that the small lock box that she had brought home with her wasn't locked anymore. She assumed that Skittles had picked the lock for her.

Wondering what was inside, she flipped open the lid. Laying on top was a picture of a man and a woman with their arms around one another. They looked young, maybe mid-twenties, and definitely appeared in love. The woman's facial features made Anna Grace take a closer look, mainly the eyes. They were more rounded than almond-shaped like hers, but it wasn't so much the shape of the eyes that drew her in; it was the color. The woman had the same violet-colored eyes as Anna Grace. And not only that, but she also had the same platinum blonde hair as her, except the woman's hair was straight, and Anna Grace's was naturally wavy. If Anna Grace didn't know any better, she would've believed that she was looking at a picture of her mother. But that was just it. Her mother, Sandra, looked nothing like the woman in the picture.

Within seconds an odd feeling started to build inside Anna Grace. She reached inside the box to see what else there was, but the only other thing in there was a thick envelope with Anna Grace's name written on the outside.

With shaking hands, she slid her finger in the seal and opened the envelope. Inside she found a letter and birth certificate which she saw was hers.

She took the letter out and unfolded it and began to read it.

Dear Anna Grace,

I am writing this letter to you as your tiny body lay pressed against mine. I fear for both of our lives, and I can only pray that you can read this someday. And, if you are reading this, then it means that something terrible has happened to me. But I need you to know the truth because I'm sure those involved in my death will make sure that you never know.

At one time, I was married to an evil man, who most likely is the reason why I'm not there with you today. While trying to escape my abusive marriage, I sought shelter with another man I fell in love with. A man with integrity and one who respected and loved me for who I was as a person. That man is also your father, who I hope you can be reunited with one day because I know deep in my heart that he will be the most incredible father any child could ask for. You will find his name on your birth certificate, which is enclosed with this letter.

Please know that I will always love you and be watching you from the stars.

Love always—your mother,
Sue Ellen

Looking through the many tears impeding her vision Anna Grace reached for the other piece of paper that lay next to her. She felt so numb and confused, not to mention deceived. Dennis and Sandra Silver deceived her. The couple who she believed for the last twenty-five years were her parents. The couple she cried over when she found their bloodied bodies. It was a lie. Her whole life had been a lie. She felt broken.

As she unfolded her Birth Certificate, her heart felt as if it was going to explode in anticipation of what the document would reveal. As she read further down and saw her mother's name typed out—Sue Ellen Edwards-DeSmith, she gasped, now realizing why her life had been turned upside down. She felt sick knowing that her own father not only tried to pawn her off to someone else, but he also tried to get rid of her. But then she remembered Sue Ellen's words. Her father wasn't Senator DeSmith. Her father was the man she sought shelter with.

When her eyes landed on the line that revealed who her biological father was, she cried out a sob that most likely could be heard from anywhere in the house. Her heart literally felt like it was going to explode. It couldn't be, she thought to herself. She never believed in fate until now.

As if sensing she was upset, Beretta rested his head in her lap. Wrapping her around his neck, she buried her face in his fur and cried. She cried for her mother that she never got to know. She cried for her father, who missed out on being a dad for the last twenty-five years. And she cried for herself.

CHAPTER TWENTY-EIGHT

Skittles was starting to get worried as Anna Grace should've been done with her shower by now. Just as he was getting up from the picnic table, he saw Anna Grace come through the back door. She was clutching something to her chest, but what alarmed him even more, were the tears streaming down her face. Apparently, he wasn't the only one to notice because as he started to run toward her, some of the others followed.

As he made it to her, she threw herself at him and cried against his chest. He'd seen Anna Grace cry before, but seeing her this upset really began to worry him. The others were all looking at him as if asking what was wrong, but he didn't know.

He held her until she started to calm down.

"A.G., you're scaring me right now. I need to know that you aren't hurt."

She shook her head but still wouldn't look up at him. She did offer him something. "My heart hurts," she told him.

She pulled away, and Skittles felt like he'd been punched in the gut. She looked totally defeated, as if someone had stepped all over her.

She turned toward Xavier, who was standing beside them. And she handed him one of the items that she had been holding against her chest.

"Is that you in that picture?" She asked him.

Xavier took the picture, and Skittles knew right away what his answer was.

"Where did you get this?" Xavier asked Anna Grace.

With a tear rolling down her already tear-stained cheeks, she answered him. "I got it from my mother, Sue Ellen." She then took a few steps until she was standing in front of Xavier. She handed him two more pieces of paper. "According to this letter I found, and this birth certificate, you are my father."

With Anna Grace's statement, Skittles felt as if the whole world had stopped moving.

She then looked at Skittles. "I found those in that lock box you opened for me. Dennis and Sandra Silver weren't my birth parents. My biological mom was Sue Ellen Edwards-DeSmith, and according to her, my father is Xavier."

Skittles didn't know what to say. He, along with everyone else, appeared to be stunned by this life-altering revelation.

Xavier stepped forward and looked down at Anna Grace. "The first time I met you in the diner, I told Melanie that there was something special about you." A tear slipped out of the man's eye, and he pulled Anna Grace into a hug. "Now I understand why. And believe me, Anna Grace, those responsible for tearing us apart will be held accounted for. You can bet your life on it."

Skittles heard Xavier take a deep breath, and everyone sort of stepped back to let the father and daughter have a moment to themselves.

CHAPTER TWENTY-NINE

Anna Grace smiled as she looked at herself in the mirror. It had been over a month since finding out the truth about her birth parents. Since then, she and Xavier have spent time together catching up on some father-daughter time. However, they had to plan around Xavier's schedule since he had been appointed by the Governor as the new Senator of Virginia, replacing the disgraced Senator DeSmith.

Senator DeSmith was caught trying to flee the country when the Federal Agents moved in to arrest him. He was charged with many offenses, including treason, murder, kidnapping, and fraud. They found out that DeSmith had ordered Dennis and Sandra killed because they tried to blackmail him for more money.

As for her and Skittles—they were living together in Skittles' apartment with Beretta. But in the coming weeks, they were going to start house hunting.

A knock sounded on the door, and when she turned around, she saw Alex standing there. She, too, was all dressed up for Arianna and Dino's wedding.

"Hey, you ready to head downstairs?" Alex asked her, and she nodded.

"I think so."

As the two started to descend the stairs leading to the living room, Anna Grace stopped in her tracks when she saw Skittles waiting at the bottom. For a moment, standing on the stairs in her cream-colored evening gown, which in her opinion resembled more of a wedding dress, she felt like Cinderella, as her Prince waited for her at the bottom.

As she took the last few steps down, Skittles held his hand out for her to take. The moment their fingers touched; she felt those butterflies in her stomach. It happened to her every time.

"You look amazing," he told her.

She smiled, looking over his navy-blue suit. "You don't look too bad either."

Suddenly, all their friends walked into the room and surrounded them. She looked around, wondering what was happening. Even Dino and Arianna were there. Wasn't it bad luck to see the bride before the wedding?

Skittles took her hand in his and looked deep into her eyes.

"Say you'll marry me," he told her.

"What?" She asked, looking at him.

He smiled. "Say that you will marry me and be my wife. Stand by my side for the rest of our lives as I will do the same for you."

Suddenly, he lowered to one knee and pulled a ring box from his pocket. When he opened it, the diamonds circling the band sparkled like tiny stars.

"Noah..." She whispered.

He grinned. "This was Arianna and Dino's idea. I was going to wait and propose this weekend, but they both wanted us to share their day with them. So, what do you say, Anna Grace Mayfield, will you marry me? Tonight?"

She tried to talk through the tears. "Of course, I'll marry you. I love you so much."

He smiled and stood as he slid the piece of jewelry onto her ring finger then kissed it.

She smiled and got up on her tiptoes and kissed him.

"I love you, Noah."

"I love you too, A.G."

EPILOGUE

Derek's phone vibrated, and he excused himself from the party to take the call. He didn't recognize the number but answered it anyway.

"Hello?"

"Derek, Fred Wilson here."

"Hey, Fred. How the hell are you? My god, it's been a while."

Derek's old SEAL buddy laughed. "Yeah, the wife keeps me busy nowadays."

"I bet. Do you guys still own that diner in West Virginia?"

"Sure do."

"Well, I know you didn't call me out of the blue just to shoot the shit."

Derek heard his old friend sigh. "Yeah, I'm calling because I need some help. Well, not me exactly but one of my employees."

Derek could hear the frustration in Fred's tone.

"What kinda help are we talking about?"

"I need to get her relocated."

"Shit. What kind of trouble is she in?"

"She's young, a hard worker, but dammit, I can't take seeing her coming to work bruised because some rich asshole thinks he can control her by manipulating her and pounding on her."

Derek was quiet for a minute. That kind of shit upset him. Before he would agree to help, he needed some clarification on some things. This woman may not want out of the relationship.

"What's her relationship with this guy?"

"There really is none. She's being forced to stay with him."

"Why doesn't she just leave him?"

"She's tried Derek, and each time she's ended up in the hospital. And, before you ask, she's too scared to press charges. The sheriff in town knows the guy is an asshole, but his hands are tied if she won't press charges. The guy has a lot of people who work for him, including really good lawyers. I

247

need a way to sneak her out of town and to stay hidden for a while. I'm hoping his interest in her will fade over time."

"What are you thinking?"

"I was hoping between you and your old team; you guys may have some suggestions. My hands are tied here, or I would up and leave town with her."

Derek thought hard. Surely Tink could provide some options, but this young woman sounded like she was important to Fred, and Derek thought it might be best to keep her close by.

He scanned the area, not sure what he was looking for, but then he landed on Diego and smiled.

"Fred, I think I may have an idea. Let me talk to some people, and I'll give you a call tomorrow morning, and hopefully, we can make some plans."

"Sounds good. Talk to you then."

Derek hung up and took a drink from his bottle. This could work out just fine. Who knows, maybe Diego would meet his match.

Diego and Campbell's story coming soon!
Pre-order available now!

248

BOOK LIST

The Trident Series

ACE
POTTER
FROST
IRISH
STITCH
DINO
SKITTLES
DIEGO *(2021)*
A TRIDENT WEDDING *(2021)*

The Trident Series II
BRAVO Team

JOKER *(2021)*
BEAR *(2022)*
DUKE *(2022)*
PLAYBOY *(2022)*
AUSSIE *(2022)*
SNOW *(2022)*
NAILS *(TBD)*
JAY BIRD *(TBD)*

ABOUT THE AUTHOR

Jaime Lewis, a *USA TODAY* bestselling author, entered the indie author world in June 2020 with ACE, the first book in the Trident Series.

With a barrage of positive reviews and a series embraced by readers, Jaime is a rising star in the romantic suspense genre.

Coming from a military family, she describes as very patriotic; it's no surprise that her books are known for their accurate portrayal of life in the service.

Passionate in her support of the military, veterans, and first responders, Jaime volunteers with the Daytona Division of the US Naval Sea Cadet Corps, a non-profit youth leadership development program sponsored by the U.S. Navy. Together with her son, she also manages a charity organization that supports military personnel and their families, along with veterans and first responders.

Born and raised in Edgewater, Maryland, Jaime now resides in Ormond Beach, Florida with her husband and two very active boys.

Between her day job, her two boys, and writing, she doesn't have a heap of spare time, but if she does, you'll find her somewhere in the outdoors. Jaime is also an avid sports fan.

Follow Jaime:

Facebook Author Page:https://www.facebook.com/jaime.lewis.58152
Jaime's Convoy: https://www.facebook.com/groups/349178512953776
Goodreads: https://www.goodreads.com/author/show/17048191.Jaime_Lewis

Made in the USA
Coppell, TX
17 February 2022

73676504R10150